Once Upon Our Time

Victoria Rocus

*For my own "Mamaw," the fiercely loving "Grandma Bernice,"
who didn't teach me anything about talking to ghosts, but made
sure I learned every bit of "kitchen magic" she had to share.
Miss you, Busia*

PROLOGUE

**SPRING HILL, TENNESSEE
NOVEMBER 29th, 1864**

JONATHAN EZRA SWEET TRADED HIS LIFE FOR A DAMN, scrawny 'possum. While he lay in the freezing mud in the middle of a darkened patch of Tennessee woods, his life was bleedin' out of him from a dang painful belly wound. Johnny Sweet didn't see no white light leadin' him off to heaven. There weren't no St. Peter and no Pearly Gates. No choir of angels sang their greetings, nor was he met by his nearest and dearest welcomin' him home to his Lord Jesus. There weren't none of that shit the Parson had promised the boys they'd get if they were to make the ultimate sacrifice for the Righteous War for Southern Independence. No siree. Johnny Sweet surely was dyin' alone, away from home and everyone that had ever cared about him.

Actin' the hero was the last thing on Johnny's mind when he'd snuck away from his regiment. 'Twas simple hunger that drove him into the woods, an empty, aching belly that was more of a rally cry than any justified speeches from the men in charge. He reckoned the woods near Rally Hill Pike must surely be home to some type of local wildlife. Even a mole or one of them large birds that constantly circled the November sky would do him good. Anything would be better than the dry, hard, chunk of cornbread that made up his rations most days.

It weren't hard to go missing. Someone in his regiment had gotten their hands on some "Sutler's Whiskey" when they'd gone through Mule Town and was doin' big business tradin' it for tobacco and whatever rations some of the fellers had managed to hang on to. Johnny was no friend of the Devil's Brew, him growin' up a good Baptist boy and such. By suppertime, most of the camp and a mess of the officers were sinfully drunk and lyin' in a stupor, leavin' the young soldier free to pursue his hunt for edible meat. He'd seen the dang 'possum scroungin' for bugs about a mile into the woods. It had done seen him as well and scuttled further into the underbrush. Bein' it was one of them dark, early, winter nights, when not even the moon felt like makin' an appearance, tracking anything was a major chore. Eventually, Johnny Sweet's eyes adjusted to the dark, and he could see more than just a few feet in front of him. Thus, it was his bad luck that from that position in the woods he caught sight of movement on Rally Hill Pike.

At first, Private Sweet thought the contingent of soldiers quietly making their way up the road had come at

General Hood's orders to stop the Yankee movement toward Franklin. He knew the General planned to keep them Union boys out of Franklin and away from Nashville so's that the Reb troops could retake the state capital and change the course of the War. Generals Cleburne, Lowery, and Forrest were said to all be in the area, but as far as Johnny knew, they wasn't supposed to be here on the Pike. Not at this time anyways. Plus, they was amovin' as quiet as church mice and dumpin' their gear all along the rutted road.

This seemed mighty strange and made Jonathan Sweet more than a bit confused. He held his position and stayed himself still. If they was a group of fellow Rebs, Johnny was away from his own regiment and out alone in the middle of the woods. If fer' nothin' else, there was a good chance that even if these men were part of Hood's contingent, he might be shot as a deserter no matter that he was wearin' the Rebel gray. As Johnny watched from his hidin' spot, a small cluster of the soldiers stopped to rest while the others spread out, most likely lookin' for a private spot to take a piss or a shit.

One man in particular climbed up the hill a mite too close to where Johnathan was hidin'. The soldier lit a cigarette, and Johnny scoffed to himself: Real men smoked cigars or pipes; cigarettes were the choice of loose women folk. But the light from the match, and then the cigarette, made one thing perfectly clear: This was a damn Union soldier, and chances were real good that the rest of them boys with him were Yanks too. That there were Yanks on Rally Hill Pike when there weren't supposed to be any meant damn trouble. This was important news. Jonathan Sweet was needin' to let his superior officers know that, somehow, the Yanks had managed to break through the lines south of Spring Hill that had been meant to keep them from movin' northward.

He leaned back to take the pressure off of his achin' right hip. That's when his trouble started. The shiftin' of his body weight caused some dry underbrush ta'crackle 'neath his feet. The man with the cigarette looked up, startled, then grabbed for his rifle. For a second, the Union boy stood in place and listened, but then he began trekking closer to the spot Johnny was hidin'. Fear replaced all of Johnny's other thoughts and he began to run. If he could just make it back to camp, he thought he might have a chance. He heard the Yank in pursuit, callin' for reinforcement, as well as the devastatin' Minié balls bouncing off of the trees around him. The good Baptist boy from Meridian, Mississippi, kept on runnin', prayin' to the Lord Jesus for deliverance from his enemies. In return, Heaven's answer came as a searing, burning pain to his gut. For a while, Johnny kept on movin' until he couldn't move no more. He dropped to his knees, then rolled on his back and stared up at the muddy night sky.

He didn't hear no more sounds and guessed that his pursuers had done given up their chase or had gone off in some other direction, but this changed nothing for the Johnny Reb. As blood poured from the Minié ball's destruction of his belly, Johnathan Ezra Sweet, a good son and brother, didn't think much about the Glory of the South. Nor did he ponder the politics of those who had brought him to this ignoble end, or whether his knowledge of the Yanks being on Rally Hill Pike might have changed future events. Instead, Johnny thought about his ma's biscuits and gravy on a Sunday mornin'.

He also brought to mind Sara Anne McKinney, the girl he loved, with his whole heart, and ole' Rolly, the loyal coon dog who'd followed him everywhere he went. These thoughts made him feel a tad better and brought him some comfort, but it weren't long before Johnny couldn't feel much of anything. His body went numb down to its very bones. He was cold. So very cold. And before the boy from Meridian, Mississippi, closed his eyes for the last time, he remembered, once again, that he'd traded his life for a damn, scrawny 'possum.

CHAPTER ONE

**Columbia, Tennessee
June 7th, 2025**

Sure as shit, my dead Mamaw is rollin' in her grave. I can picture her clear as day, she in her fancy, rose colored, casket, pinched cheeks and pursed lips, sittin' straight up in her Sunday best and waggin' a bony finger in my face for usin' my "gifts" the way I am. There's no doubt, whatsoever, that wherever my Mamaw is, she ain't much pleased with her favorite granddaughter. "So much given," she'd scold, "and thrown out like yesterday's stale corn pone. Foolish, foolish girl." Then she'd pick up her favorite conjuring broom, the one I'd snuck into her casket just before the mortician closed it, and wave it at me in a sound warning. All things considered, she wouldn't be wrong. What I'm doing is an affront to all

THINGS UNSEEN; A SLAP IN THE FACE TO EVERY GIFTED Achley woman that's come before me.

When I started to manifest signs at the tender age of eleven, it was clear that I had, indeed, inherited the "family gifts." Mamaw had taken me on as her own personal project, passing on word of mouth knowledge and skills that she herself had learned at the knee of her own grandmother. By the time I finished Junior High, I had surpassed the last three generations with my talent and skill. I could conjure, divine, and cast better than any practitioner twice my age. But that was before Caleb. Caleb changed everything. Now, I'm nothing more than a grifter. A poser. A liar. A cheat. Worse yet, I don't even feel guilty.

Today, I'm usin' the Tarot spread called a Celtic Cross only 'cause it looks more intriguing to my client. Truth be told, a simple three card spread does everything it needs to do. Past...present...future. One don't need to know much more than that. But when people visit a "psychic" to get their life questions properly answered, they're generally looking for a little more showmanship for their money, which in my case, is a lousy thirty bucks. My client today is a dim-witted, twenty-something with more discretionary cash than brains. I knew when she walked through the door of the "antique mall," aka junk store, dragging along a clueless friend for moral support, that she was looking for the same ole' boring answers to the same ole' dumb ass questions as most of my clients.

More than fifty percent of the people who come to see me want answers about their love life, or lack thereof. In almost every case, these pathetic souls already know the answers to the questions they seek. They're really comin' to me to have their angst relieved and to be told that their "one and only" will continue to be an "only." The damn signs are already there for them to see that whatever they think is "the real thing," surely ain't. Still, they hand me their money and wait for me to tell them that they're wrong. My clients don't come for the truth; they come so I can lie to them, and that's exactly what I do. Given' the customer what they want is the golden rule of business.

It's the same with questions about careers, financial issues, and health problems. No one wants to hear that… yes…the cancer they've just been diagnosed with is gonna' kill them, that the promotion they've been hopin' for will undoubtedly go to someone else, or, accordion' to the will of the Universe, they don't stand a chance in hell of ever winnin' the lottery, and thus, will struggle with financial need until the day they take their last breath. It's so much easier, and far more advantageous in gettin' enough cash to pay my rent, to tell them exactly what they want to hear. To hell with actually getting a sneak peek into the future. From my own personal experience, the future ain't always so great. It's often best not to know what's comin' for ya'.

This charade is how I've been able to keep a dry roof over my head and food in my belly. I read the cards, whip up so-called love potions, sell pretty crystals, and generally pass myself off as a new age shaman. There hasn't been much I ain't been willin' to do in the arena of fake mystic consultations. Except for ghosts. That's where I have drawn the line. I stay clear of communicating with the dead. I don't even fake it for fear that somehow a wandering soul might inadvertently sneak through and ask for help. I'm done with helping ghosts, those unlucky souls who haven't passed on for one reason or another. Caleb Nash cured me of that. Ghosts of any kind are now and forever off limits.

In this particular case, I am spot on about my current client. Her big important life question is whether the "love of her life boyfriend" has been faithful to her and should she marry him. My client already subconsciously knows the answer to this before she sits down. So do I. And so does her so-called friend who has been secretly screwing the bastard boyfriend herself. The draw of the cards in the girl's reading is proof of what we all know. Out of the ten cards in her Celtic Cross, eight of them are of the Major Arcana, several of them reversed, showing a multitude of life lessons that need to be mastered before the Universe will open itself to the client's future.

The first card in the center of the cross represents the present. In this spot sits the High Priestess in reverse, demonstrating secrets and disconnection from one's own intuition. The second card, laid over the first, is meant to focus on the challenge currently facing the client. Today, in this spot, the draw is for the Lovers Card, yet again in the reverse position.

Her two-timin' friend jumps in before I can speak. "See Stacy… it's the Card for Lovers. It's upside down. I'm pretty sure that's a sign you should break up with David." She looks at me for confirmation. "That's what it means, right?"

One don't even need "the gift" to determine what's going on here. The friend wants David for herself. Truthfully, she deserves him. They are two of a kind; energy sucking, narcissistic liars. My client would be far better off without either of them in her life. But that's not what she wants to hear. For better or worse she loves the asshole. I turn my attention to the friend. "Have you been reading cards very long?" I ask. My tone is low and chilly, and it's clear I'm being sarcastic. She starts to open her mouth but then decides better and clamps it shut.

"Actually," I explain, "the Lovers card is not just about relationships. It's a card that focuses on harmony, values, and good choices. Reversed like it is, it means that your emotions regarding the situation are not in alignment with your core values."

Both girls look at me as if I were speaking Mandarin Chinese. All of this emotional pondering goes right over their heads. "Is it possible," I ask my client, "that you are looking at this relationship with misguided values?"

"What does that even mean?" the client asks.

"It means what you think it does; that perhaps you want to marry this person for the wrong reasons," I explain.

The girl vigorously shakes her head. "Oh no! I love David. He loves me. We belong together." I obviously have hit a sore spot, because she adds, "If you're such a hot shot psychic you should already know that."

I stop asking questions and continue to turn over the cards. It's no use telling people the truth. As I said before, no one really wants to hear it. From the rest of the reading, it's obvious I've been on the right track. For whatever reasons, my client feels she has no choice but to marry the dickhead despite there being at least a hundred reasons not to do it. Her friend's false feigned concern fills my space with negative energy and gives me the beginning of a bad headache. All I want is for this session to be over. I give the girl the most basic of explanations for the rest of the spread, and when it's all said and done, I say to her, "According to the cards, you already know the answer to your question. Go with your gut feelings."

She looks at me, frowning with disappointment. "That's it? That's the answer? I was expecting it to be more of a…sure thing."

"That's not how a reading works," I explain. "It's meant to be a chance for you to focus on your inner feelings and emotions."

The girl's friend makes a face. "I once went to this psychic at the Galleria Mall. She told me I'd get a promotion, and a month later I did. That's how a real psychic works."

I shrug my shoulders. "Not this one," I say.

The client and her friend get up to leave, handing me a $3 tip, which on a thirty-dollar reading is shitty. They are obviously not satisfied customers. As they turn to leave, I stop the friend. "That's an interesting ring you're wearing."

The dubious friend looks at me, startled. I've known from the start that the ring was a gift from David, the two-timin', sonofabitch boyfriend. The girl mumbles something that sounds like "thanks" under her breath, though I know that she really wants to tell me to go fuck myself. The two girls head out into the antique mall part of the building, and I can hear them loudly complaining to the owner about their less than stellar experience with me.

The pair of girls are gone only a few minutes when the owner of the shop, Tess Porter, comes back to scold me. "Hells Bells, Delia! You're not doing this place any good by treatin' your clients poorly. This is the third complaint I've had about you this week! I thought havin' me a psychic in the place would draw customers in and then maybe, just maybe, they'd stick aroun' long enough to buy somethin'. But lately, a few minutes with you, and they can't get their asses out the door fast enough. I know you're the real thing, girl, but I can't have ya' pissin' off my customers."

"It's not my fault, Tess. I'm no genie grantin' wishes. I just channel what the Universe intends."

"Folks round here don't need no damn advice from the Universe, girl," Tess complains. "They get enough preachin' from Pastor Bob at the First Baptist Church. People that come to you are lookin' for someone to agree with them. That's all. So, when they hand over their thirty dollars, you need to just go right ahead and agree with whatever they want to hear, ya' got that?" When I don't immediately respond, the old woman adds, "Mark my words, Cordelia Mae Achley…you don't start giving my customers what they want, I hope the damn Universe helps ya' find a new place to be readin' your cards, 'cause it sure as hell won't be in my store."

Chapter Two

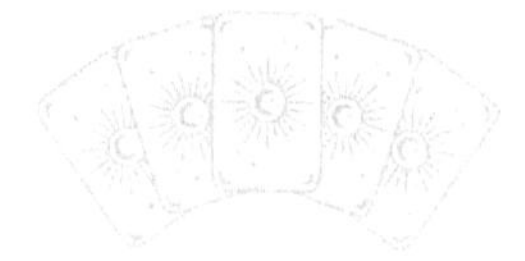

People have the wrong idea about my "gift." It don't come with an on or off switch, and I don't walk around in a constant state of pure consciousness. It's ain't the magic of fairy tales, and lightning bolts don't shoot from my fingertips. I gotta' be in the right frame of mind, and my concentration has to be channeled to the right frequency for information to come through. That's why I like using the cards. The spreads act like a conduit between me and the Universe. They let the Cosmos know that I'm here and ready for action.

My Mamaw used to smoke a little weed whenever she needed help in settlin' her head down and gettin' to the bottom of somethin', but I'm no smoker. Besides, marijuana is still illegal here in Tennessee, and I sure as hell don't need the law crawlin' all over my ass. I've had enough of that shit to last a lifetime. Truthfully, when I was younger, I had the most success and had my best results when I used deep meditation, but I've grown impatient with all of that. Sometimes it's just better not to know when the time is right.

My mind is still fuming over those bitchy girls and the scolding they cost me from Terrible Tess. That's why I don't get a cosmic warnin' in advance of what is waitin' for me when I head home that evening. I share a small, dump of a house with two other people, one that sits on the border between Columbia and Spring Hill. At one point, most of that area was rural, and it's likely the house was once home to generations of farmers. But Spring Hill suddenly has become the "new Franklin," and matchstick housing developments are poppin' up on every piece of open land. If I were to try, I bet I could hear the sound of the land weepin' under the strain and the voices of those who've gone before complaining about what's happenin' to these wild, rolling hills of Middle Tennessee.

I pull up the gravel driveway toward the house and note the stacks of boxes and bins lined up on the front porch, my first indication that something is terribly wrong. My second clue is the police car parked in what is my usual spot under the shade of a large elm tree. I turn off the ignition and get out of my car. The force of the negative energy swirling around the property just about puts me down on my ass. Whatever it is that's going down, it won't be pleasant.

Seeing me, the officer gets out of his squad car and wanders toward me. I freeze. *Deja vu* hits me square between the eyes and my mouth suddenly goes dry. "Cordelia Mae Achley?" the cop asks.

"That's me," I stammer. "What's this about?"

He hands me a paper. "You've been formally evicted, Ms. Achley. This is a copy of the forcible detainer drawn by your landlords. I'm here to see that you retrieve your belongings in a peaceful manner. I'm even willing to help you load them into your car." I feel the cop's pity for my situation, but there's also a sense of judgment there, as if he's already labeled me a loser. When I look up from the decree, I see the curtains move in the window and my anger boils over. "What the hell, Gina?" I shout towards the house. "You have to resort to this bullshit? We couldn't work this out between the two of us? If you had a problem with me, ya' should have just said so!"

Gina Cortland, owner of the house and my landlord, comes to the door and yells back at me through the screen. "I have said so, Delia! Numerous times! You've paid less than a hundred dollars towards the rent in four months! You haven't paid your share of the electric or the cable bills since February. Tyler and I have tried being patient but you just keep takin' advantage of us."

Tyler Cortland is Gina's husband. He's a cross-country trucker and not at home most of the week. That's a good thing, because when he is home, he's always putting the moves on me. My discouragement has not stopped him much. If anything, it's made me more of a challenge to him. I wonder if maybe Gina has caught wind of his "interest" and has decided it was time for the man-stealin', hoodoo woman, Delia Achley, to go. "This is pretty low, Gina. Throwing my shit out on the front porch."

"I didn't do any such thing, Cordelia Mae. I packed it nice and careful-like. I even bought those expensive packing boxes from Home Depot and I wasn't even gonna' charge you for them," the bitch says, as if anyone with a soul actually would do such an awful thing.

It's been a shitty day, and the negative energy surrounding me is adding to the throbbing in my left temple. I'm in just enough of a foul mood to scare the shit out of my asshole landlady, who I know is way beyond casually superstitious. I walk toward the front porch and begin taking the boxes and loading them in my car. The officer helps me and I don't stop him. The sooner I get out of here the better. There's not a lot to my life, so it don't take long to load it all up in my trunk. Then, I walk up the dirt pathway to the house, stopping about a foot from the bottom porch step. With my toe, I draw a large circle in the dry dirt, marking the four elements at the top, bottom, and east and west sides of the circle. I take out a little satin pouch from the pocket of my jeans and pour out a handful of herbs into my palm which I sprinkle in the middle of the circle.

Gina watches wide-eyed from the screen door. "Make her stop, officer!" The landlady begs. "She's puttin' a curse on my house."

The cop looks conflicted. Like most of law enforcement these days, he's wearing a body camera and is not keen on being caught doing anything "silly." On the other hand, he's obviously a local boy and grew up on tales of mountain people magic. "I'm sorry, Mrs. Cortland, but there ain't no law in Maury County against casting "hoodoo." He takes a few steps back from where I'm standing.

I want to laugh out loud at the irony of the moment. Instead, I spit inside the circle, hold out my hands palm up, and close my eyes. I stay this way for a full minute. Then I throw a back handed wave toward the house. "Have a real nice life, Gina," I say. Then I get in my car and back up down the driveway.

Chapter Three

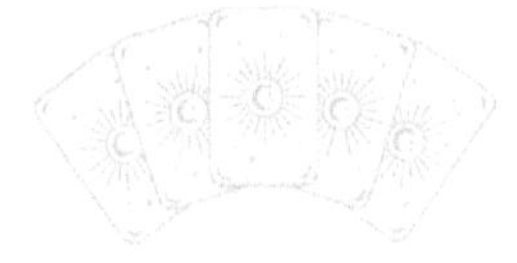

I don't really put a hex on Gina Cortland's house. Or on Gina, for that matter. It weren't even a real casting. I never deal in bad karma spells. They have a nasty way of boomeranging back at ya', and the same negative energy you send out often ends up back in your own lap. I don't need any more bad ju-ju in my life. But Gina doesn't know that, and my play acting in front of her house will give her more than a few sleepless nights. Might even make her think twice before she shits on anyone else.

Now homeless, I head down Rt. 31, Main Street in Spring Hill, to a small, local diner. I figure I'll use the $33 I just earned to buy dinner before I attempt to figure out where I'll spend the night. As an added bonus, an old friend who waits tables part time is working the dinner shift. She sees me come in the door and waves me over to a table in her station.

Liz Turner was one of the first people I met when I moved down to Spring Hill from the city of Nashville after the Caleb Nash disaster. She'd been working at the

Target Superstore in The Crossings about a month before I'd taken a job there and kindly took me under her wing. Liz was the best part of my experience at Target. Though I ended up being fired after my first month, we stayed in touch with an occasional phone call or brunch date. Lizzy is one of those truly nice people. You don't meet too many genuine ones with good souls, and I treasure her presence in my life.

She gives up a hug before seating me and hands over a menu. "It's so awesome to see you, Delia! How are things?"

I don't mean to dump on her first thing out of the box, but the words just slip out and I end up telling her about my sucky day. Being Lizzy, she immediately offers her couch as temporary shelter. "I can't impose on you like that, Liz," I say.

"Don't be silly, Delia. What are friends for? You can stay as long as you need. I know if the situation was reversed, you'd do the same for me. Now...what can I get ya' tonight. If I were you, I'd skip the pot roast and go with the chicken and dumplings."

While I wait for my dinner (obviously the chicken and dumplings...Lizzy Turner never steers you wrong), I check my bank statement and try to figure out what type of permanent housing I can actually afford. There's not enough in there to pay the necessary three month rent in advance plus a security deposit, so a regular apartment is out of the question. With the money on hand, I could probably get a motel room for a few weeks, but the ones I can afford for short stays are the types of places most girls wouldn't feel safe stayin' in.

As I scroll through ads for single rooms for rent, my friend returns to the table with a basket of biscuits and an interesting suggestion. "I was just thinking about your situation, Delia, and I had an idea."

I snatch a warm biscuit and lather it up with butter. "What idea is that?" I ask between bites.

"There's a couple that comes in here almost every morning for breakfast. Nice senior type people. Big tippers. They live over there in 'Southern Streams'...you know...that big 55 plus community off of Kedron Rd."

"Yes. I've gone by there. In back of Rippavilla, right?"

"Yup. That's the one. The Kozinskis are originally from up North some wheres. Minnesota, I think. Anyway, they still own a cabin home on a lake back there and they usually go away for six weeks every summer to beat the sweltering Tennessee summer heat."

I love Lizzy, but she does tend to ramble. Wanting to get back to my biscuit before it gets cold, I urge her along, "That's great, Hon, but how does that help me?"

"I'm getting to that. You see, last summer when they went back to Minnesota, we had that bad storm, remember?"

"I remember," looking longingly at the butter pooling on my bread plate.

"Well, it seems Mr. and Mrs. Kozinski developed a leak in their roof, and by the time they returned home, the leakage from the roof caused extensive rain damage to their living room."

"That's a shame, Liz. But again, I don't see how any of that's gonna' help me with my situation."

"You didn't let me finish, Delia! This year, the Kozinskis want to find someone trustworthy to live in their house while they're up north. Keep an eye on things. It's free room and board, plus I think there's also a stipend involved. It would be the perfect solution for you! A nice place to live for the summer while you figure out your next move, and maybe a little extra cash at the end of it all."

The idea does have solid merit, and I take this out-of-the-blue solution as a gift from the Cosmos via Lizzy Turner. "Do you think they'd consider me, Liz? They don't know me at all."

"Yes, but they know me, Delia, and if I vouch for your honesty and integrity, you'd be in like honey on that biscuit. Should I let them know you're interested?"

"Absolutely," I say. Then, smiling, at my sudden good fortune, I smear a little of that aforementioned honey on my said biscuit before poppin' it in my mouth.

LIZZY WORKS HER MAGIC, AND I GET A MEETING WITH THE Kozinskis regarding the caretaker position of their home while they spend the summer months up north. Though I've passed its front entrance a million times, I have never had reason to wander around the 55 plus community named "Southern Streams." As a life-long Tennessee native, I believe that places like these are changing the flavor of what once was charming, Southern, farm life, and not for the better. I was told that I would need my phone's GPS to find the Kozinski home; once I turn into the development, I quickly see why.

The streets curve along in an endless parade of matchy-matchy, single-level dwellings, each with the same manicured lawn and overly cutesy front porch decor made famous by Pinterest. The side streets branching from the main thoroughfare twist and turn in different directions, all with alliterative names like Cottonwood Court and Avondale Avenue. The Kozinskis live on Sprocket Springs, a small street featuring a wooded cul-de-sac and retention pond at its dead end. Their suggestion to use Google Maps is a necessary one 'cause I'm pretty sure I'd probably still be driven around the tongue twister streets without ever finding the house's location.

The two-bedroom ranch is lovely and modern, with spankin' new everything. Living here for the summer would be a slice of paradise compared to the run-down farmhouse I was sharing with Gina and her two-timin', piece of shit husband. I can't believe my good fortune, and Mr. Kozinski is just about to hand over the keys when his wife decides to show me the screened-in lanai and neatly landscaped backyard. The back of the yard ends with a rising berm which separates the couple's property from the land behind it. An old building with a fading red roof rises on the other side amidst overgrown foliage.

"Is that still part of Southern Streams?" I ask. Though I hadn't noticed anything inside, out here in the back area of the house, I detect the slightest hum of metaphysical energy under my feet and in the tips of my fingers. That's not unusual for this area. This area in Spring Hill, Tennessee, was the site of a Civil War battle in 1864, and locations that host historical traumas often contain residual negative energy. I'd felt similar physical reactions while in Franklin, especially when I visited the Carnton Plantation, where many of the badly injured soldiers had been taken during and after the battle. Lots of young men and boys from both sides lost their lives in Franklin.

"Oh no," Mrs. Kozinski explains. "The land on the other side belongs to the old Rippavilla Plantation. I think its ownership is now under the watch of The Franklin Battlefield Trust Organization."

The Rippavilla house sits on Route 31, not too far from the Columbia city border. It has a local reputation for being haunted, but down South, folks think every old house is full of resident ghosts, so I never bothered checking it out for myself on the off chance it was actually playin' host to wanderin' spectors. I'm surprised that Rippavilla's property extends so far back from the main thoroughfare on which the house sits. "Really? This far back? The property is much larger than I imagined," I say.

"Oh yes. It's massive," said Mrs. Kozinski. She waves her hand in the direction of Rippavilla and out towards the land her own house sits on. "We were told this was all a Confederate encampment before the Battle of Spring Hill took place. The Rebs were waiting for the Yank troops to come through Spring Hill. It was the Confederate boys' job to stop the Union troops from moving on toward Franklin, but somehow, the Yanks still managed to sneak by. There was a battle here in Spring Hill. You can still see the battle site down there on Kedron, next to the pizza joint."

I'm familiar with the story. It's part of the area's history. I hadn't, however, put the story together with that of the Kozinski house's location. Now the otherworldly energy I'm feeling makes perfect sense, and I consider that maybe I don't want this job after all. Bad things happened here. Suffering. Death. Heartache. That heavy shit don't ever fade. For someone with the "gift" like me, that kinda' energy can wreak havoc on your soul. It can suck you down and tie your brain all up. These places also tend to be magnets for wanderin' spectors...souls who haven't found their way to the next level. The last thing I need or want is a Johnny Reb haunt lookin' for answers. As I may have mentioned earlier, I'm done with ghosts. Forever.

I'm about to explain to Mrs. Kozinski that I've had a change of heart...that I think maybe their home here is just a mite too far from my imaginary "day job." Before I can start makin' my excuses, she tries to hand me the magnetic entry card for all of the community's activities: the outdoor pool and hot tub, the indoor fitness center and lap pool, the tennis and pickleball courts, and the free lending library. Instantly, I consider how damn fine it would be sittin' by the pool under one of those fancy umbrellas, trashy novel and a cold White Claw in my hands. Accommodations of this sort ain't a regular thing for a girl like me. I think maybe I could do a real thorough sage cleansing and keep the negative ju-ju away. I consider my other options, which at the moment only include Lizzy's lumpy sofa. Then I reach out and take the key card to my summer paradise out of Mrs. Kozinski's hand. "Thank you, Ma'am. I think this is gonna' work out just fine."

Chapter Four

I MOVE INTO THE HOUSE ON SPROCKET SPRINGS THE VERY
same day Mr. and Mrs. Kozinski leave for Minnesota.
Everything I own fits in my car, and I plan to store most
of my stuff in the corner of their garage. Before I bring a
single personal item into the house, I need to do a deep
spiritual cleansing of the negative energy I felt on my
earlier visit. I always find it ironic that Americans are so
concerned about eating clean and using natural products
on their bodies, but so few ever give notice to the metaphysical energy surrounding them on a daily basis.

All living things have a source of spiritual energy that
they spread to the environment. Negative energy begins
in your mind. There's not much we can do about it. As
many of the world religions preach, sufferin' is part of
living. The sufferin' we experience during our lives causes
dark energy to manifest itself in feelings of gloom and
doom anxiety, which then transfers over to our physical
selves in the symptoms of tight muscles, increased blood
pressure, and shallow breathing. This is the bad shit that

people expel into our environments, especially in places with such tragic history.

Before I undertake the cleansing, I spend a solid thirty minutes in deep meditation, clearing my mind of any negativity I hold from my experience with my former landlord. Instead, I focus on Lizzy's kindness toward me and this gift the Universe has bestowed upon me in the form of a lovely place to live while I sort out my future. I review the trust that the Kozinskis have placed in me, and the path that has led me to this moment. When I feel mentally calm, I take out the cleansing materials from their linen bag.

A good smudging only requires three tools; a smudging stick made of White Sage, an abalone shell to catch the ashes, and my feather fan, a gift from my Mamaw on my fourteenth birthday. This fan is one of my dearest possessions. It contains an eagle feather, the tail feather from a red hawk, and a white-tipped wing feather from a wild turkey. The feathers are bound together with a strip of soft leather with several small quartz stones worked into the braiding. It is surely a thing of pure natural energy and beauty, and I feel my Mamaw's presence every time I use it. The collection of these items incorporates all four of the earth's elements: the shell representin' water, the smoke from the burning smudge stick representin' air, the unlit sage a symbol of the earth, and once it's lit, the burnin' herb manifestin' fire.

I unlock the front door and light the smudge stick, blowing on it until the tip glows red. I place the smoking stick in the shell and step inside, leaving the door wide open to allow for the escaping negative energy. Then, I proceed to walk from room to room, using the feather fan to move the smoke into the corners of the room and towards the ceiling. I take my time, going into each room, including the closets and pantries, letting the sage smoke permeate the spaces, while asking, politely, of course, that the negative energy remove itself from this place.

The cleansing goes smoothly, and I can feel the traces of the heaviness left by negative energy disappear from the house. Some of it is newly acquired, perhaps from the building or the process of the owners moving into it, but some of it is of a much older nature, maybe from the Civil War history of the property. It's not until I step outside on the screen porch that I feel what I can only describe as "push back." Though I wave the sage smoke with the feather fan toward the backyard area, it instead wafts back towards me as if someone is blowing it straight back at me. Residual energy, positive or negative, shouldn't be able to do that. Whatever is pushing it back has teeth behind it. Which can only mean one thing. This house, or the land it sits on, has a resident spirit.

The question of whether ghosts are real or not is a hot-bed topic that's been troublin' mankind since folks began walking upright. The belief that the human spirit remains in our physical plane after death has made for some interesting reading. Folks, of course, still enjoy the ghosts in Willie Shakespeare's plays, and hell, what would Christmas be without some rendition or another of Charles Dickens', *A Christmas Carol?* There's also been a shit load of movies portraying evil or mischief-makin' ghosts like *Poltergeist, Beetlejuice* and *The Shining.* The cable channels are full of fame jockeys chasing spirits with their "special cameras" and electromagnetic measuring devices around supposedly haunted places. Even during the Victorian era, the normally reserved upper-class gentry held grandiose seances looking for the opportunity to speak with their "dearly departeds."

I don't bother debatin' the subject anymore. Most people believe what they wanna' believe, with their attitudes firmly anchored in the level of their church-goin', or in some cases, by odd, personal experiences. I've sat through more sermons about specters being nothin' more than agents of the "Evil One" then I ever care to admit. I've been told that this was one of Pastor Ernie Tuft's favorite sermon topics back home in Sevierville, 'specially during my time of trouble with Caleb Nash.

Nowadays, I just keep my mouth shut unless a client specifically asks me for my opinion about loved ones that have passed on, and even then, if I sense a spirit in the room with us, I don't share that information. I've learned my lesson the hard way. I know what I know: every human being has a soul, or if you prefer, an energy source that doesn't end when their physical body does. Most go onto the next level of existence and are gone forever from our plane of reality. A few don't; the reasons for this are as varied as the souls themselves. And the few who don't sometimes reach out to those of us who have the "gift," we "lucky," or "unlucky" individuals, depending on one's point of view, who are tuned to an entirely extra frequency of this here Universe.

I met my first specter when I was seven years old. Mamaw and I had gone into the woods to gather up some Pink Turtleheads for a neighbor suffering from digestion problems. I was already showin' some signs that I might have inherited the family "gift," and Mamaw had begun to start my training in herb lore. We was about a mile or so away from home when I saw a Cherokee brave standing near a grove of tall Fraser Firs. He raised his hand to me in greeting, and I waved back. Mamaw noticed and quietly asked, "Who ya'll wavin' at Delia?"

I explained there was an "injun man" standin' over by them firs. She told me to stand still and proceeded to draw a castin' circle around me, sprinklin' the circumference with a mixture of ground salt and quartz crystals that she always carried in a little drawstring bag in her pocket. Later, I would learn that the circle was meant to keep the spirit from takin' possession of my body, though since then, I've also learned that only the strongest of spirits could ever do such a thing.

Once protected, my Mamaw encouraged me to speak to the Cherokee. He told me his name was *Degataga*, which in his language meant "to stand firm." He said he'd been murdered by another brave in his tribe over the love of the chief's daughter and that his head and feet had been removed from his body and tossed in a nearby stream. Thus, he'd been deprived of his "life ceremony" and had been prevented from finding his rightful way to the "nightworld." I remember crying when he told me his sad story, the weight of his pain a real physical thing to me, and I'd promised to pray for him at Sunday School. Then, the brave just disappeared, evaporatin' into the mountain fog. Hence forward, my Mamaw doubled up her efforts to get me trained in the basics as quick as possible, explaining to me that when one was greatly gifted, one was expected to give even more back to the Universe.

Since that autumn day in the woods, I've met my fair share of ghosts, unfortunate souls who sometimes ask for my help in order to move on. Like livin' people, these spirits have their own personalities. Some are sad, some are resentful over their state, and others are just plain 'ole confused. None of them ever have posed a risk to my well-being, and I have had more successes than failures in aiding my spirit friends. Until the last time. What happened with Caleb wasn't his fault at all. That disaster was caused by nothing more than a general ignorance and misunderstanding of things not seen. Still, it changed my whole perspective about "the Universe's gift," and without Mamaw to talk me through my doubts, I have officially turned my back on the vocation of aiding needy specters.

Whoever is lingering here on the Kozinskis' lanai is obviously an older spirit who has learned over time to manifest its personal energy in physical manners. The newly dead are often like children, afraid and unsure, reaching out to any life source for comfort or reassurance. That is why so many people claim they can "sense" their loved ones shortly after they die; it's their loved ones trying to understand that their time here is over. Eventually, these spirits move on to the next plane, but some, apparently like the one blowing my smudging smoke back at me, linger beyond what is normal.

I inhale the cleansing smoke and try to speak to the spirit. "Wandering soul...I sympathize with your plight. But I am not the one you seek. I can't help you, and I do not want your presence in this space. Be gone from here."

I feel the energy surrounding me move away from the lanai, but it stands firmly outside the screened porch and lingers. The fact that this spirit is able to move about this way in broad daylight proves its age and strength. The reason most people see ghosts at night is because the energy of the sun during the day overshadows that of the entity. But my old friend here is able to work around this issue, again testifying to both its intelligence and afterlife experience. I know better than to underestimate a specter of this kind. I leave the white sage stick smoking in front of the door to the lanai and return to the house to retrieve some items from my metaphysical ditty bag.

Like my Mamaw before me, I have my own concoction to help keep spirits and otherworldly presences away from me. My mixture contains pure sea salt, ground amethyst, powdered sage, and cayenne pepper. I return to the lanai, glad to see that the specter has remained outside of the house's structure, though it's still very much present in the backyard. I sprinkle the mixture all around the inside of the screen porch, creating a barrier to prevent the ghost from passing through. As I turn to go back into the house with a plan to do the same to all the windows and doors, I hear a voice in my head, definitely male and surely with the same southern drawl I've heard all my life: *"Please, Ma'am, I need yar' help."*

CHAPTER FIVE

I IGNORE THE PLEA. INSTEAD, I RETURN INSIDE, CAREFUL TO be thorough with the rest of the wardin' of the house. I leave no window unprotected, including the two tiny ones in the dining area that oddly are smaller than the rest of the house. Summer in Middle Tennessee is ungodly hot, and despite doubt that I'll be openin' any of them windows, certainly not with the blissful AC running at full blast, it still ain't worth the risk to take careless chances. Lost souls can be extremely persistent, especially ones that have been hangin' on to their earthly space for longer than what's good for 'em.

Experience has taught me that most specters can move only within a small radius from where they took their last breaths. I learned this lesson the hard way. It was Caleb Nash who gave me most of my understanding regardin' the abilities of lost souls. Maybe it was his youthful age that made him so open, or perhaps it was the violent end to his life. I was never sure. All I do know is that despite Caleb's eventual move to the next plane of existence, my connection with him and everything that happened that summer, changed my life forever...

***

JULY 2ND, 2015

The week Caleb Nash went missing was one of the hottest in Tennessee recorded history. Temperatures reached well over 100 degrees for several days in a row, hitting 109 at one point, and puttin' a strain on folks' tempers along with the electrical grid. I had just moved down to Nashville from Sevierville six weeks earlier, still grievin' the loss of my Mamaw and with only four hundred dollars in my pocket.

I'd rented a long-stay room at a cheap motel on Gallatin Pike and picked up a position at the Ingleside branch of the Nashville Public Library only a few blocks away. The job paid shitty, but the library was air-conditioned, and as part of its summer program, I was given the wonderful opportunity of puttin' free books into the hands of some of Nashville's neediest children. As a poor kid myself, I knew the magic that books could provide. Not the kind of magic Mamaw was trainin' me in. No. Reading took me on adventures of the mind that a rural kid like me, livin' in near poverty, had little chance of ever experiencin' in real life. The library's low pay meant I had to watch how I spent every nickel, but surrounded by books and eager kids, I felt like I'd landed the best damn job in Nashville.

Part of my duties included tutoring local kids whose teachers had recommended them for extra help during the summer break. I was assigned to the Middle School group, a circle of 4th and 5th graders who needed help in basic math and reading skills. I didn't have any formal training as a teacher, but I was the third oldest of fourteen of my Mamaw's grandkids, so I'd had plenty of experience takin' care of young ones. All of my little "pupils" found the requirement of havin' to attend to school work during their summer break akin to bein' tossed head first into pig shit. They came to me three times a week with a chip on their shoulders, butts slumped in their chairs and eyes focused on the large clock on the wall next to us. Some of them made their displeasure a personal gift to me, dropping books and pencils on the floor, poking and prodding other students, and givin' me the complete cold-shoulder, silent treatment. Caleb Nash was the worst of them all, gracin' me with the best he had to give of pre-teen annoyance.

But Caleb Nash didn't know he was playin' against a Master Classroom Agitator. I had spent most of my growin' up years with the sacred childhood goal of drivin' my unfortunate teachers to distraction. I knew all of Caleb's tricks, plus some of my own. Instead of tryin' to change his behavior, I worked harder on makin' him and the other kids WANT to be part of my lessons. I dumped all the lesson plans and the photo-copied worksheets the public school had given us in the trash and used hands-on activities that looked more like "games" to my young charges and less like "school stuff." After three weeks of this, all of the kids in my group showed substantial gains in their weekly testing scores, and I was heartily givin' myself more than a few pats on the back.

To this day, I wonder if perhaps had I not been so busy tryin' to be "Teacher of the Year," would I have been more aware of any premonition of the tragedy that was about to befall both Caleb Nash and me.

I STEP THROUGH THE BACK DOOR ONTO THE LANAI AND throw out some metaphysical "feelers." I feel nothing other than the slight hum from the wards I set up earlier. The specter, whoever he is, no longer is around. I want to think that this will be a permanent solution, but I know better. Needy spirits, especially those with enough energy to wander about during the day, don't usually give up that easily. I don't know enough about him to determine whether he's a lost soul or one that's determined to hang around and cause havoc upon the living, though I think that if he were a "haunter," I would have felt some malevolence from him, which I did not.

For now, I simply vow to let things proceed as the Universe wills. If Mr. Specter returns, I will be determined and strong in my demands for him to leave me be. I have a few more tricks up my sleeve that I can use on those souls who don't take the hint to cease and desist, but these methods are emotionally painful both for me and the spirit, so I use them only as a last resort. Truth be told, I've only had to resort to using these "juju" spells twice in my life; once with a ghost hauntin' the abandoned Tennessee State Prison in Nashville, and once with a murder-suicide victim who refused to leave the apartment in which she died, rending it unleasable for the landlord.

I consider doing a Tarot spread to see if I can glean any additional information about my new ghost neighbor, but decide to wait until later in the evening when the sun's energy will be less interferin.' With that in mind, I decide to spend my time stackin' my packed boxes in the

Kozinskis' garage and carryin' my sparse personal items into the house's guest bed and bathroom.

It's a typical Tennessee summer scorcher, with temps hovering near the upper 80s, and humidity so high that my clothes are damp from just that little bit of effort. I think about that swimmin' pool I saw when I drove into the community, all blue and dazzlin' white, lookin' chill as hell. I resolve that after the mornin' I've had, I deserve a few hours of R and R. My situation bein' what it's been, I haven't had much use for a bathing suit, so to retrieve the one only I do have requires me to dig through one of those boxes I just left out in the garage. I find it with more ease than anticipated, though it looks in worse shape than I remember, faded and with some bad pulls in the fabric. Perhaps later this week I will consider usin' some of my house-sittin' cash to pick up a new one over at the discount store on Main Street, but today this old, ratty one will have to make due.

One of the big fluffy towels in the guest bathroom and my summer flip-flops are about all I need before headin' out to my car, the magnetic key card to the pool gate safely tucked into the back pocket of my cut-offs. As a second thought, I run back in and grab a paperback novel from the shelf in the living room, a cheerful lookin' para-normal romance about a tooth fairy who finds love with a tax accountant, the kinda' book ya' wanna' read when you're just lookin' to relax.

The pool area at Southern Streams is hard to miss, as it sits right on the main thoroughfare behind some big building called the "Lodge," which, truthfully, don't look like any lodge I've ever seen. Nary a log in sight. I park my beat-up clunker in the back so it won't stand out much among the shiny golf carts and fancy rides situated out in the front rows, and follow some people carryin' floats and towels that I assume are headin' toward the pool.

A nice man holds the gate open for me so the key card isn't even necessary. The pool deck is mostly empty, just a few people layin' around and a stack of water aerobics equipment probably left over from a class that must have gone on earlier this morning. I find a nice spot for myself with an umbrella in the far corner. Settin' out my towel, I make myself comfortable but only turn the first few pages of the novel before I begin to feel the tiniest bit of vibration underneath my chair. At first, I tell myself that I must be imagin' it, my mind havin' trouble lettin' go of the wanderin' spirit. When the vibratin' continues, I blame it on the fact that this community sits on land with a lot of active history and thus tons of residual energy. After it continues for several more minutes, I make up my mind to get into the water.

Water can either help or hamper cosmic energy. For specters and vibes of the negative kind, it's a hindrance. If this buzz is from the land's past, the water should dampen it. I don't think for a moment that this might be caused by my new-found spirit friend as we are much too far from the Kozinski's home, and specters normally don't have the power to travel long distances.

Dropping my book on the metal side table and sticking the edge of my hat into the book to hold my place, I walk to the edge of the pool and ease myself into the cool water. I am correct in my assumption. In the water, I feel no vibrations and no buzzing. I head toward the lap end of the pool and spend a good twenty minutes effortlessly cutting through the lane. The movement of muscle through water is a healing balm to my ambushed psyche, and for the first time in weeks, I truly relax, mind, body and spirit. When I'm good and tired, I pad back to my pool chair on scalding pavement, dripping wet and in need of my towel, only to find that my hat is now lying on the seat by itself and a single, full-bloomed, wild rose is bookmarking my romance novel.

Chapter Six

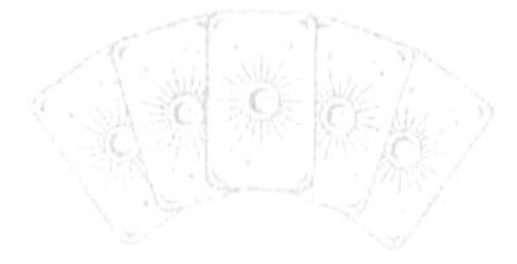

I make a 360-degree turn and see that there are only four other people here down at the pool with me, this bein' the hottest part of the day and all. There's an older couple at the other end floatin' about on air mattresses, a woman sittin' on the pool's edge, danglin' her feet in the water in the water and readin' a novel, and a maintenance guy cuttin' back a large, thorny bush hangin' well over the pool fence. None of them are anywhere near close enough to have fussed with my stuff without me seein' 'em do so. Plus, I am aware that the wild rose left for me is thought to be a bothersome weed by most Southern folks and its invasive spread is usually found in areas left undisturbed by the hands of mindful gardeners.

I throw my hat over the offending bloom, plop down on the lounger, and close my eyes. I still feel the slight vibration I felt when I first arrived, but it's far too faint to be a manifestation of a spirit. In fact, what I'm thinking right now is counter to everything I know regardin' lost souls and simply is a case of my imagination runnin' away with me. I tell myself that someone here at Southern Streams left me the rose just to play with me, either amused or annoyed that I obviously am not a true 55-plus resident of Southern Streams.

Today's impromptu trip to the pool was supposed to be the first of many relaxin' afternoons I'd envisioned for this summer, so I refuse to let any damn specter ruin it for me. I grab a bottle of hard lemonade from my bag, left as a gift for me by the Kozinskis, put the hat back on my head, and pick up my paperback. Superstition, mixed with Mamaw's training, forces me to toss the rose in the bushes behind me without touchin' it, using my towel to do so, just in case I'm wrong about where it came from.

I sip on my hard lemonade and try to involve myself in the antics of the dentist turned tooth fairy who is the main character in my book. However, no matter how hard I try, I can't bring myself to concentrate. The specter out back of the Kozinskis' property and the strange offering here at the pool keeps bringing my mind back to things I'd rather not think about...

July 2nd, 2015

The day started the same as all the others. For a better part of the mornin', my little group of students had been hurd at work on a lesson about fractions. I had spent $4.53 on a peach pie from the Food Mart near the library to use as a demonstration, with the promise that if everyone offered up their best work, there'd be a slice for each student at the end of our time together. It was also the first Thursday of the month. I remember this clear as day, because on the first Thursdays, all the kids in the program were allowed to take home a free book from a stack donated by a local Franklin charity group. For children who didn't have much, this was a big deal, even if more than likely they never actually read the books they carted home. Decisions came hard for Caleb Nash. He liked it better when he had no choices, when things were handed to him without risking the chance that he might unwittingly share a part of himself. The weight of an awful world seemed to sit on that young boy's shoulders.

Most of my students were easily able to pick out their book selections in the relegated twenty minutes. Not Caleb. I watched him pick up book after book from the stack selected for my students' below-average reading levels; he'd glance at each cover, and then put each one back on the table. It was nearly time for the children to go home, and Caleb still hadn't made his choice.

Casually, I sauntered up to him and asked if I could make some suggestions. He flatly turned me down, growling that he "didn't need no stupid baby books." Trusting a hunch, I agreed, throwing in a mention that I knew he was a much stronger reader than most of his classmates. He looked at me with a level of distrust as I walked him over to the table set aside for the Jr. High kids. "I think you should select from this table, Caleb," I told him. At first, he poked half-heartedly at the books. Then, I watched as he picked up a large volume with a particularly vibrant cover depicting two armored knights involved in sword battle. It was a collection of stories and illustrations about King Arthur and the Knights of the Round Table. I noted his wide eyes and still concentration as he turned the pages. Although I knew the text was far above his Lexile reading range, and he would no doubt struggle with understanding the medieval terms, it was the first time I saw in him the magic of anticipation one should feel when they pick up a brand-new book. "Can

I have this one, Miz Achley?" he asked in a faltering voice, setting himself up for the disappointment he expected.

I nodded my head in agreement. "Of course, Caleb! And a mighty fine choice that is! Ya'll can never go wrong reading tales about brave knights who fight for justice." Caleb Nash looked back at me and smiled with just the barest glimmer of turned up lips. This was the first time I'd seen him smile since I'd started working with the boy. He carried that book proudly out the library doors, seemingly lighter in step than when he'd walked in that morning. To this day, I can't see a book or movie with a King Arthur theme without my stomach goin' all queasy on me.

TRY AS I MIGHT, I CAN'T SEEM TO SHAKE THE DUST OF THE past from my head. That damn wild rose I threw into the bushes behind me ain't helpin' matters either, lingerin' in my thoughts like a stray kitten ya' fed just that one single time. The couple from the pool gives up on their floatin' and are dryin' off, seemingly with the intent of goin' home, and the maintenance man has moved on to other chores. I consider wanderin' over and strikin' up a conversation with the Book Lady, but she hasn't lifted her eyes from the page since I've been here, so common sense tells me she ain't lookin' for company.

I find making connections with the livin' difficult. After my Mamaw passed on, there was no reason for me to stay in Sevierville. I believe my mother is still alive somewhere, but I haven't had any contact with her since I was twelve. Last I heard, she'd moved to Alabama with some carny man, but Ma never was the type to stay in one place very long, so I doubt she's still there. When I left the Smokeys, my siblings were scattered 'cross Tennessee; four of the six had stayed within fifty miles of our hometown, while the others moved closer to the North Carolina border, but they all might as well have been on another continent. They'd never much appreciated my inheritin' the family "gift," so when they all gathered back in Sevierville for Mamaw's funeral, nothing much had changed between us. Then, the trouble that happened later with Caleb just gave them a certified reason to forever boot me from the family tribe.

When I moved down south, I tried to seek out others still practicin' the old ways. There's a whole network of us across most of the Southern states. Opal Gasper was my lifeline when I first got to Nashville. She stepped up and took Mamaw's place in my life, takin' my "hoodoo" trainin' to a higher level than I'd ever reached before. If that disaster with Caleb Nash had never takin' place, I believe I might just have stayed on with Opal. I might have even moved into a leadership role within our little group. It was Opal that warned me against bein' a crusader for wanderin' specters, always preachin' it was a thankless job that did nothin' but suck the energy from a person. Lookin' back, I guess I should have takin' her righteous advice.

I finish my hard lemonade but even the alcohol don't do anything to improve my mood. Finally decidin' I've had enough sittin' and stewin,' I gather up my things to take to the car and head back to the house on Sprocket Springs. As an afterthought, I poke around the bushes to retrieve the wild rose I tossed in there earlier. I'm again careful to use only my towel to touch it. If this really is a ghostly token, the last thing I wanna' do is make physical contact with its energy, inadvertently openin' some metaphysical channel between me and the unwelcome specter. I've only heard stories of that actually happenin', but I've learned my lesson the hard way about not takin' unnecessary chances. These days, I'd rather be safe than sorry.

The lodge is on the way to my car so I make a short detour hoping to find some definitive answers and get a little peace of mind. I pull on the lodge's door, but it's locked, which seems odd for the middle of the day. I see a woman sittin' at the front desk, and I'm pretty sure she sees me as well, but no one comes to my aid. The pool's Book Lady notices me standin' there on her way to the parkin' lot and comes over to help.

"Don't you have your key card, Honey?" she asks.

"Key card?" Then I remember the credit-card-like thing the Kozinskis left for me to use at the pool. I hold the guest card up. "Is this it?" I question.

Book Lady nods affirmatively. She takes it from my hand and runs the back of it over the electronic panel next to the door. "You need to swipe your card just about everywhere in Southern Streams. Security reasons, you know," she explains.

I hear the door click open, so I thank her for her help and wander inside the building. I don't see a single, solitary soul 'cept me and the woman at the front desk, so I can't help but wonder what's bein' kept so secure here at Southern Streams and from whom. The lodge is very fancy, very formal-like, and very quiet. The desk woman smiles politely. "Can I help you, young lady?"

"I hope so," I say. Laying the towel with the rose on the counter I ask, "I was just wonderin' if you could tell me where on the property these flowers might grow?"

She peers at the wild rose through purple-framed glasses. "Oh Sweetie, that's not a flower. It's a weed of sorts; one that's very invasive. You can rest assured you won't find that particular plant as any part of Southern Streams landscaping. Where did you get a hold of it…if I may ask?"

I certainly can't tell her I think a ghost left it for me, so I lie. "Oh…well…it was laying on the ground in the parking lot. I thought it was pretty, is all."

Concern marks her face. "You didn't see anymore, did you?"

"No," I say, continuing the fib. "Just this one."

"Well, if you do find any more, Sweetie, you come tell me, okay? We would need to nip this in the bud…literally," she says, then laughs at her own joke.

This was the answer I expected to get but also the one I dread to hear. On my way home I have only one thing on my mind. I don't even stop to peel off of my wet bathing suit. I race through the house and out the back door, through the lanai and into the yard. Wearing my pool flip-flops, I scramble up the side of the berm. This gives me a good, overall view of the plantation property that butts up to the Kozinskis' yard. There, on the Rippavilla side, just beyond that big 'ole barn, is a sea of pink and white wild roses, a perfect match to the one wrapped up in my pool towel.

CHAPTER SEVEN

THIS IS PRECISELY WHAT I EXPECTED TO SEE WHEN I RUSHED home from the pool. Still, the sight of all the seemingly endless numbers of wild roses on the other side of the berm sucks the air directly from my lungs. As much as I want to, I can't deny that the flower left in my book most likely came from here, or that it was given to me by a lost soul. What truly blows my mind is that the spirit was somehow able to travel nearly a half a mile to accomplish the task. In broad daylight. With the sun at its highest point of the day. Everything I know about specters says this is impossible, yet the proof is there, plain as day, still rolled up in that damp towel.

As I stand on that incline, my first thought is to try and pinpoint where this soul might currently be. I'm not feeling any energy vibrations strong enough to indicate that he is anywhere currently close to where I'm standin', but I have little doubt he's been here recently. However, unlike my ghost buddy who seems not to be much affected by the noon-day sun, my energy gifts are butting right up against it, thus leaving my skills far from their most productive.

There's a good reason why most folks experience specters at night. Everything in the universe is created from energy. As Albert Einstein discovered, energy can neither be created nor destroyed; it can only shift and change from one form into another. As with all matter, this also applies to those whose earthly bodies have ceased to function. Their personal energy doesn't cease to exist; rather, it moves on to the next cycle. For spirits who are trapped in this earthly plane of existence for one reason or another, this energy lets us know they are still here. During daylight hours, the energy of the sun far outweighs any energy emitted by other sources, living or deceased. Therefore, it's mainly at night, when the sun's energy is lessened, that we're able to experience the presence of ghostly energy.

Most people don't even know when they're sharing their space with a lost soul. Most earthly specters go about their wanderings without any fuss, content to remain quietly in the space they feel most comfortable. It's only when they purposefully call attention to themselves that anyone notices them, like when they turn lights on and off, open cabinet doors, knock stuff off countertops, and other similar types of things. The reasons they attempt these activities are as varied as their personalities; but for the most part, ghosts have limited physical abilities and rarely are powerful enough to move uninhibited among the world of the living. Except, of course, the one who's made it clear he wants my attention.

If connecting with this lost soul is what I decide I want to do, then I'll need to wait until this evening. The question is…do I want to make contact? That's an answer I don't yet have as I'm standing on top of this incline with the sweltering Tennessee sun beating down on my head. Also, though wild roses usually don't have a strong scent, this many, in such high heat and humidity, causes the fruity, lemony scent to be overwhelmin', thus makin' me slightly light-headed. I turn back and tread back down the berm more carefully than I'd gone up, feeling lost and somewhat confused at how to proceed.

It takes a nice, long shower and a light lunch of fruit and cheese before I feel well enough to dig deeper into the who and why of my spirit stalker. Common sense says I should start slow when dealing with a ghost possessing the strength of abilities I presume this one has. For that reason, I decide to go with the most basic form of spirit communication…tarot cards. This will allow me to communicate with the spirit without him needing to be physically manifested, and thus allowing me to break any psychic connection should it become necessary.

I begin by brewing a cup of herbal tea with the plan that it will help ground me to the earthly plain. I take my cards, the tea, and several protective crystals out to the lanai. The last thing I want to do is inadvertently invite the lost soul into the Kozinskis' home. Once a specter is "officially invited" into an enclosed space, it's extremely hard to send them on their merry way if they decide they don't wish to leave. The screened porch makes for a much better meeting ground, a sort of neutral territory for both me and my new lost soul friend.

I sweep out the protective mixture I put down earlier, dispersing it onto the grass outside the lanai while leaving it in place at the door that leads directly into the house. I put my tea and cards down on the patio table, along with a chunk of smoky quartz and black tourmaline that I hope will ward off any negative energy Mr. Ghost might bring along with him. Then, I take a seat in one of the comfy chairs and try to settle my mind while I open it to any information the specter wishes to impart through the cards. I am careful to communicate that I do not want any physical contact, nor am invitin' the lost soul to take up residence in my head. This meetin' on the lanai is akin to the livin' world's habit of exchangin' emails or texts before a possible first date.

As I always do, I use the simplest three card spread. I take a sip of the tea, feel its warmth in my mouth and taste the flavor of dried cherries and chamomile, reminding myself of my very real presence in the physical world. I call upon my Mamaw to guide my reading and protect me from metaphysical harm. Then, I shuffle the cards until I am urged by the wandering spirit to stop. I cut the deck into three piles then pull the top card from each stack and lay them face down in front of me on the table.

It isn't hard to feel the specter's presence. There's a hum of energy under my feet, and the temperature on the lanai drops fifteen degrees to a now comfortable alternative to the swelterin', late afternoon heat. I also detect a woodsy scent, the smell of fresh soil and the slightest trace of the citrusy, wild roses; a more physical aspect of a "first meetin'" that's a bit beyond my comfort level. I remind the spirit that we are communicatin' through the cards alone and if he should attempt to force his will on mine, I will immediately end the communication and deny any further attempts at contact.

The woodsy scent grows fainter, and I assume that the lost soul now has put some space between him and me. He still is present on the lanai but is no longer in my personal energy space. I ask him if he is ready to begin, and my mug with the tea rattles on the metal patio table. I take that as an affirmative and ask my first question. "Who am I speakin' with?" I give it a second before I turn over the first card.

The use of Tarot is not a game, and the results are based solely on the practitioner's deep understanding of the symbols and possible meanings of each card along with the strength of their metaphysical intuition. I have been studyin' the Tarot since I've been fifteen years old and have come to trust in both myself and the higher purpose of the metaphysical divination of their meanings. I clearly know better than to take the card's image at face value, but the drawin' of the hanged man is startlin' and my emotions are runnin' high, which leads me to the plantation's sordid history of enslaved people. I wonder if this lost soul possibly is seeking justice for an unjust lynching.

"Spirit...are you the victim of unfair justice?"

The mug on the table stays still, but the vibration under my feet quickens, and I feel a great sense of frustration from my ghostly visitor. I mentally scold myself for jumpin' to such general conclusions. The Hanged Man card in this upright position symbolizes consequences, stagnation, and a situation that must be waited out. With my next question, I backtrack and go in a completely different line of questionin'. "Honorable Specter…have you been 'lost' a long time?"

The mug rattles in the affirmative, so I continue. "More than a hundred years?' The mug rattles again. "More than two hundred years?" The mug stays still so I make the conclusion that the soul probably met its end sometime between the mid 1800s and our current date. I know it's a very wide range, but considerin' the history of the land I'm sittin', I make a reasonable guess. "Spirit, did you meet your end durin' the time of the Civil War?" There is no reaction, and I'm a bit confused. I was sure I was on the right track. Then, I rethink my words and change the question. "Spirit, did you meet your end as a result of 'The Righteous War for Southern Independence?'" I ask. The cup shakes violently, splashing some of the tea up out of it. It's clear now. My ghost friend most likely is a departed Rebel, a sympathizer to the Southern cause.

This is a very good start. Pinpointin' the period and reason for the specter's death will help me analyze the rest of the draw while pointin' me in the right direction if I decide I need further research. I proceed to my next question. "Is there anythin' more you want to tell me about yourself?" I place my hand on the Hanged Man and open my thoughts. Images form in my head of a dark night, a heavily wooded spot. Of Confederate gray and serious hunger. And pain. A seerin', burnin' physical pain that I feel deep in my own belly. In shock, I pull my hand away from the card, breaking the connection between the spirit and myself. Openin' my eyes, I have no doubt that I am now alone on the lanai, the spirit gone from my reach.

I swear at my stupidity and begin to pace the small screened porch. It's damn obvious that I am ridiculously out of practice; that these lost years have turned me into nothin' more than a damn amateur. Ten years ago, I would never have let a specter take the upper hand in a connection attempt usin' the cards. Not like this one apparently just had. I blame my experience with Caleb Nash for the decision to neglect my metaphysical health for as long as I had, but the honest truth is…I'm the only one to blame for screwin' up this first important contact I had with the lost and sufferin', Johnny Reb.

Right now, I'm more than a little disgusted with myself. I consider taking another shower to rinse any remaining negative energy from this past encounter with the hopes of tryin' the cards again. But I sense that the soldier specter was just as alarmed by our connection as I was. Experience tells me that nothing I do will allow me to connect with him again this afternoon. Disgust turns to regret. I should have turned down this house-sitting job when I first felt the energy vibrations and learned of the property's history. I most certainly should have ignored the rose token completely, or at the least, burned it when I got home, and I most definitely should not have removed the wards I set up on the lanai. Finally, from my own personal experience, I should have never, ever, attempted to communicate with a specter that was obviously desperate enough, and powerful enough, to track me in the middle of the frickin' day. There was a very good reason that I had given up helpin' lost souls, and for ten

long years, I had been successful at avoiding gettin'
involved with ghosts. I suppose my luck was bound to run
out at some point.

JULY 2, 2015

THURSDAY WAS MY SHORT WORKIN' DAY, SO I WASN'T FAR
*behind Caleb and the rest of the kids out the door and ready to
enjoy the freedom of a beautiful summer afternoon. I had plans
to head to Hidden Lake State Park on McCory Lane with the
desire to spend the afternoon tubin' on the Harpeth River. It was
the perfect day for some chill time on the water. I had nothin'
important to do and no one I needed to see, so I just went about
enjoyin' the float, in no particular hurry to do anything else.
My car radio had been busted for goin' on two years and I
didn't stop nowhere on my way home, so I never did hear the
terrible news and thus had no damn idea why two of Nashville's
finest was waitin' for me when I arrived back at the motel in the
early evening.*

*Detective Pritchard was a small man with a short-guy-atti-
tude who didn't much care for the fact that he had been required
to wait on me. I got the distinct impression he'd already gone
and made his judgment call 'bout a single woman livin' by
herself in a motel on the seedier side of East Nashville. But as I
had been taught by Mamaw to always respect the law, I was as
polite as polite could be and invited Pritchard and the other
baby-faced patrolman into my room. I heard the news that
Caleb Nash was missin' from them. Apparently, the boy had*

never made it home after his tutorin' session at the library, and no one had claimed to have seen him since.

I recalled the boy's pride as he carried the King Arthur book out the library door. Rememberin' his lighter step and shy smile made my stomach turn at the thought that somethin' terrible might have happened. I didn't dare put out any psychic "feelers." Not with them officers standin' there actin' as if they might get cooties just from sittin' in the chairs I'd offered them. They asked me the same questions several times, takin' turns bein' the hard ass. This weren't no good cop, bad cop thing. Both of 'em disliked me equally. They questioned me about the exact time Caleb Nash left the library. They asked who left with him and was he with any other children. Not wantin' to appear like I was holdin' back information, I relayed the story about the free books and how Caleb had had a hard time choosin' one, tryin' to explain' why he left about ten minutes after the other kids. The two officers exchanged looks between 'em and Pritchard wrote everything down in his little notepad.

Then, in the manner of every police drama I'd ever watched, the short cop asked me what time I left and where I was the whole afternoon and early part of the evening. On TV, this is when the "perp" always asks for a lawyer. But I weren't no perp, and so I told them all the details. Baby Face asked me if anyone could verify my location. I said I was tubin' alone, but that I'd waved to other floaters. He made a face, but then I remembered the receipt for the tube rental I had in my pocket. I showed them the receipt with the time stamp. Pritchard only grunted, then wrote the time in his notepad with a chewed-up pencil.

Chapter Eight

For the rest of the afternoon, I sensed a deep and unsettling mode of guilt concerning my experience with the Johnny Reb. It's a feelin' I haven't had in a very long time and not one that I'd ever planned to repeat. When I finally feel metaphysically strong enough to deal with the ghost again, I unroll the damp towel that's been holdin' the wild rose its prisoner. The bloom is in surprisingly good shape for bein' all scrunched for the past few hours, Still, its lemony scent reminds me of how just how badly I handled my specter friend's presence earlier on the lanai.

I can't explain why the initial contact 'tween me and the soldier boy was so intense, nor why I now continue to feel so badly about it. My feelings are similar to those I'd felt over Caleb Nash, but in that instance, I had personally known Caleb before he'd shed his earthly body. I'd spent time with the boy and had gotten to know him as much as he'd let me. In this case, I don't know the first thing about the personal life of this Johnny Reb, and because he'd probably met his end on this plane of the Universe over

150 years ago, I'd obviously had never met him. Still, I have enough of the "gift" and enough knowledge in me to understand that there must be some type of mystical thread between the two of us. However, "why" is the all-important question I can't answer.

For several years after my Mamaw passed, part of me hoped that someday she'd come aroun' from the Afterlife and let me know how she was doin'. I missed her like nobody's business and some contact with her would have been a true blessin' for my achin' heart. On the other hand, if I actually had been able to make contact with her, it would have meant that she was lost and unable to move on to her next stop, and I loved her too much to wish that for her. A lost soul is a very lonely soul.

So why in the hell is everythin' I have always held to be true tellin' me that this Johnny Reb's seekin' me out' is in some way important to my own earthly journey? Not havin' the answers frustrates me. I waver over what to do with the rose token; previously it had been my plan to burn it, but now after what had happened on the lanai, I find myself unable to do it. Though I had read much on the subject of ghostly gifts, and been directly warned against them, I'd personally never received one, which up until now, I'd always considered a darn good thing.

Specter tokens are often both a blessin' and a curse. Once Mamaw realized I could connect with the departed, she took me to train with a wisewoman practitioner she knew in Pigeon Forge, since Mamaw herself did not have knowledge of that particular gift. Beatrice Flushing was a harsh taskmaster who liked to smack my hands with a hickory stick when I gave her wrong answers, but I'm pretty sure she knew more about specter life than any other livin' person in Tennessee. Her gravelly voice comes back to me as I stand in the Kozinski kitchen, contemplatin' what to do with the wild rose. *"Girl, yo' never, ever, takes a specter's token fo' granted, yo' hear me? If yo' find yo'self thinkin' 'bout keepin' one, then yo' better understand that as long as that soul be walkin' this plane, yo' never gonna be free of 'dem. Whether or not yo' decide to keep it, a token from a departed soul must always be acknowledged…with proper 'tanks and somethin' in return, less yo' wanna make yo'self a ghostly enemy."*

I decide to put off making my final decision regardin' the rose token, but Miz Beatrice was right. I must thank my Johnny Reb for leavin' me the gift and think of somethin' proper to leave him in return. But just what the hell does one get for a soldier boy who's been dead for 158 years?

JULY 3RD, 2015

CALEB NASH'S WANDERIN' SPIRIT WAS THE FIRST TO INITIATE direct contact with me. Prior to him, that had never been my experience with lost souls. I'd always been called in when a lost soul was makin' a nuisance of him or herself, and the living residents of the space were at their wit's ends to have it end. My "services" weren't advertised on billboards or seen on TV commercials mixed in with them ads for personal injury lawyers. I didn't have any kind of social media presence, and I sure as hell wasn't lookin' for no five-star reviews on Yelp. My assistance usually was found by word of mouth from folks who'd had their own little ghost problems solved and were more than happy to pass my name along.

I solved my first "official" specter problem back in Sevierville the month after I'd turned sixteen. A neighbor down the ways from my family farm had found himself bothered by a lost soul causin' havoc in his barn day and night. That specter had scared off two hired hands and upset the hens so much they'd refused to lay. When the stressed birds finally did produce, the end results weren't of the proper size or quality to sell to the local markets. My Mamaw already had a long reputation 'round those parts for bein' a local "wisewoman", so it was no surprise that Fred Thompson sought out the advice of Aurora Achley. Truth be told, he weren't all that excited when my Mamaw insisted that her teenage granddaughter, Cordelia Mae, was truly was the right Achley for the job.

As I've said before, I come from a long line of women who've been blessed by the Universe with gifts most people don't possess. Those of us who inherit this branch of the family genes go by the surname, "Achley," no matter who our daddies might be. This was particularly helpful in my case 'cause my Mama weren't never really sure which man's DNA I carried. I was named Cordelia Mae Achley from birth, my Mamaw bein' convinced from my first breath I was "special" and my Mama not much carin' one way or other. I suppose it was a good thing my Mamaw was right about me. I would have felt pretty bad 'bout myself if I had ended up with a name I didn't deserve.

Fred Thompson agreed to let me try to rid him of his haunt. I was equally parts scared and excited 'bout gettin' my first big chance to show what I could do. As it turned out, it was an easy *fix. The blusterin' specter first attempted to frighten me away by throwing various barn material at me, but I could tell that the he or she didn't possess a very strong energy. It turns out the lost soul was just a boy about the same age as me who had once attended the old Island View, one- room Schoolhouse near Boyd's Creek Highway. He'd been actin' the fool and his teacher, a rather large man by the name Mr. Fulton, had threatened to whoop his behind. The boy ghost, who never did give up his name, fled the school when the teacher wasn't lookin' and hid in the surroundin' woods, afraid to go home and face expected punishment. Unfortunately, the boy ended up coming up against a mama bear protectin' her young that fateful day and thus found himself on the other side of the livin'.*

It didn't take much convincin' to persuade him to go towards the light when it presented itself. He weren't a very smart boy, either before or after his demise, and when I told him I was absolutely sure that if he went into that light he'd be absolutely free of school, chores, and any more whoopins', he was more than happy to oblige. I asked him real nice-like not to scare the hens as he went 'cuz it was cruel to them and I said that he didn't seem like a mean boy. He agreed, and then he was gone, just like that. In the blink of an eye.

Fred Thompson was mighty glad to have gotten himself rid of that ghost, and he paid Mamaw for my services with two fine laying hens. I felt funny 'bout takin' payment for my "ghost work," but Mamaw scolded that if I didn't charge somethin', folks wouldn't take me seriously or give me the respect I deserved. Thus, from that day forward, Cordelia Mae Achley always took payment for her "hoodoo work." Little did I know that someday in the future I'd end up gettin' punished for it instead of paid. Life's funny that way.

When Caleb Nash sought me out on his own in the early mornin' hours of that July day, showin' himself in my crappy motel room, I should have severed our metaphysical connection immediately, no matter how pitiful the boy's pleas were. The fact that he'd come lookin' for me rather than me lookin' for him should have acted as a big warnin' that somethin' awful was afoot. But in that regard, Cordelia Mae Achely was a bigger fool than that boy ghost I helped in Fred Thompson's barn.

Chapter Nine

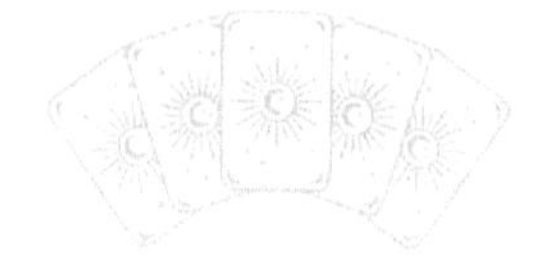

I don't own a laptop, and doin' research on my old phone with a cracked screen turns out to be a giant pain in the ass. I'm pretty sure Spring Hill must have a library, and that would undoubtedly be my best bet for figurin' out the proper token to leave my mysterious specter, even though I have mostly avoided libraries since…well…Caleb Nash, I decide that's what needs to be done. A quick check of Google maps verifies that the town does indeed have a public library further down on Kedron Parkway, a little less than two miles from the Kozinski house. It's too far to walk in this heat, so I decide to drive myself there.

The Spring Hill library is like every other smalltown library here in the south. I am greeted and offered help by the head librarian, a pleasant lady in her 60's, who shows me to the section that holds all their books on the area's local history. She reminds me that I'm also able to use the library's computers for research and leaves me to my work. I set myself down in front of a computer and type the words "Confederate Soldier" into the search bar.

It's a broad topic and I am faced with over 35,000 possible links. I narrow down my topic and find a few websites that describe daily life for a low-ranking "Johnny Reb." I don't know for sure that my lost soul isn't an officer, but somethin' about his demeanor during our brief encounter leads me to believe he's on the younger side at the time of his demise and not very worldly. I also believe my specter ended his earthly life somewhere in the area around the house where I'm stayin', despite his unique ability to travel around the property. I could very well be wrong in all my assumptions, but this seems like a logical place to start my research.

Born in Tennessee, I grew up knowin' all about my state's role in the Righteous War for Southern Independence, but for some reason I find myself now especially drawn to the history surroundin' the Battle of Spring Hill and the subsequent tragic Battle of Franklin. I lose myself in the rich passages describin' them, and before I realize it, the afternoon has slipped away from me. I still don't have a token to leave for my dead soldier boy; but I do have a solid idea. I check Google Maps again and am pleased to find my planned destination is not far from the library and has late evening hours.

I also find several books I want to take with me, but unfortunately, I don't have a library card nor can I apply for one without a permanent address. I throw caution to the wind and seek out the same lady that helped me when I walked in earlier. I explain to her that I am house-sitting for a couple who live in Southern Streams and that I really want to learn more about the history of the town while I'm here for the summer and that I don't have a library card. She looks at my Community Guest Card and notes the resident's name. Lucky for me, the library lady also lives in Southern Streams and knows the Kozinskis. She swipes her own card and pushes the books my way, making me promise to learn all I can before I "return home." This pleases me, but I am not surprised at her kindness or generosity. People down South are just this way.

My library research leads me to decide on a gift of tobacco. I know full well that spirits do not have the ability to physically enjoy the things they'd once treasured, but from first-hand experience, I have found it to be true that the lost souls still deeply carry the memories of these items. My decision wavered between Tennessee whiskey and a pipe and tobacco, but rememberin' how some people down South feel about the consumption of alcohol, I err on the side of caution and choose the pipe.

The Tobacco Station is a one-stop destination for anything smoke related. I wander about the large store a bit, unsure as to what exactly I want. I know that someone like my "Johnny Reb" would most probably have used a corn cob pipe, but which one? I end up asking the gentleman behind the counter which of the six corn cob pipes look most like those used during the Civil War. I explained to him that my grandpap is involved with a reenactment group and that I want to gift him with a real nice pipe to add to his costume. He picks me out a fine one called, "The Diamondback," which was pretty pricey in my mind at $35. When I hesitate, he throws in a can of flake tobacco for free, expressin' his gratitude to my grandfather for keeping the "Dixie Spirit" alive. As he packs up my purchases, I smile to myself wonderin' what that gentleman might have thought if he knew that an actual "Dixie spirit" had never left Spring Hill.

I drive back to Southern Streams with the pipe and tobacco on the seat next to me and a bellyful of optimism. If the specter takes my token like I hope he does, perhaps he'll be comfortable enough to let me help him move on. Truthfully, I'm more than just a little curious to understand how he is able to do the things that are beyond the reach of most other lost spirits. I ignore the warning bells clanging in my head scoldin' me over connectin' too intimately with a wandering soul. I sure as hell should have learned my lesson with Caleb Nash. But there's something about this Johnny Reb that draws me to him, and I know I won't be satisfied unless I find out what that is.

When I get home, I make myself a turkey sandwich, courtesy of the ever-hospitable Kozinskis, and take it out to the lanai to enjoy. It's mid-evening and the setting sun is casting long shadows on the berm in the back of the yard. I don't feel the specter's presence, not even in the slightest. No vibration, no chill...nada. I worry that perhaps he's decided not to seek my attention any further. Still, I've gone to so much trouble and expense to secure a proper token, I decide that I will leave it and accept whatever occurs.

There's a great deal of truth in the old stories regardin' the so-called "witchn' hour," the time between 3:00 and 4:00 AM. Historically, psychic phenomena can peak during these hours. Nothing I've ever read has ever pinpointed the exact reasons why, but I've found that my metaphysical abilities do seem especially potent during that sixty-minute span, so I figure that'll be the best chance of making my next contact with the lost soldier boy.

I'd originally planned to stay awake until I deemed it late enough, and dark enough, to leave my token on the berm and not be seen doing so by any of the neighbors. However, after a long day of moving in, paddling around the pool, and traveling all over town, I quickly doze off in front of the T.V. I awake much later with a terrible crick in my neck, a puddle of drool on the throw pillow, and the only light in the room coming from the television's glow. I panic for a second, thinking I might have gone and slept through the whole damn witchin' hour, but a quick look at my phone reveals that it's only a little after 1:00 AM, which allows me plenty of time to get my gift ready and leave it on the berm.

As I have said, most departed souls have limited physical abilities, but this particular one seems to have more than most. Still, within the range of knowledge I have about him, I can't be sure of what he can or cannot do. Therefore, I don't want to make my token too hard for him to access, which means no wrappins' or gift bags. On the other hand, I don't want to just leave it in the weeds as if it's just trash. My goal is to make him understand that it's a gift from me to him. Thus, I find a used Amazon box among my hosts' recycling items, remove its labels and cut the flaps off its top, making it easier for the specter to remove my token from it in whatever way he's able. I take a sheet of paper from the printer in the sunroom and write the words, "THANK YOU FOR THE ROSE. I WANT TO HELP YOU. CAN WE PLEASE MEET

AGAIN?" I place the note in the box along with the new pipe and the can of tobacco.

The houses in this community are very close together, so I try my best not to make unnecessary noise when I leave the house and the lanai. The sound of the screen door latching shut seems crazy loud to me, and I freeze for a second, waiting for lights to go on in the houses surroundin' me. Since everything stays quiet and dark, I make my way to the back of the yard and up the small hill overlooking the Rippavilla property. The grass is high and it's dark meanin' I'm careful where I step, grateful I chose to wear my cowboy boots lest I step on somethin' slitherin' 'round up here. I decide on a spot between two small trees that will give me a specific vantage point to watch, and I place my token there and return to the lanai to wait it out.

And wait I do. It's nearly 4:00 AM and the sky is turning from smooth black velvet to the darkest shade of purple when the hair on my arm stands up and I feel a definite prickle of energy under my feet. I peer into the darkness through the screen of the lanai walls at the space between the two trees. At first, I see nothing. I know from the vibrations that something metaphysical is out there, but there's no apparition. Then, as I squint and stare hard, I see the slightest flicker of an electrical charge that slowly materializes into a standing figure of a man right there on the berm. With both excitement and curiosity, I stand and reach for the lanai door so I can see more clearly without the interference of the screen, but as soon as my hand hits the latch the image disappears and the energy I felt only a second ago evaporates like rain on a hot pavement.

I whisper under my breath "Wait...don't go," but I already know that my Johnny Reb is no longer there. Disappointed, I leave the lanai and head up the berm to see whether the specter at least had accepted my token. The box is right there where I left it, looking very much untouched, and my heart sinks. I pick it up and the item in the box rolls around, but it's not my token. The pipe and tobacco are gone, and something else is in its place.

CHAPTER TEN

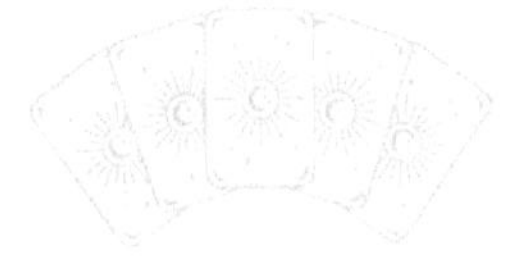

I PEER INTO THE CARDBOARD BOX, BUT IT'S MUCH TOO DARK on the berm for me to determine what's inside. I know better than to make skin to skin contact with anything recently handled by a specter, 'specially if I'm not sure what it might be or how much metaphysical energy it possibly may hold. Carrying the box back to the house so's I can get a better look, my heart thumps in my chest so fast I can feel it in my ears. To have this much physical interaction with a lost soul is highly unusual, and I am in brand new territory as far as my understandin' of what souls can do after they leave their earthly body.

I go on into the house, careful not to let the noisy screen door slam shut behind me, and flip the light on in the kitchen. I learn that the item rollin' about in the old Amazon box is a rock: a crystal actually, and a beautiful one at that. I still don't want to handle it with my bare hands, so I hunt under the sink, looking for some rubber gloves. Sure enough, I find a pair that will work perfectly as a barrier between me and the ghost token.

Once I pick it up and am able to examine it closely, I see that the token is a natural quartz crystal. I've used many crystals in my spirit work, but this one is an especially beautiful specimen; it's so clear it's earned the appropriate nickname of "field diamond." Made of silicon and oxygen, clear quartz has been used for thousands of years as an energy amplifier and a purifying stone, while bein' especially good for manifestin' your desires to the Universe. My collection of spiritual stones contains several of them, but none of them are of this quality or strength.

I am a whirlwind of questions. Where did the crystal come from? How did it come to be in the possession of this lost soul? Does this Johnny Reb understand the metaphysical benefits of his token? If so, is that why he gave it to me?

It's not yet 5:00 AM, and I should be dead on my feet from lack of sleep, but this new token has me buzzing with excitement. I need to do more research on the property my Johnny Reb calls "home," countin' on it to lead me to the answers I seek. Placing the crystal back in the box, I dig through the stack of books I brought home from the Spring Hill library. I find the one I'm looking for, a thick volume containing several chapters on the history of the Rippavilla Plantation. I make myself a cup of tea, pull a few cookies from the jar on the island, grab the library book, and make myself nice and cozy in the guest room.

And cozy it is. Mrs. Kozinski has made the room so warm and invitin' that even though I am a complete stranger, I am surrounded by positive, welcomin' energy the moment I enter. The room's decor is soft and feminine, and it would be hard to imagine anyone having anything but sweet dreams in such a peaceful, calming place. I place my tea and cookies on the side table and am about to curl up in the extra wide armchair next to it, when a thought crosses my mind. I find a glass vase in one of the kitchen cabinets and add water to it. Then, using the rubber gloves, I stick the wild rose token inside. I take the vase with the rose, grab the crystal from the box, along with my cards, and head back to the guest room.

My experiences with this particular lost soldier boy have been unlike any previous encounters with any other spirits, so I feel as if I'm travelin' this road more than a little blind. Still, if this lost soul wishes to make further contact, then I plan to surround myself with metaphysical boosters that will help give him a little "leg up" and allow him to understand that I'm interested in further communication. I place the vase with the rose and the crystal on the table. Then I remove my gloves, settle my focus, and quickly do a three-card spread.

The first card once again is The Hanged Man in the upright position. Somehow, I'm not surprised. My specter friend is in a type of waiting pattern, unable to move forward. The next card I turn over is the Eight of Swords in the Reversed Position. This card typically signifies some form of imprisonment or the feeling of being trapped. It's bein' reversed means that persistence and ingenuity will be necessary to become free of it. Superficially, this card makes perfect sense to me in this particular case: the Johnny Reb is imprisoned in this earthly domain, and it requires my perseverance to help him move on. Yet, I feel somethin' ain't right with this interpretation, and I deeply perceive I'm missing something of grand importance. Impatient, I flip the last card to reveal The Lovers. This probably is the most misunderstood card in the Tarot deck. Although it sometimes can be related to romantic and sexual relationships, it's more often a sign of emotional or physical healing. Tonight, I'm convinced that I'm making generalizations about all of these cards' meanings that my soul knows are far too shallow. I have an overwhelming feeling of frustration that I'm not sure is coming from my own psyche, from my Johnny Reb's, or from the two of us combined.

This is a far more confusing spread than I'd anticipated, but my lack of sleep and the adrenaline caused by the prospect of seeing my specter's physical manifestation have thrown me totally off kilter. I leave the cards in their positions and pick up the library book instead. I find the chapters on Rippavilla and begin to read. Sadly, I don't get too far. After only a few minutes, the words on the page begin to blur, and before I even can close the book or crawl into the bed, I fall into a deep, dream-filled sleep.

JULY 3RD, *2015*

I'M PRETTY SURE THE PART OF MY SOUL THAT HOLDS MY "GIFTS" knows Caleb Nash is dead the moment those policemen tell me he's gone missing. A cold shadow of foreboding settles about my person, which only adds to my general uneasiness about talkin' to two of Nashville's finest regardin' the last time I'd seen the boy. I also git' the distinct feelin' that though neither of the officers like me much, Pritchard's animosity towards me goes beyond the fact that I am a single woman, non-native to the area, and livin' in a transient motel in the seedier part of East Nashville. Their visit causes so much negative energy to gather in my room that I am forced to do a thorough sage cleanse once they leave to rid my space of it.

After the conversation I just had with Baby Face and Pritchard, there is no chance I will be able to rest peacefully this evening. I set out a few of my stronger crystals and light a purple and black candle: the black is for further cleansing and protection, and the purple for encouraging psychic abilities and spiritual crossovers. I close my eyes and work to calm my racing heart and mind.

I am not at all surprised when I feel a metaphysical pull in my motel room. Instinct I neither can understand nor verify has predicted that Caleb might reach out to me, and this vibe in my motel room is proof. Initially, I only feel his presence. I don't see any type of physical manifestation at all. "Is that you, Caleb?" I ask out loud. "Don't be afraid. It's just me here, Caleb...Miz Achley from the library. You can show yourself, Honey. It's ok. I want to help you."

A spot across from my bed loses solid clarity, and the temperature in the room noticeably drops a few degrees. I hear the faintest sound of a child's whimpering. "Caleb...Sweetheart...I know you're here, Honey, but I can't see you. I want to help. I truly do. Tell Miz Achley what's wrong, Caleb."

A specter mist I've seen countless times before gathers in that same spot. I can make out the faintest image of the boy along with a pungent, unwashed, fishy smell. This isn't unusual. I have found that lost souls hang onto their personal odors far *longer than any other physical aspect of what was once their earthly bodies. The smell of unwashed body and clothes is not unusual to the Caleb I'd been teaching. The moldy, fishy smell, however, is new.*

Very slowly, the undefined mist begins to take on a more solid shape. I keep quiet except to murmur little bits of care and encouragement. Not surprisingly, child spirits are the most upset to find themselves separated from the earthly plane. In fact, most lost souls labeled poltergeists have turned out to be child specters who are confused and frightened, lashing out in frustration and seeking intervention and help. In truth, they often are also the easiest types of souls to re-direct toward their afterlife if one is careful to remember that they are, in essence, simply lost kids. They are seeking someone to help them find their way home. Unlike adult souls, who often carry a heavy load of life baggage and unfinished business, child spirits eagerly follow directions. Convincing Caleb's soul to move along to the Afterlife shouldn't be all that difficult...

I wake up in a cold sweat, the tea on the table beside me ice cold and the book I had in my lap now upside down on the floor. The leg tucked underneath me for the past several hours is now completely numb, and I need to walk around the room for a few minutes to get the feeling back. The time on my cell phone reads 9:46 AM, meaning that I've been asleep in the armchair for over four hours. Memories of Caleb Nash are the last thing I need or want right now. I wonder if my dreaming of him is a sign from the Universe that I should avoid gettin' tangled up with this lost Johnny Reb spirit. I look at the spread I cast earlier this morning, and my heart jumps into my throat. I clearly remember that when I laid the cards out in the wee morning hours the Hanged Man was in the Upright posi-tion. Now the card is reversed, signaling an entirely different meaning. None of the other cards have been moved, nor does it appear that anything else on the table was touched. A million possibilities of what this could mean hits me all at once, and when the Ring Doorbell chimes, loud and shrill, I literally jump.

I peer through the front window and see a woman holding a plate. Finger combing my sleep tangled hair, I open the door and ask, "Can I help you?"

The woman smiles and holds out the plate toward me. "You must be Delia! So nice to meet you! Emma said you'd be house-sitting for her. I'm your next-door neighbor, Sylvie Weathers. I thought you might like a sweet treat, so I made these cookies for you. Welcome to Southern Streams."

I want to offer my thanks but the experiences of the last several hours have left me not functioning on all mental cylinders. I must look like a complete nut to the nice lady next door, because her smile turns to a look of concern. "Are you alright, Sweetie? You look like you've seen a ghost."

Chapter Eleven

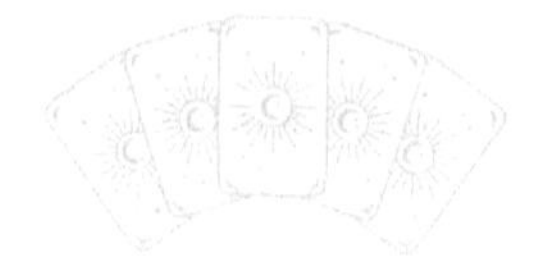

I WONDER HOW THE NICE NEIGHBOR LADY WOULD REACT IF I looked her straight in the eye and said, "Why yes, Ma'am…as matter of fact, I HAVE seen a ghost. A mighty talented one at that! A Civil War type specter that's wanderin' 'round your very own backyard." But of course, I don't say this to her. Not out loud anyways. Miz Weathers seems like a right friendly sort of person, bringin' over these homemade cookies and all, so there's no reason I can think of to go on and frighten her like that.

I have discovered over the years that when it comes to the subject of haunts, there basically are two kinds of people in the world; those who believe in them and those who don't. Personal attitudes about specters vary greatly dependin' on one's experience and general disposition, but folks are always divided by whether they think that the souls of dead folk can stick around after their hearts stop beatin' or whether they hold to the conviction that dead means gone for good. I have found it to be far too frustratin' to try and change which side of the fence they sit on, so I no longer spend any energy tryin'. I have no idea where Sylvie Weathers might stand on this topic, and right at this very moment, I, myself, am as confused as a bagel in a bucket of grits over that newly reversed card in my Tarot spread and not ready for a ghostly debate.

Thus, I simply say, "I'm fine, Ma'am. Thanks for askin' after me. I just woke up with a start in a strange bed and found myself a tad confused, is all." I immediately change the direction of our conversation. "This sure is a real nice neighborhood. So quiet and peaceful-like."

Miz Weathers waves her arm in the direction of the street. "Southern Streams is just THE best place to call home. Everyone is always so friendly and welcoming, and its wonderful amenities are a big bonus. Have you been down to the Lodge yet…Miss Delia?"

"Yes Ma'am. I stopped there yesterday after visitin' the pool. Very impressive. And secure," I say.

"That it is. That it is," the neighbor repeats proudly. "Well, Delia, I should let you start your day. I hope you enjoy your stay with us. Tom and Emma Kozinski are wonderful people, and I promised them I'd make sure you have everything you need while they're gone. If there's anything I can do for you, just come on over and ring my bell, okay?"

"I will do just that, Ma'am. Thanks so much. And thanks for the cookies. They look good enough to bring tears to a glass eye," I say.

Sylvie Weathers gives an odd look to my reference of a glass eye and tries to appear as if she's not staring at mine, but smiles regardless. "You are most welcome, Delia. I hope you have the best summer at Southern Streams. Make sure you try and meet all the lovely people here on Sprocket Springs. We all just love Emma and Tom." She waves at me as she heads across the small piece of lawn to her front door.

I'm sure she's right about all the folk livin' on this street bein' friendly and all, but there's only one neighbor I'm hopin' to get to know better, and that would be the Johnny Reb who has managed to shake my determination to be forever done with interferin' specters wreckin' my life. I carry the plate of cookies into the house and fix myself a fresh cup of tea. Starin' out the sunroom windows at the mule barn on the other side of the berm, I can already feel the heat of the Tennessee summer sun shinin' in through. It's the kind of day perfect for sittin' in one of them comfy lounge chairs by the pool. But I got no time for piddlin' my day away soaking up a lizard scorcher.

I need to dig deeper and get a handle on the reasons this particular haunt can do things he ain't supposed to be able to manage. I get the feelin' that maybe some of the answers lie beyond the mule barn sittin' on the property buttin' up to against the Kozinski's yard. I consider climbin' over the berm to the other side to do some meta-physical exploration, but I ain't sure there's no security cameras keepin' an eye on Rippavilla's back property. Folks 'round here seem to wanna' make extra sure to be keepin' strangers out from where they think they don't belong and I don't need any particular notice by the Spring Hill police, 'specially after my experiences with that damned-to-hell Detective Pritchard.

Like most historical sites in Tennessee, I'm bettin' that for a small fee, Rippavilla Plantation is open to visitors. A tour by a book-taught local yokel might save me hours of tedious research. Plus, I'm hopin' it probably also will gain me access to all of the grounds, 'specially the remote spots out back I figure to be home to my specter neighbor. A quick Google search of the historic site proves me right; tours run all day. A guided 90-minute tour costs $25, but tickets are only sold in pairs. I am momentarily frustrated, until I recall my cookie-baking neighbor's offer to help me out. I think it's the perfect time for me to get to know Miz Sylvie Weathers, along with the history of Rippavilla Plantation, a little bit better.

It don't take much proddin' to convince Miz Sylvie to join me for the Rippavilla tour, though my new friend makes me agree to lunch afterward as her treat. I'm not sure what I expect to find at the old plantation. The South is full of these imposin' keepsakes from a different time and mind set, but for the past ten years I've kept clear of settin' foot in one for fear of encounterin' a lost soul. Lots of old buildings play host to wanderin' specters, but there seems to be an especially large amount of them south of the Mason-Dixon line, and just like livin', breathin' folks, Southern ghosts seem a right more social.

Though the back of Rippavilla is just a few feet from our backyards, we are required to drive out of Southern Streams, over to Rt 31, and through the plantation's main entrance, which stands as testament to how large the property is. Miz Sylvie and I are booked for the 1:00 PM tour and are sent to the gift shop to meet our docent. While we wait, the two of us browse the array of books, tourist souvenirs, and period-style collectables. I thumb through a few paperbacks focusing on The Battle of Spring Hill, all the while puttin' out metaphysical feelers hopin' for signs of my mysterious Johnny Reb.

As soon as Miz Sylvie pulled up the driveway to the landmark, I'd felt a shift in the property's natural energy. The hair on the back of my arms reacted to unseen static electricity, and I suddenly got itchy all over, which don't surprise me none. Rippavilla played its part in a tumultuous period of American history, and undoubtedly, still contains a large amount of trapped residual energy. However, somethin' is different 'bout what I'm feelin' here as compared to other historically tragic locations. It's an energy current that feels much older and richer than that of any of the specter visited places I'd previously experienced.

Other tourists join us in the gift shop until our little group swells to just under a dozen people. The docent is a middle-aged woman with a surprising British accent who seems comically out of place in her tweed skirt and long sleeved, high collared blouse. However, there's no denyin' she knows her shit. We're led to the mansion's front porch where Priscilla Bagley gives us an overview of the house's history as well as that of the Cheairs family who were the property's original owners. I do my best to focus on what the woman is sayin', but as we get closer to the home's entrance, I develop a stabbin' pain in my left temple.

I stick my hand in the pocket of my jeans where I'd

placed two, small, drawstring bags. One bag contains a variety of crystals meant to balance various types of energy, and the other holds the beautiful quartz that my lost soul left me as a token. I rub my thumb over my Johnny Reb's gift and an unusually cool breeze blows across Rippavilla steps. It is strong enough to cause the small American flag attached to the tour sign board to flutter gently in the hot stagnant air, which, in turn, causes the visitors to look at each other questioningly. Docent Bagley smiles. "It appears our resident ghost has decided to welcome us this afternoon. No worries. He's proven himself to be most hospitable."

Her use of the pronoun "he" makes my heart race. Could she be referrin' to my Johnny Reb? I realize that this hypothesis might be a stretch. In a house with as much history as this one, it isn't inconceivable that more than one lost specter might be wanderin' 'round. But the fact that the breeze appeared just as I touched my new buddy's token gives me sudden hope that I might make a stronger connection with him here at Rippavilla.

Miz Sylvie grabs my arm. "Did you hear that, Delia? We might actually see a real ghost today! Isn't that just so fun?" She stops a moment and adds, "Do you believe in ghosts, Delia?"

I look her straight in the eye and say, "I sure would like to believe that there's an Afterlife, Miz Sylvie. It would seem to me to be a comfortin' thought to anyone at the end of their days. So, in answer to your question, I can honestly say I certainly do believe that ghosts exist on this plane." As I say these words I feel a cool breath on the back of my neck, and all the hair is standin' straight up on my arm. 'Course when I turn around there ain't nobody there, but I will swear on a stack of holy books that I hear a low, male laugh right next to my ear.

The docent leads the group inside the house while I linger on the porch a mere second longer. Rubbin' my thumb over the quartz again, I whisper under my breath, "Well ain't you just the cheekiest haunt. By the way...I love the quartz ya left me, but I sure would like another peek at ya'. Will ya' go ahead and show yourself to me?"

There's no response. Disappointed, I follow the group inside just as the tour continues into the parlor. Rippavilla has recently changed ownership from the City of Spring Hill to the Battle of Franklin Trust, a non-profit designed to keep the history of the area safe and respected. As such, the house is getting a much-needed overhaul designed to return it to its original glory. Therefore, most of the rooms are currently empty of furniture. Still, it's not hard to imagine the stately elegance the space once held. As Priscilla Bagley continues with her lecture about Nathaniel Cheairs, I see something from the corner of my eye. Next to the room's fireplace a dark mist is gatherin'. The longer I stare, the clearer the mist becomes as it slowly begins to take shape. I see a filmy apparition of a young man in Confederate gray casually leanin' against the fireplace, his arms crossed with a smile that goes from ear to ear. This specter's got the bluest eyes I've ever seen in a man, either livin' or dead.

My heart is poundin' so hard in my chest that I am surprised no one around me can hear it. The other tourists all are focused on the docent's lecture about the architecture of the house. No one else seems to be aware of our ghostly eavesdropper. I smile back at the manifestation of the spirit I believe to be my gift-givin' Johnny Reb, and he in turn gives me a most un-ghost-like, saucy, wink. I blush and take a step towards him, only to watch the handsome specter disappear into thin air.

Chapter Twelve

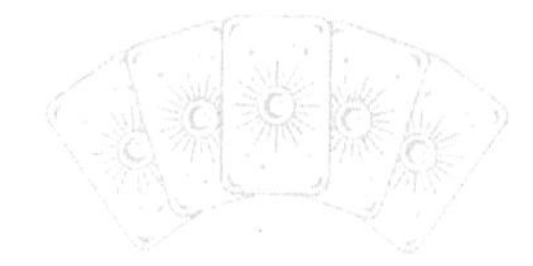

WHEN I STAND IN THE SAME SPOT NEXT TO THE FIREPLACE where I last saw my specter friend, the floor is still vibratin' with energy, but on a very low frequency. The temperature is normal, and there are no other signs that the ghost is still here. This Johnny Reb has me as confused as a blind dog in a meat factory. On the one hand, he seems to desperately want my attention, but on the other, he also appears to be workin' overtime to keep me at arm's length. More importantly, this lost soldier boy seems capable of metaphysical shenanigans I've never seen manifested by any other wanderin' soul, and the practitioner in me is itchin' to learn the hows and whys of it all.

I put a hand on the mantle but am instantly scolded by the multi-tasking Miz Bagley, who stops her lecture on the social customs of the South in mid-sentence to say, "Pardon me, Miss...but we ask that guests refrain from touching the period pieces. The natural oil on your hands is detrimental to preservation." I pull my hand back, but not before a slight tingle runs up my arm courtesy of "eau de ghost" residual energy.

The docent herds us all up the grand staircase to the second floor, relating the history of the house and the various remodels, mostly terrible, of this historic property. She then ushers us into a bedroom that is one of the few rooms in the house that still contains a handful of period furniture. I try to focus on the lecture about the Cheairs Family history, but I'm distracted by someone gently tugging on the back of my hair. As before, when I turn 'round, no living person is behind me. The quartz in my pocket is warm enough for me to notice, and the bottom of my feet are itchy and tinglin', a normal sign of the presence of ghostly energy. I know he's here in this room. I also know that he can manifest himself to me if he so chooses, but that for whatever reason, he is currently not choosing to do so. If I were alone, I'd try to speak to him, but talkin' out loud to an empty space would just get me unwanted attention.

Miz Bagley moves the topic of her talk to the lovely carved, four-poster bed on the opposite side of the room. As she continues, a defined mist forms on the mattress, growin' stronger a lot quicker than the mist downstairs. When the shape firms up, I see my insolent ghost reclinin' on the antique bed, muddy boots and all, his arms crossed behind his head and grinnin' at me with a smile that would melt butter in an igloo. I'm a lot closer to him this time, so I get a real good look, and Lord have mercy, this damn specter is genuine, movie-star handsome. Dark curly hair pokes out from under his old-time planter hat, while June-sky, blue eyes look at me from under dark arched brows that grace a face with a chiseled jaw and full, expressive lips. He is the prettiest damn ghost I have ever seen and far younger than I'd originally guessed.

During the Righteous War for Southern Independence, recruits were taken from every walk of life and every age group, so it's not far off that this Johnny Reb might have been just a boy when he met his sad end. Far too many sons, brothers, and husbands lost their young lives in that tragic period of American history. However, in all our previous encounters, this same lost soul held the seriousness of someone much more advanced in years, so I am more than a little confused. Is this the same specter who left me the tokens and spoke of his belly pain on the Kozinski's lanai, or have I somehow run into yet another Confederate ghost?

The quartz in my pocket feels strangely warm, and I hesitate to touch it, afraid I might open a connection I may not be able to control in front of a living audience. Sensing my apprehension, the ghost momentarily looks disappointed. Then, he suddenly gets on his knees and crawls over to the corner of the bed where the docent is pointing out the intricate carvings on the bedpost. Using the index finger of his left hand, he flips up the collar of her prim cardigan sweater. Unconsciously, she flips it back down without losing a beat. My Johnny Reb repeats the action, and once again Miz Bagley puts it back in place. On the third round, the tourists begin to notice and poke at each other wide-eyed. This makes my Johnny Reb smile so widely I see a mouthful of straight, whiter-than-expected teeth, a not-too-common occurrence during that period in history. The docent never misses a beat, nor does she appear ruffled by his paranormal teasing. She tells the group, "It appears our resident ghost is in a mischievous mood today. Perhaps we should move on in our tour and give him some space."

By now, every visitor, including my new neighbor Sylvie Weathers, is in an all-fire hurry to leave that room. A few of the guests decide to leave the house completely, but the majority are both frightened and excited to have been party to such strange goings on. I hesitate to move myself. There is so much more I want to know about my lost specter. He has me intrigued in so many ways. Too many. My training suggests I should probably leave the house until I can get a better handle on my racing emotions. Personal feelins' are a surefire handicap when dealin' with lost souls, a lesson I learned the hard way with Caleb Nash.

I glance over at Miz Sylvie who looks more flushed and thrilled than frightened, and I decide I don't want to ruin this experience for her. Only a handful of the livin' ever get a chance to witness the proof of ghosts, and I'd hate to deprive her of such a moment. I decide to complete the tour and promise myself that if I should see my Johnny Reb again, I will simply ignore him and not engage his spirit.

Only seconds later, I carelessly break that promise. Something makes me turn around and look back at the doorway of the bedroom through which I just passed. I catch the ghostly soldier boy leanin' on the doorframe. He smiles at me in a sad, longing way and then waves good-bye. Against better judgment and every bit of knowledge I have about dealin' with errant lost souls, I lift a hand and wave back.

The tour continues throughout the rest of the house and outside onto the grounds, but I don't physically see my Johnny Reb again. I do, however, feel his presence. The air is noticeably cooler, so much so that my neighbor shudders and says, "Do you feel that, Delia? Something cold just passed us by. I actually got goosebumps. When I was a kid, we'd always say that someone walked on our grave when that happened." Sylvie grabs my arms. "Maybe our ghost friend is following us?" She laughs, but I don't miss her nervous edge. "I'm so glad you invited me, Delia! This is the most exciting thing that's happened to me in years! I can't wait to tell the girls at water aerobics that there's an actual, real, live ghost at Rippavilla."

I smile back at her and don't explain that the term "real, live ghost" is an oxymoron. A ghost literally requires that the soul's physical body no longer is functioning, so it's not really "living" in the normal sense of the word, although my specter pal does appear to be unusually animated for a long dead, wanderin' spirit. I wish I had gotten the opportunity to speak one on one with him while he was physically manifested, but the situation wasn't ripe for a meaningful conversation 'tween the two of us.

The guided portion of the tour ends outside in front of a large white oak that the docent calls a "witness tree," a living, growing remnant of the past. I place my hand on its rough bark but quickly pull it away as hundreds of images and voices fill my head. Phyllis Bagley isn't exaggeratin' when she says that this old oak tree has stood witness to a monumental amount of American history. There's little doubt that I am in a heightened state of metaphysical awareness. I'm not sure if it's being on this property, the power of the quartz in my pocket, or me experiencin' such a vibrant manifestation of a specter as I just did. What I do know is that I'm not in any hurry to have the energy of a thousand different memories gain entry to my head.

To see the back of the property, including the cemeteries and a still-standin' cabin once belonging to the enslaved people who lived here, we need to take the car, as it is much too long of a walk for my senior neighbor friend. I am particularly anxious to see this area, as it's the property that butts up against the houses in Southern Streams, particularly the ones belongin' to the Kozinskis and Miz Weathers, along with the spot beyond the berm with all them wild roses. As Sylvie heads for the car, I am stopped by Phyllis Bagley, the docent my Johnny Reb teased so publicly. "I hope you enjoyed your tour, Miss…"

"Delia," I say. "Delia Achley. And yes…I found the tour fascinating. This old house sure does have a rich history."

"That it does," she says. "I hope you found the answers you were seeking."

My heart just about stops in my chest. How in Hades does this docent lady know I had a specific purpose in comin' to Rippavilla? Is she psychic, or does she have some kind of connection with the Johnny Reb as well? A pang of jealousy hits me from way out in left field, an idea that somebody else knows about my lost soul. I immediately push that thought out of my head. The biggest mistake I can make is gettin' emotionally involved with any wanderin' specter, 'specially one that could steal buttons from a Parson's wife and charm her nonetheless. I figure I most likely have misconstrued what the docent just said to me. Still, I'm not inclined to share any of what I know with her. "Oh, I wasn't seekin' anything in particular, Ma'am. I'm new to the area and I've made it my business to try and educate myself about my state's history, is all."

The woman raises an eyebrow and smiles with a sense of self-amusement. "I see. Well, knowledge is certainly the key to most things." She rummages in the pocket of her cardigan and hands me a small white business card. "Just in case you have any further questions, you can contact me at the email address on this card."

"Thank you," I say with hesitation. Then, I reach out to take it from her, and when I do, a cool breeze blows over us both.

Chapter Thirteen

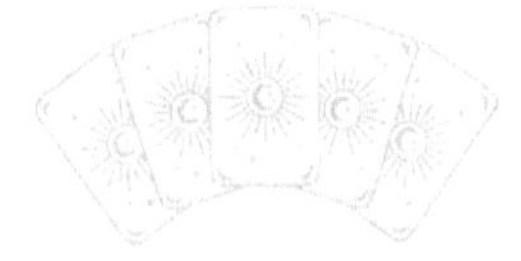

JULY 3RD, 2015

Caleb, the lost specter, is drippin' water all over the carpet of my rented motel room, but I know it's just part of his spiritual manifestation. When he disappears, so will any trace of dampness. I decide his wet state is an opening to conversation. "Caleb, Honey...why don't we start off by you telling Miz Achley why you're standin' here soaked to the bone. What got ya' all wet, Sweetie?"

The shakin' ghost opens his mouth to speak, but no words escape. This weren't totally unexpected. Without the physical body parts to make actual sounds, specters struggle with communication. If they stick around this plane long enough, they learn to communicate telepathically, but only on a very basic level and only recognizable to those of us livin' folks with the ability to pick up their messages. When I hear people claiming to have recorded the voices of ghosts on tape, I am always skeptical, though I suppose it's possible. It would take a lot of metaphysical energy for a specter to produce enough sound to form a whole word. I suppose that's why those so-called recordings only have the ghost saying a single word. On the other hand, the multi-talents of lost souls continue to surprise me, so I ain't rulin' out speech as impossible.

My ghost is becoming increasingly frustrated with his inability to explain to me what happened and how I can help. An idea forms in my head as to how I can try another method. I've never tried this technique before, but I have studied the writings of other practitioners who have, and, for the sake of this distraught, shiverin' child ghost, I am willin' to try. I use my most soothin' "mama style" voice to call out to him. "Caleb, Honey, can you come a little closer and put your hand on the end of Miz Achley's bed?" I pat the spot to give him a target of sorts. "Come on, Sweetheart...I know it's all scary for ya', but ya' gotta' trust me. I can help you go where ya' need to go. Be brave like those knights in the King Arthur book you picked out."

At the mention of the book, the ghost panics, his blood-shot eyes goin' wide and his mouth opening as if he were bawlin' without the accompanin' sound. For the life of me, I can't figure out what the hell is goin' on here, but the King Arthur book Caleb selected from the library give-away obviously plays a role in his sorrow and discontent. "It's okay, Sweetie. Whatever is wrong with the book, it'll all be fine. Just come here a bit closer like I'm asking. Put your hand here on the bed."

The boy specter stands firmly in the same spot, wiping imaginary tears from his bruised face. I consider getting up and movin' closer to him, but every bone in my body tells me he'll just bolt, disappear without a hint to what's happened to him. Then I would just have to wait around until he decides to re-appear again. That is surely not what I want, so I bide my time and wait for Caleb to make the first move.

Eventually, he ends his ghostly sobbin', wipin' his face with a drippin' sleeve. He takes a tentative step towards me, then another. When he gets closer, the smell of him is so overwhelming I have to work hard not to gag at the foul odors. Caleb Nash reeks of mold and standin' water, as well as piss and shit. This close up, I can see the ring of dark marks around his neck and somethin' inside me goes stone cold. Even without direct contact, I suspect that the end of the poor boy's life was traumatic...and not just an unfortunate accident.

I remain silent while I pat the end of the bed, not wantin' to scare him off with the wrong words. He puts one mottled, bruised hand on the spot I direct him to. Sensin' this is the best shot I have at gettin' to the truth and eventually helpin' his poor soul, I place my own hand over his ghostly one, not exactly sure of what will happen. There is a feeling of ice-cold energy, and without any warnin' or lead-in on my part, the connection between us is immediate. Visions fill my head...awful, terrible flickers of the child's last terrifying moments on earth. If these images weren't bad enough on their own, our connection goes even deeper, allowing me to physically feel the horrible emotions and physical pain the child bore as his breath was cruelly choked out of him. In my own fear, I panic and pull my hand away and Caleb Nash instantly disappears.

I reach for the wastebasket near my bed and vomit into it, but even after I purge the entire contents of my stomach, all the mental images...the pain and sufferin'...shrouds me in an emotional cloak of despair as the realization of the situation hits me like a solid brick to the head. Caleb Nash didn't just die. He was violently murdered.

I DON'T EVEN LOOK AT THE BUSINESS CARD; I JUST STICK IT in the pocket with the crystal while thrownin' a quick thank you the docent's way and head toward Miz Sylvie's car. My new neighbor don't miss a thing. I don't have my ass on the seat before she's givin' me the third degree. "What did that nice tour lady want, Delia? She was talkin' your ear near off."

"Nothin' in particular," I fib. "She was just askin' if I enjoyed the tour, is all. She seems real 'gung-ho' on the subject matter. Wants the plantation's visitors to get the full story, I suppose."

"Well, she does seem to be quite knowledgeable on the subject," Miz Weathers interjects. "Very passionate as well, though she was cool as a cucumber when those odd things were happening with her sweater collar. At first, I wondered if she was just tryin' to pump up interest…you know, so we'd give her a nice tip an 'all, or spend a little money in the gift shop. But, in truth, Delia, call me crazy, but I swear something spooky is walking the halls of Rippavilla."

I feel the need to defend my Johnny Reb. He's nowhere near what I'd call "spooky." I've seen spooky ghosts, Caleb Nash bein' one of the most alarmin' ones, coming to me all pale and wet, with his bloodshot eyes and all that brusin'. My soldier boy ain't at all frightenin'. In fact, I'd say he's as pretty as a speckled pup and just as charmin' to boot. But this ain't somethin' I can talk about with Miz Sylvie. "From what I've read, most ghost are nothin' more than lost souls, lookin' for answers and a way to move forward. I expect that if they wasn't mean when they were breathin', then they ain't lookin' for trouble when they're not," I comment. Last thing I want is for her to be sendin' hordes of Southern Streams seniors over to the plantation in search of a "real live ghost," so I quickly add, "And I also agree with ya'll when ya' mentioned that the docent might just be wantin' to increase visitors to the house. I expect it's gonna take a lot of cash to fix that old place up. Loads of payin' customers comin' to see spooks would surely help with those costs."

Sylvie sighs. "I guess you're right, Delia. I shouldn't go around believin' in that stuff anyway. I'm sure the Reverend Michaels wouldn't approve." She starts the car's engine. "C'mon…let's go see the stuff in back."

We drive to the back of the property, visitin' the Cheairs Family cemetery, and the old cabin and restin' place of the enslaved people who once worked the plantation. I stay as far away from both places as I can without lookin' ridiculous and make a specific point of not touchin' anything. In my current heightened state of metaphysical awareness, I'd prefer not to make connections to events and people I'd rather not have in my head right now. The whole property back here has a vibe of deep melancholy, while the sea of wild roses makes me feel an overwhelming sense of loss. I am more than happy when Miz Sylvie says, "I don't know about you, Delia, but I'm truly starvin' right about now. If you think you're done seein' what you want to see, how 'bout we go have us some lunch?"

I was hopin' for some clear sign that my Johnny is back here, but I don't feel even the slightest bit of cool air, nor do I have any "ghost" alerts tinglin' anywhere on my body. We walk back to the parked the car on the road near the cemetery, and I see something pink stuck underneath the windshield wipers. Sure 'nough, there held down by the wiper blade is a large wild rose bloom.

Unfortunately, Miz Weathers also sees it before I can grab it. "Now who would go and do something like that?" the lady asks.

My lyin' self instantly jumps to action. "Well, ain't that funny, Miz Sylvie. Those folks in the other car probably just wanted to joke with us and all. I guess all that talk of ghosts put everyone in a silly mood."

"Well, I don't think it's very funny at all! I have a good mind to chase them down and give them a piece of my mind," Sylvie huffs.

"I don't think they meant anything by it, Ma'am. Just havin' a little fun is all." I tuck the bloom behind my left ear while a cool tingle the strength of Jericho's trumpet runs down the length of my entire body. This soldier boy has the strongest aura of any ghost I've ever known.

Appeased by my words, Miz Weathers and I drive into the center of town to the same diner where my friend Lizzy works. She's on the evening shift, so I don't get a chance now to tell her how well this new gig is workin' out for me. We place our order with a different waitress, and my neighbor trots off to the Ladies room. Now finally alone, I remove the business card the Rippavilla docent handed me and somehow, I am not much surprised to read what it says:

PHYLLIS WORTHINGTON BAGLEY, PhD
KOESTLER PARAPSYCHOLOGY DEPARTMENT
UNIVERSITY OF EDINBURGH
EDINBURGH, SCOTLAND

CHAPTER FOURTEEN

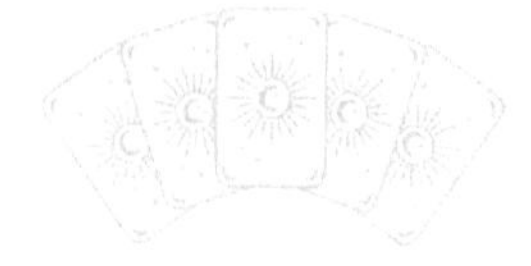

THERE'S ZERO CHANCE I'M DISCUSSION' MY JOHNNY REB with Phyllis Bagley. I don't have any doubt that she's an honest to goodness "believer," but I also realize that her intentions regardin' this Confederate lost soul are likely not altruistic. These science research types always seem to have their own agendas, and the comfort of lost souls usually ain't part of them. Plus, the fact that she came all the way here from Scotland to look for this ghost tells me she's got a very specific agenda for huntin' him down.

Miz Sylvie and I have a very pleasant lunch. I carefully turn the topic away from lost spirits, and she is more than willin' to do her part by regalin' me with funny stories 'bout her six rambunctious grandchildren. It's a topic I welcome over sweet tea and "meat and three" 'cause it works to take my jumbled mind off the monumental problem of what to do next to help this soldier boy. Truthfully, I don't quite understand why this particular lost soul has piqued my sympathy and interest as much as he has. Since that awful time dealin' with Caleb Nash, I have successfully ignored pleas from a handful of other confused specters, not willin' to put myself in that same, vulnerable position. Though I always feel a bit guilty for not usin' my special gift as it was intended, my metaphysical self and my inner-confidence are too raw after Caleb, so I just turn away from any interaction with poor, needy ghosts.

But this Johnny Reb is different, and I can't rightly say why. Maybe it's just that I finally am ready to move on from the events of that awful summer. Still, something inside me tells me it's more than that. From our first contact that afternoon on the lanai, there's been an intensity to the energy the two of us exchange that goes beyond any I've ever experienced. Plus, his easy goin' temperament and boyish charm is well...appealin'. The average lost specter, denied the proper afterlife for as long as this one, is traditionally moody and dismal; but there's nothin' gloomy 'bout this good ole' southern boy specter, which makes me strangely drawn to him.

After lunch, Miz Sylvie drives us back to Southern Streams. She's off to a watercolor class at the lodge, and I have high hopes of a visit with my soldier. I'm glad that my neighbor isn't home 'cause I don't relish explainin' why I'm sittin' on top of the berm in the hot June sun.

The land on the Rippavilla side is buzzin' with the energy of livin' things. Birds roost on top of the old mule barn, a community of bees are humming a genuine workin' tune as they feast on the patch of wild roses, and a pair of red foxes eye me suspiciously from behind a dense grove of butternut hickory. There is plenty of life, but no sense of the type of metaphysical energy that specters give off. After nearly two hours of waitin' without a single sign of my ghostly friend, I am tired, hot, and frustrated. Because of all those interactions during the Rippavilla tour and him leavin' me another rose token, I was confident my Johnny Reb would follow me here to this spot. The fact that he does not is a stinging disappointment.

I get up from the berm and head into the house intendin' to keep myself busy until I can try again later in the evening. I reason that the full manifestations of earlier today have likely weakened the specter's energy and perhaps he'll show himself again during that "sweet spot" time between 3:00 and 4:00 AM. As I get closer to the house, I see something stuck into the screen door frame fluttering in the slight, late afternoon breeze. I admit to quickenin' my steps to get there faster, and when I reach the lanai, I realize it's a finely detailed tarot card, though not one from my own set. This card belongs to a collection much older than mine, faded and worn. I pluck it from the screen door, and I can feel the slight hum of metaphysical energy. But it's the image on the card and its usual meanin' that gets my heart beatin' faster.

The vintage tarot card depicts The Wheel of Fortune; it's a major Arcana symbol of fate and destiny, a reminder that the universe always moves in a cyclical pattern. Within a readin', if it's in the upright position, it typically signifies that a positive change is comin' with the realization that life moves as the Universe directs it. I've done hundreds of spreads, for myself and for others, and the Wheel of Fortune only has shown up a handful of times. Bein' that it's so powerful and rare, it always gets my attention. But this card ain't part of any readin; it's a message…left where I'd be sure to see it. Fact is, I can't determine if the changes this card indicates are meant for me, the lost Johnny Reb, or the both of us.

Up and down the block, the backyards of Southern Streams are empty and quiet. There'd be no way anyone could have snuck up and put that card there without me havin' seen them. Not a person that's livin' anyway. The card in my hand is warm, though it's hard to decide whether it's from bein' handled by a specter, or just because it's been sittin' out in the brutal afternoon sun. Energy is energy, and it's impossible to distinguish whether this is from the natural kind or that which is produced by a metaphysical source, especially during daylight hours. With that in mind. I believe my original plan to look for the lost soul in the wee mornin' hours is the most reasonable, so I head into the house takin' the mysterious card with me.

For the rest of the afternoon, I keep myself busy by unpackin' my sparse belongins' and putterin' about in the modern kitchen. My hosts were generous in stockin' the fridge and pantry, and discoverin' a batch of ripe peaches, I decide to treat myself and Miz Sylvie to some home-made cobbler using a recipe my Mamaw taught me. I think about her while I slice and stir, wonderin' what she'd make of this peculiar Johnny Reb ghost. I almost can hear her in my head, *"Delia, child, you'd have your answers if ya'd just trust what ya' feel inside rather than flip-floppin' about like an 'ole catfish on land. Rely on your soul, girl."* I miss my Mamaw so much right now that it hurts, but I finish the cobbler thinkin' 'bout her the whole time.

Later, I try takin' a nap so I'll be fresher thinkin' tonight, but sleep eludes me completely. I've placed the vintage Wheel of Fortune Card on the bedside table in the guest room with my crystal token and the roses, and every now and then I look at them and concentrate, hopin' the answers to all my questions will magically pop into my head. Of course, they don't. My Mamaw is right. Answers to questions pertainin' to ghosts never come from the brain. They are always "felt" and never "knowed."

The sun sets, and the moon comes out, castin' shadows on the berm behind the house. When midnight rolls around, I settle myself on the lanai with a cup of tea, the found tarot card, and my gifted crystal. The hum of the crickets, the warm night air, and my herbal tea lulls me into an undesired light doze. The tour of Rippavilla replays in my head as a dream, but this time I see the house as it was in its heyday, before the war, new and beautiful. As I walk its wooden floors, the house changes around me, slowly aging and fallin' into disrepair, and I'm filled with a deep sense of sadness. I eventually wander into a room I saw earlier in the day that was painted a garish rose color, out of place in such a genteel home of a by-gone era. There is a woman there, dressed in 1950's attire, her hair teased and sprayed in the style of the day, eyes shinin' behind cat-eyed glasses. She smiles and says to me, "Lordy, girl, it sure took ya' long 'nuff."

I wake with a start, my hand flaylin' all over the place and knockin' over my now cold tea. I grab the tarot card before the spilled tea can damage it and swear over the mess I've made and the clanking of china hittin' the metal table, a sound that echoes in the nighttime silence. I mutter to myself, "You are as smooth as a porcupine in a silk factory, Delia Achley." A cool breeze settles around me, and I look up from the mess on the table. Standin' there on the berm in the June moonlight is my Johnny Reb.

Of all the questions I should be ponderin' at this serious moment, there bein' a 158-year-old ghost fully manifestin' in my backyard and all, how my hair looks shouldn't be foremost on my mind right now. But sure 'nough, I think just that, along with the worry that I might have sleep drool dried at the corners of my mouth from dozin' in a chair. This just further proves how damn out of specter practice I've grown these past ten years. Why in blazes should I care how I look to a ghost?

I take a deep breath to try to center myself. I don't want to appear too metaphysically strong and thus scare him off, which might require me to court him all over again. That's when it suddenly hits me right square between the eyes: true fact...I haven't been just "courtin'" him. My Johnny Reb has been courtin' me as well; the little tokens, the cool, unexpected breezes, the brief moments of fully showin' himself to me alone, all seem more of a flirty dance than the expected behavior of a bereaved lost soul lookin' for help to move on. This thought throws me totally off my game and so I hesitate at the screen door. What the hell have I gotten my meta-physical self into?

However, the pull is too great, and my curiosity wins out over any hesitation. Treading across the backyard, my shadow looms enormous in the light of a nearly full June moon. My heart is beatin' fast in my chest, but I don't think it's from fear. I haven't a bit of concern that this soldier boy plans on doing me poltergeist harm. Still, I keep my distance, lest I scare him off, or even set off any type of an undesired reaction. This specter is different from any I've dealt with before, so I am walkin' into this connection totally blind as far as my trainin' goes.

I stop on the berm about two feet away from the ghostly apparition. Though this Johnny Reb is more solid than other specters I've dealt with, there still is a wispiness to his form. If I squint hard enough, I can see right through parts of him, verifyin' he is spirit and not flesh and blood. He's got the biggest ole' smile on his handsome face, dressed all in Confederate gray, and holdin' my gifted pipe unlit in his left hand, though I can't for sure figure out how he's goin' about such a remarkable feat.

My specter friend shows no signs of the injury that ended his life, which, again, is not all that unusual. If specters have enough energy to manifest physically, they usually present themselves in the manner they remember appearin' before death took them out of this world. Caleb Nash was the only lost soul I ever met who showed himself to me as he was in the moments right after he left the world of the livin'. I'd surmised that the confusion and shock of being murdered in such a sudden and violent manner is the reason. The Cherokee ghost I saw when I was a child appeared to me in his full native dress and not in the image of the butchered corpse he'd ended up bein'; and gratefully, the boy torn apart by a startled black bear manifested as the healthy school boy he was before his most traumatic death. It makes sense then, that this must be the way my soldier boy looked before a Minnie ball tore his belly apart, and, as I probably have mentioned before, he's a right pretty ghost.

I wave to him, and he waves back, and I can't but help grinnin' to myself. Vocalization is extremely difficult for specters, as this is just a mirror image of what they looked like in life. They don't actually possess the body parts for natural speech, so I assume if we do end up communicating, it best be mentally goin' forward. I start with a simple mental *"Hello."*

For a full minute, I hear nothing in return, but then, inside my head I hear him, clear as day. He speaks with the deep southern drawl of the bygone past, but his words don't make a lick of sense to me. *"Saints be praised! I'd always knew ya'd come, Sara Anne. No matter that it's taken so long, darlin'...I never stopped believin'."*

Chapter Fifteen

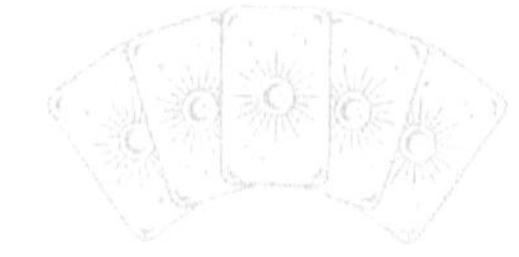

The "gifts" I was born with aren't an exact science. There ain't no data on the hows and whys of what I can and cannot do. Although I've had premonitions and dreams that have come fully to fruition, I can't explain why I didn't see in advance all the things that would happen to Caleb and myself. Perhaps I did sense that things wouldn't go well for me, but ignored it all in the name of doin' what I believed was right. It might have been false pride thinkin' I was blessed with a divine purpose; it may have just been a sign from the Universe that I wasn't, nor ever would be, in charge of how things proceed in the cycle of life. No matter the reason, on the day I was arrested for murdering Caleb Nash, I never saw any of it comin'.

In hindsight, it probably was incredibly stupid and naive of me to think the Nashville Police Department would believe me when I said I knew where Caleb's battered body could be found because his ghost had personally told me so. Had I been in my hometown of Sevierville, or anywheres in the shadow of the Smokies, the law would at least have kept an open mind to the possibilities of "mountain hoodoo," as there'd been a long history in the area of such things that could not be explained. But Nashville, Tennessee, wasn't rooted in the same culture and traditions of the Appalachian Mountains, and my pleas of innocence fell on deaf and wholly unbelievin' ears.

Confusion must register plainly in my expression, 'cause I see the smile slide from the specter's ghostly face. *"I reckon ya' don't remember me, darlin'. Miz Ruby said that might happen, but I had still hoped ya' might. Maybe these things just take time, and Lord knows, I'm a patient man."*

I am so confused by his words that I don't know how to respond. The last thing I want is for this lost soul to disappear in malcontent. But I have no inklin' of how to reply to his comments. It's obvious my specter thinks I am someone he once knew and for whom he cared. I'm not sure why he has this notion, but now, his leavin' me tokens makes more sense, and there's no doubt that this Johnny Reb sought me out for a specific reason. I also ponder who is this "Miz Ruby" he speaks of, and what does she have to do with this lost specter not movin' on? I force myself to seem cordial and relaxed, though I'm feelin' anything but. Perhaps additional conversation will reveal more information. *"Ya' have me at a disadvantage, Mr...?"*

My specter looks disappointed. *"It's true then. Ya' don't recognize me at all, do ya', Sara?"* He shakes his head, and a sense of deep sadness and longing rolls over me. It's so terribly profound, I feel an ache in my throat and the sting of tears in the corners of my eyes. The connection between this specter and me is unusually strong, a situation I haven't felt the likes of for ten long years…

JULY 5TH, 2015

I didn't expect miracles when I went to see Pritchard. I never expected the detective assigned to Caleb's case to believe me at my first words. Strangely enough, when I told him that Caleb Nash's spirit had come to me and told me where his body could be found, Pritchard grabbed his suit jacket from the back of his chair despite the swelterin' July temps, and slippin it on, asked me to show him the location of the child's body.

We took the officer's unmarked car to Shelby Avenue and 20th Avenue to Shelby Park in East Nashville. The 300-acre, multi-use recreational center was a mecca for the residents of Nashville lookin' for some R and R away from the grit and grime of the city. Situated on the Cumberland River, the park offered boating, fishing, playgrounds, dog parks, walking trails, and even a few baseball fields. On that day, it also played witness to the evil humans often hold in their hearts. I led the detective along the river path to mile marker 193 where a boat ramp provided access to the river. "He's somewhere along this spot," I explained, "caught up in some tree roots hangin' over the banks."

Pritchard and I walked the ramp side of the river for nearly ¾ of a mile. We almost missed Caleb the first time, so overgrown was the spot where we found him. Instructing me to stay on the shore, the officer took off his shoes and socks and rolled up his pant legs before wading into the murky water. He poked around the collection of branches, river muck, and garbage that had been caught there in the river's current. Then he went quiet, and I heard him swear under his breath, "Aww, shit. Sonofabitch."

He climbed out of the water without sayin' a single word to me and then pulled off the radio clipped to his belt. "This is Detective Pritchard, Shield number 6453...I got a 10-55 at Shelby Park about half mile east of the boat ramp on 20th Avenue. I'm gonna' need the coroner and a CSI team ASAP. I think I've found the missing Nash kid."

MY GHOSTLY SOLDIER BOY SITS HIMSELF ON THE GRASS AT the top of the berm and pats the spot next to him. *"I suppose the best place to start is at the beginin'. Could be somethin' I says will shake your memory,"* he speaks to my head. The fact that I can converse so easily with him is another sign that this lost soul is different from any of the others I've encountered...well...besides Caleb Nash.

I sit myself down, close enough to see his face clearly in the dark but not close enough that I inadvertently come in direct contact with his personal energy. The specter puts his hand out for me to shake but instantly drops it when I involuntarily pull away. Another wave of forlorn sadness fills the space between us. *"Private Jonathan Sweet,"* he says, *"Company C of the 9th Tennessee Infantry Regiment and formerly of Meridian, Mississippi...at your service Ma'am."*

I smile. *"Your name is actually Johnny? Like in 'Johnny Reb'?"*

This statement instantly brightens him up, and I see his face so clearly that I make out a tiny scar above his left eyebrow. Somethin' about it makes me want to reach out and touch it, but I don't. One never touches specters. It's the most basic lesson I learned in my hoodoo trainin'. Preachers always are screamin' about the possibility of spirit possession, but there might actually be a grain of truth to their warnins'. I don't mean a devil with horns and a tail kind of possession like they show in them silly horror movies. It's a certified fact that spirits of all kinds can transfer energy through touch. If a person willingly lets a specter touch 'em, they run the risk that the ghost will like their space so much they'll set up shop and not want to go, not to mention the physical response similar to touchin' a live wire. Best not to welcome contact in the first place.

"Saints be praised! See... Ya' are rememberin' things already, darlin'!" the soldier says. *"The irony of my name always did make ya' smile, Sara Anne. Ya' used to call me your 'Sweet Johnny Reb' before I left with my regiment."* I watch him as he tenderly rolls the pipe token I gave him in his hands, but then I have to look away 'cause I feel as if I'm losing the upper hand here. This lost soul is breakin' all the rules I've known regardin' what a specter can and cannot do, and I try to imagine what advice my Mamaw would give me in this same situation; but just like she did when I was involved with rescuin' Caleb Nash, my beloved grandmother stays silent from the great beyond. I am left alone to use only my own metaphysical devices. I take a deep breath and compose my own mental questions. *"So, Private Sweet...suppose you tell me how you came to be settled*

right here in Spring Hill and why ya' didn't move on after your earthly life ended?" I ask.

He stays quiet for a long time, and I worry that I'm losin' his ghostly attention. Then, without lookin' at me, he begins to tell his story with the same sense of overwhelmin', achin' sadness that's been fillin' the space between us. "I know I made a promise to return to ya', Sara Anne." Lord knows, I done tried my very best to stay out of the line of fire. To know that I broke my sacred promise to ya' over a lousy chunk of possum meat and the call of hunger shames me to my very core. Not a day goes by that I don't wish I had just stayed in the camp like I'd been ordered. If I hadn't gone out on my own, perhaps we might have had a life together...just like we planned." He turns and faces me. "To this very moment, I regret that stupid decision...but there's not been one single day that I have ever stopped lovin' you, Sara Anne McKinney. I carried that pocket watch with our love token tucked inside...the one Big Lucy made for us the night 'fore I left...until my last dyin' breath. Now that watch and that token are outta' ma' reach, darlin', but my true feelins' for ya' have not lessened ... not one little bit...in all this time."

Chapter Sixteen

This is a surreal moment for me. Not only 'cause I'm sittin' on the grass in the middle of the night mentally communicatin' with a dead soldier boy from the Civil War, but also because it's the only time in my life I can recall anyone ever tellin' me that they loved me, even if it's mistakenly. I know that sounds sad and pathetic to most folks, but in my case, I guess I never gave it much thought. Until now.

It might be that my Mama cooed those words to me when I was a wee babe, but I don't rightly know since she left me with my grandmother when I was less than a year old. Since then, she hasn't been much of a factor in my day-to-day life. It was never made clear to me who my daddy was, and even if I had known, I doubt he was the type of man lookin' to be a father. My Mama wasn't drawn to no family-man type. And though I am entirely sure that my Mamaw cared for me in her own way, she weren't one for cooing or coddlin' over the multiple grandchildren my Mama left in her care, especially ones who required her special trainin'.

The Johnny Reb's words touch me; and in this moment, I wish with my whole dang heart I actually was this Sara Anne person whom he so desperately loves, clinging to his feelins' for her even after his earthly life ended. There's no doubt that he truly loves this woman. All teachin' on the subject states that the feelin' of love is one of the strongest types of energy in the Universe, so it ain't no surprise that a lost soul might linger around because of love long after it should have moved on. I am filled with the need to help this young man, but I am currently lost as to how to go about it. He's quiet after his passionate admission and undoubtedly waitin' for my reply.

"Private Sweet..." I begin.

"Lordy, darlin'...I wish ya' would just call me 'Johnny.' I have had my fill of wearin' that dang army title."

I start again. *"As you wish...Johnny."* Even though I've been callin' this specter "Johnny Reb" to myself for some time now, usin' his given Christian name oddly pulls at my heart. *"I am so very sorry to tell you I am not this Sara Anne that you think I am. As much as I wish I could be who you're lookin' for, my name is Cordelia Mae Achley. I'm a livin' soul in the year 2025. I know this might come as a shock to you, but I'm afraid you're no longer part of the livin' community anymore; you haven't been for nearly 160 years. You're a ghost, Johnny- a lost soul who hasn't moved on."*

Sometimes wanderin' specters don't realize they're dead, or they're not willin' to come to terms with the finality of their earthly life. Most ghosts I've worked with, like Caleb Nash, respond with a heart-breakin' display of grief and fear. Some are plain angry, and others are confused. But not a single one has ever reacted in the manner of this handsome young man. Upon hearing my solemn declaration, Johnny breaks out in jovial giggles and knee-slappin' laughter, as if I've just told him the funniest of jokes.

When he's done with his chucklin', he looks at my shocked face and grins. *"I wish ya' could see your own face, darlin'. Ya' look like you've seen a ghost."* This comment gets him laughin' again, and after he finally catches his breath and wipes invisible tears from his eyes he says, *"I'm sorry, Sara Anne. Ya' know how I like a jolly good laugh. I promise I'm not laughin' at ya, darlin'. It's just that ya' got all serious... like ya' was afraid to break some terrible news to me. Truth is, Sweetheart, I am well aware that I'm dead, and that I'm what we used to call 'a haunt,' so don't go worryin' your pretty little head about somehow hurtin' my feelins. In fact, it's been the best belly buster I've had in years."*

Johnny's cavalier attitude about bein' dead throws off my concentration. I'm used to consolin' and counselin' these lost souls, not given' them "belly buster" fits of laughter. *"So, it don't bother you none that your time on earth has ended?"* I ask.

My soldier boy specter lays back in the grass, with his arms behind his head and the unlit pipe stuck between his teeth. It's a strange sight, this specter bein' all misty and smokey-like with the solid pipe danglin' from his ghostly lips. He pulls it from his mouth and says, *"As you said, darlin'...it's no big secret. I've been gone from my earthly life for a long time. Not much I can do 'bout it. What's done is done, though I will say it gets a mite borin' at times. I do what I can to liven' things up. 'Course...now that you're here, things will be a whole lot better. We're back together agin', Sara Anne...just like we promised we would be...all 'cause of Big Lucy's conjurin'."*

His use of the word "conjurin'" gets my whole attention, and I want nothin' more than to stay right here on this berm and listen to Johnny Sweet tell me why he thinks I am this Sara Anne person. I desperately want to hear the details surroundin' the implied metaphysical actions of "Big Lucy," guessing they might have somethin' to do with this lingerin' spirit's reluctance to move on to the Afterlife. But the sky is gettin' lighter in the east, and I see some lights flick on at the back of Miz Sylvie's house. I surely don't want to be caught sittin' on this berm talkin' to myself in the pre-dawn hours.

"I'm sorry...Johnny, but it's gonna' be light soon, and I don't want any of my neighbors catchin' me out here. It would raise too many questions." Suddenly I feel extremely vulnerable, like a young girl on her first date...but with reversed roles. I stammer out my next words. *"Can I see you again? Tonight maybe?"*

The specter is losing shape in the comin' daylight hours, and I can barely make out his whole face, but I can hear the echo of happiness in his mental voice. *"Course darlin'...I was hopin' ya' would want to come back. This evenin'...for sure. I'll be here in this very spot. I'm excited for it already. I got somethin' very important I need to show ya."* And then, before I can turn and leave, the ghost of a dead Confederate soldier kisses my cheek.

There's a very good reason one doesn't touch specters. Their levels of personal energy can vary dependin' on a whole lot of things, but the fact remains, spirits are simply remnant energy. Because they have no physical body to contain this vitality, touchin' one is like makin' contact with a low voltage, live wire. It ain't likely ta' kill a person, but once that person's gone and done it once, they ain't likely ta' want ta' repeat the experience any time soon. This particular Confederate lost spirit has energy levels that are off the chart for reasons I've yet to determine, and the kiss he leaves on my cheek is akin to me puckerin' up for a smooch from a potent bug zapper.

I wasn't expectin' him to do anything of this sort, and thus, I am wholly unprepared when the current runs from my face and travels down my entire body, suckin' the breath from my lungs and causin' my knees to buckle underneath me. I tumble down to the grass, and it takes every bit of my conscious will power not to holler out in shock lest I call the attention of my neighbors. I got no good explanation for bein' out here on the berm in the early mornin' hours. Johnny obviously had no idea regardin' the consequences of his stolen kiss, and now he shimmers with agitation like a Tesla coil gone crazy. He bends down to help me off the ground, but I scuttle a few inches away on my butt, putting a hand out to stop him and mentally pushin' out the few words I can string together in this state. *"Don't! Can't touch you. Hurts!"*

The sun is over the horizon now, and I can barely make out his face, but there's no missin' the ghost's shock and sorrow over his accidently causin' me such pain. His genuine sadness and angst is a thick blanket of energy surroundin' us both. *"I am so, so sorry, Sara Anne. It's been so long, and I thought...maybe..."* His thought fades away along with his form, and I close my eyes and try to breathe normally. *"Tonight...please come, darlin'. Please..."* These last words are just a mental whisper, and then I feel that Johnny is gone completely from this spot.

I push myself up and stumble down the berm and across the yard to the house, voicin' my desire to the Universe that none of my neighbors are up this early and viewin' a crazy woman wanderin' out back of their property. I flop on the sofa and take some deep meditating breaths to try to bring my body back into normal, workin' order.

I'm only on the sofa a few minutes before the first "memory" appears in my mind from out of nowhere. It's the briefest of flashes...a fuzzy sensory overload of visuals, smells, and sounds: the twitter of evening birds at call, the rushing of water over rocks, dappled light through a canopy of green, the smell of damp earth...and wild roses. My mind struggles to put everything together into a cohesive, comprehensible package, but before I can make sense of who, what and where, it fades to mere nothingness. I ponder whether this is my own memory or something transferred from my physical interaction with the lost soul. I close my eyes and wish it back to no avail. It's gone, and no matter how hard I try I can't summon it back again.

The past hour spent with my Johnny Reb has left me with more questions than answers. Why does he still insist that I am this Sara Anne person even after I've made it clear that I'm not? What gives this lost specter the considerable energy he possesses despite being gone from this plane of existence for nearly 160 years? And how does the old Rippavilla plantation and grounds fit into all of this?

I begin to feel a bit steadier on my feet, so I leave the safety of the sofa and head to the kitchen to make myself some tea and toast. Realizing I am voraciously hungry after my ghostly encounter, I add two soft boiled eggs to the menu. While I munch, I peruse a few more chapters of the Spring Hill history book, but there is nothing there to explain my specter's ties to this place other than the fact that the grounds surrounding Rippavilla were used as a Confederate encampment for the troops General Hood brought up from Atlanta. I am now convinced, more than ever, that my lost soul's reluctance to move on has little to do with the ensuing battle; his commitment to stay here is a personal one.

Despite his encroachment of my physical person without my consent, I do not hold any fear or animosity towards my Johnny Reb. What he did was done out of pure longing and devotion and was in no way an act of violence against me. I believe that this specter is as confused about our connection as I am, and his inability to "move onto" the next phase is something he himself can't help. I think about my commitment to get out of the "specter helpin' business" after the events surrroundin' Caleb Nash's rescue, and I push it out of my mind. I believe that if I keep my "hoodoo" work with this specter a secret just between the two of us, I can avoid the trials and tribulations that occurred the last time. Stayin' private when workin' with wanderin' spirits is the best course of action for me; regular folk don't understand things from beyond, and ghostly stuff frightens 'em, 'which then causes all kinds of unfair assumptions and lots of finger-pointin'.

Right now, I need more information, the kind I won't find in the books I borrowed from the Spring Hill library. I need access to the web, but without a computer of my own, I'm forced to, once again, rely on the public ones available at the library. The more information I'm armed with before meetin' with my specter tonight, the better for the both of us. I put my dishes in the sink and hurry off to shower and dress. I gotta' busy day ahead.

Chapter Seventeen

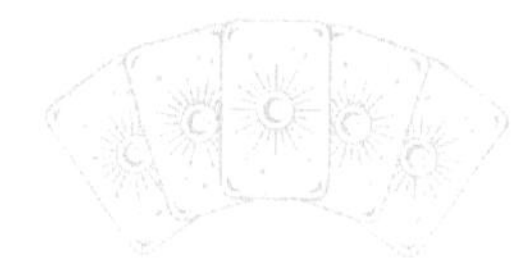

I'm filled with anticipation as I walk through the doors of the Spring Hill library, lookin' forward to gettin' information to help me fill in some of the blanks after my meetin' this mornin' with Private Jonathan Sweet. The irony of his name still makes me smile, and I'm a little envious of the young woman who called him her "Sweet Johnny Reb," the mysterious Sara Anne whose love keeps him tethered to this earthly plane.

The same librarian I met a few days ago is here again. Seein' me walk in the door, she gives a friendly wave. I smile and wave back, not for the first time thinkin' what a pleasant and friendly place Spring Hill is, part of a vanishin' breed of Southern hospitality. I head straight for the bank of computers at the back of the buildin' and settle myself behind one. There's so much I need to research but decide to start with my specter himself, or at least any possible information about him. I recall he said he was from Meridian, Mississippi, so I start there, lookin' to access any information in the city's archives. Unfortunately, though the Meridian website has lots of information on tourism, it doesn't go back far enough in its history to help me any. However, I do discover that Meridian is in Lauderdale County, so I check the county site next. There are hundreds of archives going back to 1790, so I just jump in and start scrollin' through deeds. It's a tedious job. They're arranged by dates and not in alphabetical order, so I am required to go line by line looking for the name "Sweet." After 'bout an hour of leanin' over the monitor, I sit back in my chair, my eyes tired from starin' so hard at the screen. I have located only one reference to anyone by that name, a William J. Sweet, who purchased a plot of land on the east side of Meridian in 1847, and, just by chance, I find another deed in the name of Thomas Turnboldt McKinney, who bought his land in 1853. There's no way of tellin' if these people are in anyway connected to my specter, though it's definitely a possibility. Before I can continue on to the death certificates, the librarian walks by pushing a cart of books. She sees me and stops, asking, "You findin' everythin' you need, Honey?"

I don't want to get too specific on what I'm searchin' for, so I explain, "I'm lookin' for some information on some specific Confederate soldiers who fought here in Spring Hill and were mentioned in the books I borrowed the other day, but there's so much to go through. I feel like I'm lookin' for the proverbial needle in a haystack."

She thinks for a moment and then says, "Have you checked the Library of Congress? They have a huge collection of images and documents from the Civil War era. Perhaps you might get some solid information there. I know our local historians use the LOC site all the time."

"That's a wonderful idea, Ma'am! Thanks for suggestin' it," I say with honest enthusiasm.

"No worries, Honey. If you need anything else, just ask. I'll be around all afternoon." Then she pushes the cart off in the opposite direction.

The Library of Congress website is a treasure, and the librarian wasn't kiddin' about their extensive collection of Civil War material. There are hundreds of pages, neatly organized by keywords and topics. I type in the name Pvt. Jonathan Sweet and immediately an old photograph, yellow with age, appears on the screen. I can't help but gasp out loud as an image of my ghostly specter stares at me from my computer. He is dressed in crisp, new, Confederate grays, a pistol and bowie knife tucked in his belt, looking solemnly at the camera. Though he looks younger in the photograph than he did on the berm last night, there's no doubt the two are one and the same, those piercing blue eyes and strong jawline exactly alike.

I sit and stare at the photo for the longest time, and when I am sure no one is lookin' my way, I take a finger and touch the screen, runnin' my finger over his face and imaginin' what it might be like to have touched him when he was a livin', breathin' soul. Out of nowhere, I'm filled with an incredible sense of melancholy, and tears fill my eyes, threatenin' to overflow and run down my cheeks. I quickly brush them away before anyone can see. How could I ever possibly explain why I'm sobbin' over a photo of a long dead confederate soldier? Hell...I can't explain it myself!

Suddenly, I feel absolutely exhausted, the events of the last twenty-four hours finally catchin' up with me. I pay my ten cents and print out a colored copy of the photo of Pvt. Jonathan Sweet. Then, tuckin' it carefully inside my oversized tote, I head home to contemplate everythin' that's happened to me in the past few days.

WHEN I RETURN HOME FROM THE LIBRARY, I MEET MIZ Sylvie outside tendin' to her flowers. I really don't wish to make polite small talk; I could barely keep my eyes open during the short drive home, and all I can think of is kickin' off my shoes and catchin' forty winks. I want to be awake and fresh for tonight's meetin' with my Johnny Reb. But my neighbor has been entirely too nice for me to ignore, so I stop when she waves to me.

"Hey there, Delia. How ya' settlin' in?" she asks as she waters her geraniums.

"I'm doin' just fine, Miz Sylvie. Southern Streams is a lovely place," I answer.

"Are ya' sleepin' okay, young lady? I could have sworn I saw ya' wanderin' around in the backyard durin' the wee dawn hours this mornin'," she says.

I don't want to be caught in a lie. When I saw the lights go in through her kitchen windows, I kinda' figured she'd seen me. "I'm an early riser, Ma'am. I do like to hear the mornin' birds and watch the sun come up. It's sort of the way I like to start my day…with mornin' meditation and prayers…if the weather allows."

Like all good Christians in the South, Miz Sylvie

heartily accepts the notion of talkin' to the Creator one on one. "Of course, dear. What a lovely practice. It's good to see young folk communicatin' with the Almighty. So rare today. You just go ahead and do your own thing, Miz Delia. Folks here are very acceptin' of religious practices."

I feel a mite guilty lyin' to this nice lady, but it's not like I can tell her what I was really doin' up on that berm. Folks 'round these parts might be acceptin' like Miz Sylvie says, but I'm pretty sure they'd be less cordial if they knew I was mixin' it up with dead spirits.

I offer my thanks and change the conversation to the fine appearance of the roses that line the walkway to her front door. She's happy to give me the hows and whys of her success with the plants. Their scent perfumes my way back into the house, and I am more than relieved when I shut the door on further conversation. I kick off my sandals in the foyer and head for the guest room. Taking the photo of Pvt. Jonathan Sweet from my tote, I prop it against the vase holdin' the two wild rose tokens and place the crystal in front of it. Satisfied, I stretch out across the bed for what I expect to be a twenty-minute cat nap.

I fall into a much deeper sleep than anticipated, and my dreams are filled with a collection of unfamiliar places and people. This could be said about most dreams: people's brains creatin' visual clues from bits and pieces of all kinds of memories. However, in this case my head tells me I should know and understand what it is I'm dreamin, but try as I might, my sleepin' head isn't making any sense of the entire collection. Even stranger, I know for a fact that I usually dream in black and white, but the mental images now runnin' in my head are all in color. I wake up with a start, my last subconscious thought bein' somethin' about hair that I'm struggling to retain. I awake groggy and disoriented. The shadows across the room telling me that it's already early evenin' and that I've been asleep for several hours.

I grab my phone and see that it's nearly 7:00 PM. This is gratifyin' as I now have less time to fill until I see my soldier boy again. I fix somethin' to eat, watch a lot of mindless TV, and when 3:00 AM rolls around, head out to the lanai to watch and wait. Happily, I don't need to mark time for very long. Up in the same spot as the night before, I see a faint figure materialize in the pale moonlight. If I didn't know what to look for, I might think that what I'm seein' is nothin' more than shadows from the small trees lining the berm. But I know that figure ain't no tree, and so I head out to the backyard, carefully closin' the screen door quietly behind me.

I climb up the small incline to the top and am greeted with a heart-stoppin' smile on my soldier boy's face. *"I was so worried ya' wouldn't come back, darlin'. I'm ever so sorry 'bout kissin' ya' like that. I shudda' known better. Are ya' feelin' okay now?"* he says to my mind.

I'm okay, Johnny," I say shyly. *"It just caught me off guard is all. Spirits have a certain energy that don't mix well with the livin'. We need to be careful about not makin' physical contact."* These words leave me sad. Crazy as it sounds, I want nothin' more than to touch this lost soul, even though I am aware that doin' so would entail tremendous risk.

"I promise no more touchin', Sara Anne. At least until we figure this all out."

His promise leaves me melancholy, but I got work to do here and I push myself to shrug off any romantic feelins' that might be crossin' my mind. *"I don't know what there is to figure out, Johnny. We both know you've been here far too long already. You need to move on. It's the way these things are supposed to go. If anythin', I need to find out how to help you do so, but to be perfectly honest, I'm more than a little confused 'bout all of this. I keep tellin' you I'm not this Sara Anne ya' believe I am, and you keep insistin' otherwise. We have to get past that if I'm to offer ya' any help at all."*

My specter's face darkens a bit, more out of frustration than anger. *"I need to show ya' somethin' important darlin'. Maybe it will help ya' make sense of what I'm tryn' to tell ya.'"* He puts out his hand for me to take, but then rememberin' his promise not to touch me he pulls it back. *"I guess ya'll just have to follow me on your own. I'll try to stay as bright as I can for as long as I'm able."* He begins to head down the other side of the berm...the Rippavilla side; when I don't instantly follow, he stops and turns around. *"Please, Sara Anne. I really need to show ya' this. I think everythin' might make more sense once ya' see it for yourself."*

I decide I have officially lost my ever-lovin' mind as I follow a Civil War ghost onto private property...in the middle of the night...in the dark. I have no idea whether the historical site has active security cameras around the grounds. Plus, there could be all kinds of critters and snakes out at this time of night. But none of this matters at all, since there's no way I'm not followin' my Johnny Reb after he's asked me so nicely to do so. I cautiously make my way down the side, catchin' up to my ghost at the bottom. *"So just where are ya takin' me, Johnny Sweet?"* I ask.

"We need to go over to the big house, darlin'. What I gotta' show ya' is inside."

I stop walkin'. *"Wait...you plan on takin' me inside Rippavilla? At night? Surely, it's gonna' be all locked up. How are we gonna' get in?"*

He smiles again, all dimples and amazingly straight teeth. *"You just leave that to me, darlin'"* he says with a wink. *"There are some advantages to bein' a ghost."*

CHAPTER EIGHTEEN

THE SIZE OF THE RIPPAVILLA PLANTATION PROPERTY IS deceiving. One can view the grand, old house from the main road that weaves through Southern Streams, yet from that vantage point, it doesn't seem nearly as immense as it does while I'm walking from the very back of the property where it meets the berm, all the way to the front where the house is situated facin' Rt. 31. Thankfully, there's a stone path that runs the length of it, so I'm not forced to tramp through knee high grass and overgrown shrubs with the chance of steppin' on whatever might be hidin' in 'em. My specter walks in front of me. At least I think he does. Sometimes his manifestation fades to near nothingness, and if it weren't for the spark of electrical energy I feel in the air surroundin' me, I wouldn't even be sure he was still around.

After walkin' for what seems a very long time, I ask Johnny if we're gettin' close. I hadn't prepared myself for a three-mile hike, and my flip flops are beginnin' to rub in between my toes. *"Almost there, darlin'...just past that old barn there."* The barn he's referrin' to looks to be 'bout another half mile away, and I make a face I hope he don't notice. When the back of the house finally comes into view, I am totally pooped and need to sit on an old step to catch my breath and rub my achin' feet. I try not to think 'bout havin' to walk back when the time comes.

Closer to the house, I get the clearest view of Private Johnny Sweet I've ever had. I guess him to be about 5' 11", which is pretty tall for the time, and of solid build with wide shoulders and a narrow waist. He leans against a pillar, arms folded 'cross his chest, with one booted foot on the ground and the other bent back and restin' on the base of the pillar. He smiles down at me, and suddenly, I'm filled with an eerie sense of deja vu, as if I've been in this same position before…me sittin'…him standin' over me with that same grin. My head suddenly feels funny and there's a strange hummin' inside my ears. These symptoms must be showin' on my face, 'cause Johnny drops his smile and sits down next to me…close but not touchin', with an expression of obvious concern. *"Are ya feelin' unwell, Sara Anne? Maybe the walk was too much? I sometimes don't figure things out like I did before I ended up dead. Do ya' want to go back, darlin?"*

The thought of walkin' all the way back to the Kozonski's house without seein' what I came for is enough to shake the "heebie-jeebies" from my head. I stand up and consider tellin' him about the odd dream and memories I have no personal recollection of, but I worry I could be gettin' his hopes up over somethin' that might be nothin' more than my overactive imagination. Instead, I say *"I'll be fine, Johnny. Why don't you just show me what it is ya' wanted me to see?"*

His smile returns, and he stands as well. *"You was always up for an adventure, Sara Anne. I'm glad that hasn't changed 'bout you. You wait right here. I'm gonna' go open that door to let you in,"* he says, pointin' to a heavy wooden door, obviously a modern build to replace the original. Then, my Johnny Reb walks directly through the wall as if the bricks were made of smoke. It's not the first time I've seen a specter defy the physical world, but because it's my Johnny doin' it, I can't help but let out a nervous giggle.

After a minute or two, I hear the door rattle and then watch it swing open. I get up and cautiously enter as the door closes behind me. There's a light mist, and then he's back, lookin' as real to life as he did outside. *"Follow me,"* he says. He leads me to the wide, central staircase, and up two flights we go. He looks at me sadly. *"I sure wish I could hold your hand, darlin'."*

Without thinkin' 'bout it, I reply, *"I wish I could hold your hand too, Johnny."*

"Truly?" he asks.

It's probably a huge mistake, gettin' all sweet on a specter, but I can't seem to help myself. I'd love nothin' more than to hold his hand...and to have him kiss me again. It don't seem fair to lie 'bout it, 'specially knowin' that once I help him move on, that'll be the last I'll see of Pvt. Jonathan Sweet. I'd like to think he'll remember me when he finally gets to the Afterlife. *"Truly,"* I reply.

"That makes me so very happy, darlin'. It means that what Big Lucy promised is comin' true, just like Miz Ruby said it

would. When I show you what I gotta' show you, you're gonna' believe it too!"

Johnny turns and enters a small room on the left of the hallway. I remember it from my tour, which seems to have occurred a lifetime ago, but really was just a few days earlier. It's the room that was painted a garish raspberry color, the one with the same woman that showed up in my dream...the one with the beehive hairdo who scolded me 'bout "takin' so long." I stop short and stare up at the paintin'.

"That there is Miz Ruby," Johnny says. *"She could see me too. Just like you. She's the one who drew the picture for me. She was a kind old soul. I sorely missed her when she moved on."*

I'm now totally confused. Someone else saw my Johnny Reb? This so-called "Miz Ruby" drew him a picture? None of it makes sense to me. *"What picture, Johnny?"* I ask.

The Civil War specter removes the portrait from the wall and gently peels away the brown paper that's covering the back of the canvas to reveal a large piece of folded white paper inside. The ghost removes the paper and leans the painting against the wall. Unfolding it, he hands the paper to me. *"Miz Ruby drew me a picture of you, Sara Anne, straight from my mind...so I'd have somethin' of ya' to hang on to. She's the one that told me you'd be comin'. That I just needed to give it more time."*

I take the drawing from his hands, and my knees almost buckle right out from under me. There, staring up at me from the paper is my very own image.

It now makes perfect sense to me why my Johnny Reb keeps insistin' that I'm his beloved "Sara Anne." The face in the drawin' bears a remarkable likeness to the same one that faces me in the mirror every mornin'. I do notice little differences here and there; the woman in the drawin' has a tiny birthmark on the left side of her chin that I lack, her hair is longer than mine and worked in an old fashioned, tight bun at the back of her head, and it's fairly obvious from the delicacy of her features that my doppelganger is much smaller in height and build. Nevertheless, there's no denyin' that "Sara Anne" and me could be twins.

My knees feel shaky, so I back up against a wall and slide my way down to the floor. My lost specter plops himself down in front of me, his face again registerin' his concern. *"I'm guessin' ya' might be a tad shocked, darlin'. I figured ya' would be, but I was hopin' that this here drawin' would spark some memory inside ya'."*

"When was this drawin' made?" I ask, not sure I'm ready for the answer.

"I'm a little mixed up on dates that happened after my life ended, Sweetheart...one day moves into another and it's hard to keep track, but as far as I can tell, Miz Ruby lived here in this big house at the same time some fancy pants senator from the East came and spoke to the Tennessee legislature...a Mr. John F. Kennedy. Miz Ruby held that man in high regard, she did, and she was plumb besides herself when he came to Tennessee. It was around that time that we met and she drew that 'pitcher of you for me."

Of course, I recognize the name of John F. Kennedy. He was elected our 35th president in November, 1960, beatin' out Richard. M. Nixon. If he was still a senator when he came to Tennessee, then the drawin' was made sometime before then; most likely somewhere in the late 1950s. It'll be easy enough to find out for certain on the internet, so I vow to do just that on my phone when I return home. Unfortunately, none of this helps me understand why I look like this Sara Anne person. I prod my Johnny Reb to feed me more information. *"Well, that does give me an idea when this drawin' was made, but I still have no idea why your Sara Anne and I look so much alike. Can tell me more, Johnny? Earlier you mentioned that this all came about because of someone named 'Big Lucy.' Are Big Lucy and Miz Ruby both somehow connected to this house and, therefore, connected to you? I need your help in making some sense out of all of this."*

The lost spirit looks frustrated at my lack of understandin'. He glances out the uncovered window at the night sky and then back at me before answerin'. *"I su'pose it would be best to start at the beginnin', darlin. Some part of this story just gotta' go ahead and shake up your head so you'll remember...least that's what I'm hopin'. I'm guessin' we got about an hour before daylight, so I'll try and get it all out before then."*

This is exactly what I want to hear. Once I get to the bottom of how me and this specter are connected, I hopefully can find a way to break the chains that keep him here. I make myself comfortable on the floor of this garishly pink room, ready to hear the whole story.

Johnny Reb crosses his legs and props his elbows on his knees. *"I would have to say it all started between me and you..."* He sees my startled face and changes his verbiage. *"Between me and Sara Anne McKinney, that is, the summer before I signed up to be part of the Righteous War for Southern*

Independence. That would be during the Full Buck Moon in early July. I seen you...I mean her... standin' with her folks watchin' the fireworks at Meridian's annual 4th of July celebration. I remember it distinctly 'cause I thought that the show seemed less spectacular than previous years, and I considered it might be 'cause of all the talk regardin' the possibility of Mississippi secedin' from the republic. At the time, I truly didn't think it would happen like it did, but folks did seem pretty riled up 'bout what was bein' done to the Southern States. What I do remember clearly was Sara's face by the light of them fireworks. She was just about the prettiest girl I ever laid eyes on. I even said so out loud, and a few of my pals teased me into goin' up and talkin' to her. I took the dare and meandered over to her and said somethin' silly, I'm sure. She laughed but she didn't turn away, and told me her name was Sara Anne, despite the fact her mama kept givin' me the 'ole evil eye the whole time.

Next day, I went over to her place, 'bout a mile down the road from our land. I dressed in my Sunday-goin'-to-church clothes even though it was Saturday, and brought along some of Big Lucy's warm 'benyays'(beignets) to take to her mama. Them puffy fry cakes could charm the horns right off the devil himself, they was so tasty, and I knew Mrs. McKinney would feel it rude not to invite me inside. She introduced me to Mr. McKinney, and puttin' all my eggs in one basket, I asked the gentleman's permission to court his daughter. He was gruff but fair and said he would consider it after he talked to Sara Anne herself. He said he knew my Paps and considered him a just and God-fearin' man and hoped his boy was of the same stock. I nodded my agreement so hard I thought my head would fall dang off, but I guess it was enough to sway the man 'cause the next day I was allowed to walk ya'...I mean Sara Anne...to *church services at the Methodist church. I didn't go inside for the services themselves though, 'cause my Ma would've had herself a fit, us bein' dyed-in-the-wool Baptists, but I waited outside until the services were over, and walked her back home again."*

Johnny's tellin' me a charmin' story of a buddin' romance, and I'm hangin' on every word, picturin' everything in my head as if I'd been there myself. I try not to let this distract me…how real it all seems…'cause as much as I'm enjoyin' my time alone with him, the clock is tickin' closer to sunrise and I'm no closer to understandin' any of this than when I first walked through the back door. *"I love this story of yours, Johnny,"* I interrupt, *"but it ain't helpin' me figure out what you want from me. I'm afraid it's gonna' be sunrise soon, and we'll have to leave before I get the information I need. Perhaps ya' could skip the parts that don't specifically include Big Lucy?"*

This makes my specter laugh out loud, and he says, *"You was always the impatient one, darlin', always teasin' me 'bout my long-winded tales. In fact, as I remember it…it was your lack of patience that got Big Lucy involved to begin with."*

CHAPTER NINETEEN

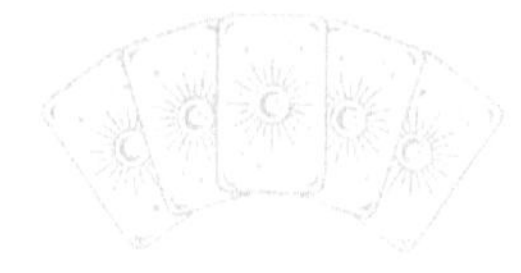

Gettin' the whole story from my Johnny in an expedient manner is like tryin' to pry a bone away from an ole' hound dog. *"Sara Anne's lack of patience is the reason you haven't moved on, Johnny? I'm sorry, but that don't seem very plausible. This ain't makin' a lick a sense to me. Who is this Big Lucy person you keep goin' on 'bout?"* As I'm sayin' these words to Johnny in my head it occurs to me that my speech patterns have slowly been takin' on a more… antiquated, Southern tone. I don't recall ever usin' a simile about a hound dog or Jericho's Wall before.

The specter frowns. *"If you ain't rememberin' any of this, darlin, then this story's gonna take a lot longer than we have here tonight,"* he reciprocates, clearly frustrated by my…I mean "his" Sara Anne's…lack of recall. *"Big Lucy was our cook…a free Creole woman from Louisiana that done followed my Mama to Tennessee when she married my Paps. Best damn cook in Lauderdale County, Big Lucy was. Her gumbo could make a person cry tears of joy."* He must sense I'm gettin' impatient again about his goin' off course again, 'cause he squares up his shoulders as if he's bound and determined to stop embellishin'. *"Big Lucy was also the best spell caster and 'hoodoo practicin' wise woman that ever come from the bayou. Even my Mama, who was totally committed to our Savior, Lord Jesus, sought Big Lucy's help from time to time, like when my baby sister had a bad case of the flux and the time she lost her favorite jeweled hat pin, the one her Daddy gived her when she'd married my Paps. That Creole woman could talk to spirits like nobody's business and was always able to git' them to do whatever it was she wanted."*

A chill runs down my spine when Johnny describes Big Lucy's "hoodoo." It ain't the same kind I inherited from my Mamaw. Our mountain metaphysics is born within an individual's soul. It's a gift from the Universe, mixed with a good deal of learnin' 'bout the folklore surroundin' the medicinal and practical uses of the local flowers and fauna. We don't call upon any paranormal spirits or entities to help achieve our goals, divine or otherwise. In fact, our work is centered firmly on returning spirits to where they rightfully belong, not callin' the out-of-world ones to this plane of the Universe.

I can't be sure, but since she was from the bayou and used spirits to achieve her goals, my guess is that Big Lucy was a *Vodou manbo*, a priestess of the diasporic religion that mixes parts of traditional West and Central African religions with Roman Catholicism. It developed from the slave trade in Haiti during the 16th to 19th Century. My own people consider it black magic, and we stay as far away from it as possible. Nevertheless, it's still widely practiced and found in more places 'round the world than one would think

My sudden realization that this spirit's inability to move on to the Afterlife is tied to a *Vodou* castin' alarms me. I know next to nothin' 'bout breakin' spells forged by dark spirits, if there's even a possibility of such a thing. Anxious for more information, I again interrupt him. *"So...what exactly did Big Lucy do for you and Sara, Johnny? Did she create a spell of some kind? Do you remember exactly how she did it? The words she used?"*

He looks at me and tilts his head. *"Now who's doin' the interruptin', darlin?"* He laughs, and I can't help notin' how the sound of it makes me happy. *"I'm gittin' to that part,"* he says, *"I promise. But I got to tell it my own way, 'else I might forget an important part."*

"Sorry," I say. *"Go on. I promise I won't interrupt again."*

Johnny nods his head and continues. *"Anyways, me and you..."* He doesn't stop to correct himself, and I just let it pass. *"...we fell in love as sure as the sun rises in the east every mornin'. But by then, I had already enlisted to fight them damn Yankees, and I was due to ship out at the end of September. We wanted nothin' more than to join our lives in holy matrimony, but your Ma was dead set against you marryin' a soldier boy who might not make it back alive. She was as stubborn as a Columbia mule over the decision that her daughter not become a widow at the tender age of seventeen, with the possibility of a fatherless baby on her hip and little chance of makin' another decent match. Your Pa didn't like to go against his woman, so he agreed and told me that if I came back to Meridian alive after them Yankees were vanquished, he'd throw us the biggest darn weddin' party Lauderdale County had ever seen.*

Neither of us wanted to wait. Much as we didn't like to talk about it, we knew too many good Southern boys already had given their all to the Confederacy. I begged ya' to run off and elope, but you was always a good girl who obeyed her ma and pa, and so ya' refused my offer time and time again. It got to be September 23rd, and I was only a week away from leavin' when you hatched this plan to have Big Lucy help us make sure the two of us would never be parted. I knew it might be a sin... me seekin' out spirits to change the destiny the good Lord had planned for me, but I loved ya' so much I couldn't say no.

I met with Big Lucy one day as she was dressin' some hens out by the barn and told her what you and I wanted from her. She didn't say much at first, jest' kept pluckin' them feathers one by one. Then, she looked at me and said, 'Pigeon Toes'... that's what she always called me on a count of the way my feet pointed inward, 'Pigeon Toes'...ya' sure this is what ya' both want? You talkin' 'bout a spell that ain't easily broken. This ain't for no 'puppy dog love', no 'scratch an itch' kinda feelins'. This be powerful magic we talkin' 'bout here.'

I done my best to convince her it truly was what we both wanted with all our hearts. She just grunted and shook her head, then said to me, 'This kinda spell castin' don't come cheap, boy. But 'cause I've known ya' since ya' slipped out from your Mama, I'll give ya' my very best price. I'll do what ya' is askin' in exchange for that gold cross ya' is wearin' 'round your neck.'

Truth be told, darlin', it was a hard bargain. My Ma gave me that cross when I 'cepted Jesus as my Saviour, on the day of my baptismal dunkin', and I wore that thing night and day. But I pulled it over my head as fast as I could and handed it to Big Lucy, lest she suddenly change her mind. She told me and you to come meet her two nights from that day, when the moon was at its highest point in the sky, next to the grove of white oak near the stream that runned at the back of our property. And just like that, we set everything in motion."

There's little doubt left in my mind that it's a Vodou castin' keepin' my Johnny Reb stuck here on this earthly plane where he don't belong anymore. Every bit of information I can gather will increase the chances that I might be able to help him move on. *"So...just what did Big Lucy do with ya'll down by that stream, Johnny? Can you remember the words she used?"* I mentally ask him.

"Lan' sakes, darlin'...Big Lucy was usin' her Creole language like she always did when she was doin' her hoodoo work. Weren't no words I remember recognizin'. Plus, I was nigh worried that one of those strange spirits she was commmunicatin' with would make an appearance right there in them woods. A meetin' with 'Ole Scratch weren't what I was wishin' for, 'specially 'cause I didn't have me that cross my Ma gave me no more," the specter explained.

"Surely you remember something about the steps she took, right? Did she sprinkle anything on the ground, or maybe draw a circle' round the two of you? Anything of that nature?" I prod.

My ghost removes his cavalry hat and scratches his head, doin' his best to recall what he can. *"Come to think of it, she did draw a big circle 'round me and you...I mean....me and Sara Anne. I do remember it bein' nice that we could be in each other's arms like that, all cuddles and kisses, though I didn't much care for the hair pluckin' part. Big Lucy weren't very gentle."*

"Hair pluckin?" I ask in a horrified tone. I don't know much 'bout usin' black magic, but I am savvy enough to know that the use of hair or blood in a castin' is powerful juju. *"Big Lucy took hair from ya' both, Johnny?"*

"That she did," he answers, seemingly recallin' more of the procedure the longer we chat. *"I remember me sayin' that I hoped ya'd still love me when Big Lucy plucked me bald."* He smiles at the memory, not botherin' to correct his pronouns this time. *"Then, she tied our hair together with a white ribbon 'fore pricking our fingers with a sewin' needle and havin' us smear a drop of blood over the knot. I could barely keep the giggles inside me, 'cause it was all so strange."*

His description of the castin'...the use of both hair and blood shocks me into silence. I don't need a mess of Vodou trainin' to understand the scope of what this now-dead Creole woman must have conjured up. The fact that she used both blood and hair in a closed-circle castin' speaks volumes to the strength and skill of the hoodoo she must have used. An overwhelmin' sense of hopeless-ness settles over me as I realize just how futile my attempts at freein' the Johnny Reb from his earthly confinement might be. It becomes crystal clear that If I can't undo this Vodou spell, this poor lost soul will be forced to continue to wander this space without hope. It's also evident, for reasons I can't yet understand, that as long as Johnny's tied here to Rippavilla, I will somehow always be tied to him in a way that makes my connection to Caleb Nash child's play. From seemingly nowhere, a thought pops into my head. *"So, what ever happened to those strands of hair and ribbon, Johnny? The ones Big Lucy used in her castin'? Did she give them to you? Do you, by any chance, still have them?"*

He leans over and looks at me with earnest eyes, though as the sky lightens outside the house's window, my Johnny Reb's manifestation grows fainter by the minute. *"Of course, I do, darlin! Big Lucy told us over and over 'agin that if I was to come back to you, I needed to keep this 'charm' with me. Always."*

This gives me a glimmer of a chance. *"That's wonderful news!"* I exclaim. *"Can you show it to me?"*

He slumps back against the wall in that raspberry-colored room. *"I'm 'fraid I can't, darlin. I put it in my Grand-pappy's gold watch, the one my Daddy gave me 'fore I left with my regiment, for safe keepin'. My guess is it's still there,"* he says with a sigh.

"And just where is your Grandpappy's watch now, Johnny?"

As my specter continues to fade, he says with a frown, *"Far as I know, that watch is still with my earthly bones, darlin...and I sure as hell can't get to it.'*

Chapter Twenty

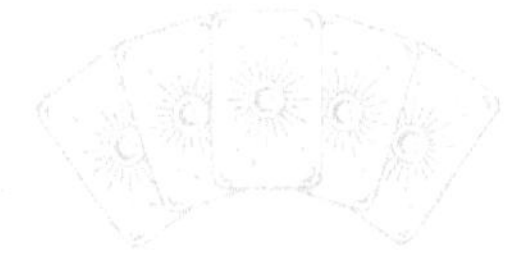

THE SPECTER'S REVELATION LEAVES ME STUNNED. BIG Lucy's Vodou charm, the one I believe is tetherin' my Johnny Reb to this plane, is buried deep in the earth along with his earthly remains. Even if I could undo a charm so powerfully cast, I still have the problem of findin' the body, diggin' it up, and retrievin' this Vodou *bijou*(charm)...all without bein' seen by my new neighbors over at Southern Streams, or worse yet, bein' arrested for trespassin' on private property. I feel a slight chill come over me that ain't got nothin' to do with a ghost sittin' across from me. This is shades of Caleb Nash all over again...me gettin' drawn into somethin' that I know sure as shit won't end well.

The room grows brighter as the dawn creeps over the horizon, and Johnny's manifestation grows dimmer. I can barely make-out the outline of his face, the blue of his eyes the only pop of color in the misty apparition. I realize he's waitin' for me to respond to his declaration that the charm is buried with him. *"I'll be honest with ya,*

Johnny," I telepathically say, "*Undoin' Big Lucy's castin' might be beyond my skills, and that's only if I can even find the bijou in the first place. I don't think the Battlefield Trust people who own this place will take kindly to me diggin' up their property on a whim.*"

"*Oh...my bones ain't here at the big house, darlin'. I can show you where they are, but that charm don't matter none to me other than the fact that it worked just like Big Lucy said it would. We're back together, Sara Anne. That's all that matters.*"

By now, the sun has completely risen, and my charmin' specter is almost entirely gone from my sight. I feel the hum of his energy, so I know he's still here, and I try to ignore the disappointment I feel at no longer bein' able to see his handsome face. I'm suddenly exhausted after the experience of the past few hours and I still have that long walk back to the house. I don't have the heart or the fortitude to again argue with Johnny that despite us lookin' the same, I ain't his beloved, long-lost Sara Anne. "*We'll have to talk about this further, Johnny, but it can't be now. It's past sunrise and people are gonna' be out and about soon. I need to get home without anyone noticin' me traipsin' through Rippavilla's back property.*" I rise from the floor. "*We need to put this drawin' back where we found it, and rehang this portrait of Miz Ruby in its rightful spot, less we raise suspicions among the staff. I gotta a feelin' that that British lady given' the tours don't miss a thing.*"

Johnny's form is no longer visible, and it's more than a little eerie watching the paper with the drawin' seemingly floatin by itself in mid-air. I hear the crinkle of the portrait's paper backin' as the ghost returns the image of Sara Anne to its hiding place, followed by the sight of the heavy frame lifted into its place on the wall by invisible ghostly hands. I look up at the confident Miz Ruby Davis and wonder what role she played in bringin' both me and the Johnny Reb to this point in time.

The brush of the specter's energy floats around me, close enough to pick up his vibrations, but not close enough to actually make contact. I'm glad for that. As tired as I am, I don't think I could easily shake off the shock of the electrical charge that would occur if my Johnny Reb physically touched me, a thought that makes a lump tighten in my throat.

The soldier boy must pick up on my feelins' cause I hear him say, *"You feel sad, darlin'. I don' know how to make it better. I'm hopin' that with time we can figure this all out."*

"I hope so too, Johnny," I say, the knot in my throat growin' bigger and my eyes burnin' at the corners with unshed tears. I blame my racin' emotions on my exhaustion and the constant bombardment of the specter's energy I've been exposed to these past few hours. I don't want to contemplate that my feelins' might be something entirely else.

"I'd like to walk ya' home, if ya' would allow me to, Sara Anne," the ghost says, and the feel of lovin' devotion in that mental message threatens to undo me. All I can manage is a nod of approval, anything else bein' too much to handle at this moment.

The specter and I wander down the hallway and take the main staircase to the ground floor. We make our way toward the back door where I entered. Suddenly, I hear my specter curse in my head, so very out of character for the ultra-polite, Southern boy of a different era. I look up to see the reason for his rare expletive. There in the door-way, in the wee hours of dawn, is the peculiar Rippavilla docent, Phyllis Bagley.

It appears that I am a lot more surprised to see the elderly, British woman standing there in the doorway to the old plantation house than she is to find me here at this ungodly hour. In fact, she seems entirely nonplussed to find a stranger wanderin' 'round the historical landmark when it's supposed to be locked up good and tight. She leans against the door jam, her arms folded across the front of her fussy, button-upped cardigan. "Good Morn-ing, Miss Achley. I hope I didn't give you a fright. Excuse me for saying so, dear, but you look as if you've seen a ghost." Then her lips turn up into the slightest of smiles.

It takes me a second or two to realize that she's messin' with me. I return her sentiment with a fake nonchalance of my own. "I'll be happy to excuse you, Ma'am...if ya'll are willin' to excuse my expressin' the opinion that it's a mite too early in the day for such witty repartee."

This makes her laugh outright. "Perhaps a cup of morning tea would balance this exchange, don't you think, Miss Achley? Why don't you follow me, my dear. We can have ourselves a nice, little chat over a cuppa. Your poltergeist friend is welcome to join us...should he be so inclined."

I can feel my Johnny's angst over that idea, so I say to him mentally. *"You go on Johnny. I'll handle Miz Bagley myself. Maybe the two of us can meet again tonight? On the berm?"*

I no longer can make out any of the features of his manifestation, but the gratitude in his voice is hard to miss. *"Thank ya', darlin'. I find this one to be more persistent than Old Scratch, himself. She's right determined to make me the subject of her schoolin' work. As to this evenin', ya' gotta know that I will be countin' the hours until we are together again. You be careful 'round that Pond Yankee, Sara Anne. She's a force to be reckoned with."*

His ghostly energy fades away and I am left alone with the very much alive, Phyllis Bagley. Havin' little choice and hopin' to avoid bein' arrested for breakin' and enterin', I follow the British woman to the back of the house where it meets up with the visitor's center and the small gift shop. She leads me to a small space off the entrance that's set-up as a break room, complete with a table and three chairs, a mini fridge, coffee maker, microwave and hot plate. There's a kettle already restin' on its coils. Miz Bagley cheerfully fills it with a gallon jug of bottled water before turnin' the hot plate switch on. She pulls out two mugs with drawings' of Rippavilla on the front of them from a small cabinet and sets them down on the table, then signals me to take the seat across from her.

I slide into the chair, tryin' my best not to show just how damn nervous I really am. Images from my terrible experience with Caleb Nash float around in my head, and I get a certain *deja vu* feelin' that, once again, I've gotten myself in a whole heap of trouble by tryin' to help a lost spirit. When the docent remains silent for an uncomfortably long time, I decide to start the conversation. "So how did you know I was here?" I ask her. "I was pretty sure I didn't see any security cameras...unless of course, they've been carefully camouflaged."

"Frankly, I'm surprised you'd take such obvious risks, Miss Achley," she replies. "Especially given your past history with law enforcement. However, I do understand, better than most people, how powerful the pull of the paranormal can be."

My heart freezes on the spot when she mentions my history with the police, and she must read the panic in my face, or perhaps the negative energy associated with that period in my life, 'cause she quickly adds. "There's no need to panic, young lady. I fully respect what it is you do." She sees the shock on my face and explains without being asked. "Ah, the internet is a wonderful tool. Rest assured, I did my due diligence regarding your talent, Cordelia." She stops and thinks to ask, "May I call you by your first name dear? There's no reason for us to be so formal. We have more in common than you realize."

I shrug. I'd let her call me anything she damn well wants if it meant keeping her from dialin' up the Spring Hill police. "As you wish, Ma'am," I reply.

"Good. And you must call me Phyllis from now on, Cordelia." The teapot whistles and the docent rose. Using a dish towel to grab it, she places the teapot on a metal trivet that she's set in the center of the table. She removes a canister from the cabinet, along with a plastic bag containing a handful of sugar cubes. "I hope English Breakfast is acceptable, dear. And I'm afraid I'm out of milk, so we'll have to do without," she apologizes.

"It's fine," I say, then repeat the question I asked earlier. "So…how did you know I was here…Phyllis?"

The docent fixes her own cup of tea. "The Battle Trust people don't much believe in wastin' money on security measures of that nature. Like most people here in the South, they believe in the general, good natured, honesty of people. Plus, they believe the presence of cameras 'ruins' the historical feel of the house, and there isn't much of anything worth stealing right now. However, as part of my approved sabbatical here at Rippavilla, and for gathering information for the academic paper I'm writing, they've allowed me to put in hidden paranormal, electro-magnetic devices, including a specially made video camera, that pick up spectral energy. Of course, it was also able to pick up your own metaphysical energy, so I knew someone of the living kind with special gifts was here along with my resident ghost. Based on my research, I was pretty certain it would be you I'd find here."

Making a face, I respond, "I find it a little disconcerting that you looked up information about me Ma'am," I say, sounding more defensive than I had planned. It makes me heartsick that even after ten years, the Caleb Nash experience clings to me like a bad smell that won't disappear no matter how hard I try.

She adds additional tea leaves to the strainer and places it in my cup, then adds the hot water, as if I am a child who can't do this simple task for myself. "There's no need to get your dander up, Cordelia. Heaven knows, I am your biggest fan. I don't believe for a minute that you had anything to do with that unfortunate boy's demise. In fact, I am most intrigued to hear your side of the story...not only regarding the dead child, but just how it is that you can make contact with Rippavilla's elusive, resident ghost."

Chapter Twenty-One

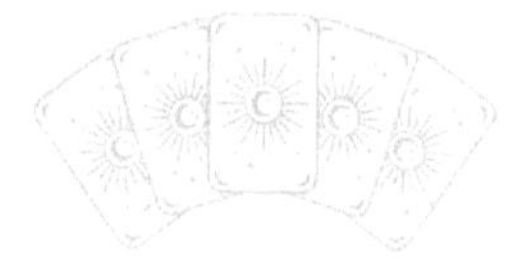

I watch the steam rise from my cup, unwillin' to meet the docent's eye. "If it's all the same to you, Ma'am...I'd rather not talk about that part of my life."

Maybe British type people don't understand the boundaries of what is considered polite down South, 'cause Phyllis Bagley acts like she don't even hear my request to drop this particular line of questionin'. She blows on the rim of her cup and takes a sip before sayin', "My research says you spent three months in jail awaiting trial until a new break in the case proved you innocent, but there wasn't any information about what exactly occurred before or after your release. Surely you sued the City of Nashville for falsely imprisoning you, didn't you?"

I look at the crazy professor as if she has two heads. Sue them? Hell! All I wanted was to relinquish my role as the Music City's #1 Freak and disappear into obscurity. Sitting in that tiny room, so similar to the interrogation one from my memory, it all comes back to me...every terrible, heart-wrenching moment. For reasons I can't begin to understand, the story comes pourin' from my lips like water over the rocks of McCutcheon Creek...

JULY, **2015**

After they pulled poor Caleb from that river in Shelby Park, Detective Pritchard asked me to come to the station to give a statement. It never crossed my mind to ask for a lawyer, and even if I had thought to do so, there weren't no one I knew to call. I was brought to the East Nashville Police Precinct and set in a small room with just a table and a few chairs where I sat by myself for what seemed like hours. When Detective Pritchard finally joined me, he was accompanied by another detective, a tall woman with a face that expressed her complete disgust with me. They asked me the same questions over and over again: How did I know where to find Caleb Nash's body? When was the last time I saw the boy? Could anyone vouch for my where-abouts on the day the boy disappeared? Why did I kill Caleb Nash? I do my best to answer, but I could tell they had no patience for my explanation about Caleb's spirit visitin' me at the motel. In fact, the lady detective outright laughed in my face at the story. I reminded Detective Pritchard about the receipt for my float on the Harpeth River, but he claimed that despite me havin' the receipt, no one could say for sure they'd actually seen me there, includin' the young kid at the cashier stand, and just 'cause I had a receipt it didn't mean I'd actually done the float. This questionin' went on for what seemed like an eternity. I was hot, thirsty and tired, but I refused all their attempts at forcin' me to sign a confession for something I didn't do. Eventually, I was arrested and booked on what my public defender called "trumped up" charges. The following day at my arraignment, the judge refused my lawyer's request for bail, as I was deemed a "transient" for livin' in a motel and considered a flight risk. I was remanded and thus spent the next three months in a temporary detention center awaitin' trial.

I can say, without a doubt, those ninety days were some of the worst of my life. I knew no one in Nashville, and my siblings' back East were ashamed to be related to the "Murderin' Ghost Girl" as the newspaper had taken to callin' me. The only visitors I had in those long days were my public defender, who had hit the media jackpot when he took my case, and various journalists and new age spiritualists who were only lookin' to exploit my nefarious claim to fame.

My freedom came about by a sheer chance, a strange coincidence that I always thought was designed by the Universe to right a wrong. One early October evenin', a certain Nashville policeman happened to stop a beat-up minivan drivin' erratically down Gallatin Pike. It belonged to a local handyman, one Winston Frazier, who had a few outstandin' warrants for check fraud and one for indecent exposure. When the patrolman stopped his van, he smelled the distinct aroma of marijuana and decided to search the vehicle. In the back of the van, under a pile of old tarps, the officer came across a book marked "Summer Reading Program- Nashville Public Library," its cover titled, "King Arthur and the Knights of the Round Table." The patrolman, who by chance had worked the Caleb Nash case, recalled that the murdered boy had been in possession of such a book at the time of his disappearance, and took Mr. Frazier in for questionin'. When the DNA of mysterious skin found underneath the nails of the dead boy matched that of the unemployed *handyman, authorities took a revived interest in the case. A few days later, Winston Thomas Frazier confessed to the murder of Caleb Nash on that warm summer afternoon in July, and I was free to go, without so much as the slightest apology from the Nashville Police Department.*

"After all that happened with me tryin' to help Caleb Nash, I gave up any desire to aid wanderin' spirits, and for ten years, I successfully avoided makin' contact with any specters," I explain to Phyllis Bagley. My tea has gone cold while I relate my story, so I stand up and head to the microwave to warm it. I hope that now that the nosey docent has heard the terrible tale straight from the horse's mouth, she'll leave well enough alone and not involve herself with my connection to the Johnny Reb.

Unfortunately, I have apparently only wet her appetite for more diggin' into my personal business. She waits until I sit down, then leans across the table, and puts her hand over mine. "I've been waiting my whole life to meet someone like you, Cordelia Mae Achley. You're just the one to help me prove the existence of an afterlife."

Her statement is so absurd I'm not sure how to react. Lacking any polite response, I force a bland smile to my face and say, "I'm afraid you're gonna have to go on waitin' a bit longer, Miz Bagley, 'cause I sure as hell can't help ya' with that project."

"Can't? Or won't?" the British woman asks over the rim of her tea cup.

Johnny was right about one thing. The docent is as

stubborn as a Tennessee mule. Now that she's caught me where I weren't supposed to be, she's got me by the proverbial "collar," and I don't figure she'll give up on me so easily. "I'm tellin' you the God's honest truth, Ma'am, when I say I don't know a lick about the 'afterlife' 'cept what the preachers describe; when your journey here on Earth is over, and you've accepted Jesus as your Lord and Savior, you are welcomed into Paradise. Other than that, there's nothin' more I can tell ya'."

The elderly woman leans back in her chair and crosses her arms over her chest. "Please, Cordelia…let's not play these games. It's beneath you. I understand you might be hesitant to share your special knowledge with an outsider, but we both know that you are blessed with abilities most human beings can only dream about. I am absolutely solid in my belief that you can not only see the ghost that wanders this house, but that you have some kind of special connection to him." She reads the shock in my face and adds, "You're not the only one who can recognize spirits, young lady. Though I don't share your level of ability, I've been sensing wandering ghosts since I was a young girl in Devonshire, England. It's not by chance that the paranormal is my field of academic study, and I'm no charlatan. I am a well-respected authority on lingering souls moving through the natural world. In fact, I've come specifically to Tennessee to study this particular spirit in this specific location. I would guess you are familiar with ley lines, Cordelia?"

I nod. Anyone who taps into the metaphysical world as far back as the Native American peoples understands the energy grid surrounding the earth and the idea of there bein' so-called "global hotspots" for paranormal activities. My home in the Smoky Mountains was an especially powerful location and thus was home to so many practitioners. "I am aware."

"Even the Native American Cherokee Tribe understood the energy pull of this area in Middle Tennessee, and their shamans often traveled here for religious ceremonies. That level of natural energy, combined with the tragedy and extreme emotion that went on here during your Civil War, makes this a highly charged metaphysical location. It's no wonder your young ghost is centered here."

From what I already have learned from Johnny, his refusal to leave this plane and move into the light is more complex than just an attraction to energy. I believe he's been tethered here waitin' for his "Sara Anne" and unable to go onward because of the castin' by Big Lucy, although the docent's information about the ley line energy pull of this location explains why Miz Ruby was drawn to Rippavilla as well and how she came to interact with my Johnny Reb. It's perhaps also the reason my Johnny's ghostly abilities are so unusually strong here. I say none of this to Phyllis Bagley. I tell myself it is because I don't trust the woman and her intentions, but I can't deny that part of me is possessive of this unique specter, and the thought of sharin' him with someone else rubs me the wrong way.

Suddenly, I'm beyond tired, and I still have a long walk back to the house. Continuing this back and forth with the British professor is getting me nowhere. I place my tea cup on the table and rise. "I don't want to be rude or unhelpful, Ma'am, but I'm so tired I can hardly see straight. If ya'll intend to call the authorities and have me arrested then I suppose I can't help that. I can't deny I was here at Rippavilla in the wee hours without permission. But I hope ya' can see it in your heart to let this slide. I promise I will consider talkin' to ya' about our mutual specter friend, but right at this moment, I'm just not up to it."

The docent stands as well, and I'm reminded of what a tiny thing she really is. "I have no intention of calling the police, Cordelia. I'm saddened that you think I'm capable of such a ridiculous thing, especially after all you've suffered at the hands of law enforcement. However, I admit that I continue to hope that you will be willing to introduce me to Rippavilla's ghostly resident and stand as a go-between interpreter between the two of us. You have my card, and you certainly know where to find me during the day. I look forward to working with you and your specter, young lady."

CHAPTER TWENTY-TWO

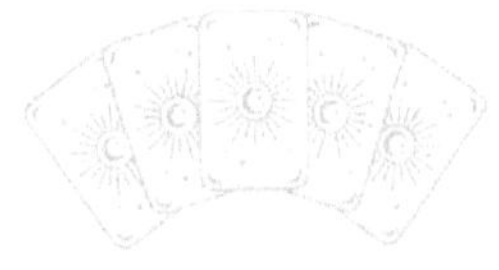

NOT SURPRISINGLY, IN THE PREDAWN HOURS, THE HIKE BACK to Southern Streams feels twice as long as my earlier walk to Rippavilla. Maybe it's because it's daylight now and I can clearly see the long, wooded path stretchin' out for miles in front of me. Or maybe it just seems longer because I'm trekin' the whole way back without the benefit of my Johnny Reb's company to distract me. No matter the reason, my energy tank's runnin' on empty. I can barely put one foot in front of another, and I almost cry tears of joy when the old Mule Barn on the other side of the berm comes into sight, signalin' I'm almost home.

I stumble down the hill and into the lanai, floppin' onto the nearest patio chair to catch my breath. Around me, I hear the sounds of the community comin' to life and wonder how many of them folks just saw me come up over that berm at this ridiculous hour of the mornin'. Some of the houses have kitchens at the back of the property over lookin' the quiet green of their yards and the little incline separatin' Southern Streams' property from that belongin' to the plantation. It would be naive of me to think I've gone completely unnoticed, and I remind myself to start workin' on a plausible story as to why I was wanderin' on the Rippavilla side so early in the day. But the creation of that whopper of a tale will have to wait until later. Right at this moment, I'm too tired to even remember my name.

I kick the flip flops off my blistered feet and flop face first into bed without takin' off my clothes or turnin' down the linens. Despite all the excitement of the past few hours, I fall asleep instantly. But even in slumber, my mind don't rest. I have vivid dreams, one after another, of people and places I feel I should know but don't. Some of them are sweet, some funny, and some are even highly erotic, but it is the last one that eventually jars me awake; a wave of grief so painful it washes over me like a drowin' wave, suckin' the very breath from my lungs. I awake in a sudden panic, panting, with my cheeks wet from tears over a tragedy I can't remember now that I'm fully conscious. I sit on the side of the bed, a little dizzy, somewhat nauseous, and work to slow my heart rate. 'Cause of my gifts, I'm no stranger to full sensory-style dreams, but the ones I've just now experienced felt more real to me than any I have ever had before and I find myself extremely disoriented. On the bedside table next to me, the vintage clock radio shows it's 1:00 PM. I notice that the crystal Johnny gave me a few days back seems darker than I remember it, and when I pick it up to take a closer look, it's crazy hot in my hand. I instantly drop it, and it falls to the floor and rolls under the bed.

In this moment, I'm too wobbly to crawl on the floor to go after it. Instead, I make my way to the bathroom, holding on to the door jams and wall as I go. I barely make it in there before being sick, but strangely enough, I feel much better after a hearty bout of vomitin'. At last, actin' more like myself, I take a long, hot shower, lettin' the water jets work their magic on sore calf muscles which haven't done that much walkin' in ages. I shampoo and condition my hair, and once in front of the sink mirror, decide to put it up in a bun thingy at the back of my head 'stead of leavin' it long and loose like I usually do. I don't own no hair clips, as that ain't my normal look, so I search around the kitchen drawers until I find the chop sticks I saw a few days ago and use them to hold my hair knot in place. The reflection in the mirror looks like me and someone else all at the same time, and for the slightest of seconds, I feel another overwhelmin' sense of deja vu.

I'm also so dang hungry I could eat the hole from the middle of a doughnut. I haven't been to the grocery store since I moved in, and the fridge is as empty as my belly, so I decide to treat myself to lunch out. I lock up the house and head down to Main Street to the diner where my friend Lizzy works. She sees me come in and points me to a table in her section. I study the menu while I wait for her, intendin' to order a simple burger until the special of the day catches my eye. Before I can figure out why this odd entree attracts my attention, Liz saunters up to my table. She gives me the once over and says, "Girl...you look fabulous! That 'stay-cation' at Southern Streams must be agreein' with you." She points to my head, "I like the new 'do.' It makes you look ten years younger…like an old-fashion', sweet, young thang."

"Thanks, Liz. This house-sittin' job's been the best thing to happen to me in years." I think 'bout my experiences with Johnny and can't help but smile as I say, "It's like a whole new chapter's gone and opened up for me. I can't thank you enough for introducin' me to the Kozinskis."

"Oh, honey. I am so happy for you. You deserve some good things in your life. And speakin' of good things, the smothered pork chops are top-notch today."

I shake my head, "Ya' know, for some odd reason, I got a hankerin' for somethin' completely different today. I think I'll try today's 'special.'"

My friend looks at me like I've grown two heads. "You want the country ham and grits?" she asks, making a face. "Girl, you always told me that you thought eatin' grits was like spoonin' up wet sand. And I ain't never seen you eat country ham before. It's surely an acquired taste."

I shrug. "I know. But for some reason it sounds delicious today. Like I said, whole new chapter and all. Oh… and bring me a sweet tea as well."

Lizzy puts her hands on her hips. "Well, now I've seen just 'bout everythin'. Cordelia Mae Achley, who abhors all things saccharine, wants sugar in her tea? Girl, you ain't kiddin' when you say things are changin' for ya'll. It's like you're a whole new person."

After lunch, I struggle to fill the time until I can meet with my "specter crush" again. I wander around some stores in the Crossings, but I've never been much of a shopper and nothing in any of them catches my eye. Plus, I'm horrified by the cost of women's clothing, which to my eye, is nothing more than a plethora of mass-produced junk with crazy price tags affixed. For most of my life, I've been a simple jeans and t-shirt kinda' gal, shunning the rapidly changing styles and cultural expectations put on females down here in the south. Growin' up, I usually had two "goin' to church dresses," which I was expected to alternate, both of which were handed down from the family's older females and tailored to fit me by my Mamaw, who weren't much for the art of sewin'. The rest of the time, I wore faded farm clothes cast-offs from my siblins' and cousins, be they male or female, which was par for the course in rural Sevierville.

When I became a young adult responsible for my own needs, I filled my closet with thrift store treasures, an eclectic selection of whatever suited my fancy at the time. This hasn't changed much as I've aged. Suddenly, I feel an urge to find somethin' new to wear tonight for my visit with Johnny, so I head north down Main Street to the Spring Hill Goodwill store, which I discover looks like every other Goodwill store I've ever shopped.

The racks are chocked full, and I congratulate myself for arrivin' on a day the staff most likely has restocked inventory. I bypass the housewares, books, shoes, and used handbags, focusin' on several racks of women's clothing. I find myself specifically drawn to the selection of Ladies dresses, which is highly unusual for my typical, faded-jean-lovin' fashion sense. Not for the first time today, I feel that the Delia I've always been is takin' a back seat to new aspects of my alternative personality. With my metaphysical gifts and trainin', these feelings should cause all sorts of warnin' bells to be goin' off in my head, yet I am oddly calm about this strange shift of my psyche. I flip through the rack, ignorin' anythin' with spangles an' sparkles, garish colors, or modern cuts. Instead, I'm drawn to the cotton and linen dresses in soft colors and longer lengths, which definitely are in the minority. I gather up a handful in my size and enter the lone dressin' room at the back of the store which, illogically, doesn't have a mirror inside, forcin' me to step outside to use the full-length one hanging there. Of the five dresses I bring into the changin' room, three are either too large or too small and one has a large stain I didn't notice earlier. I slip on the last one, a lightweight cotton gauze, taupe in color, with a faint rose print and tiny buttons goin' all the way down, from neckline to hem. Though it has a modern label, it definitely looks vintage, as if it's come straight out of someone's attic.

I slip it on and begin to button it up, stoppin' at the knee, then step outside to look at myself in the mirror. An elderly woman is browsin' some blankets near the dressin' room, and when she sees me, she says, "Lordy, don't you look like a pretty pitcher', young lady! Like ya'll just stepped out of some romance story. If I was you, I'd snap that frock up right up. No boy gonna' resist you in that dress, honey."

I look at my reflection in the mirror, and my heart jumps in my chest. With my hair up like it is, wearin' this ole'-fashioned dress, I no longer seem to be the Cordelia Achley whom only one a week ago was readin' cards for a livin', but who I am now remains a mystery.

Chapter Twenty-Three

Once home from the Goodwill store, I find myself antsy, not sure of what to do with my person until the early mornin' hours of tomorrow when I will see Johnny again. The dress I just purchased has a funky, musty odor common to resale clothin', so I hand wash it in cold water and mild soap, and hang it on the lanai to dry in the June heat Then, I do some light housekeepin' chores and even try to get involved in the tooth fairy romance I started when I was at the pool, a memory that seems like it happened years ago. Around suppertime, I make myself a soft-boiled egg and toast, an adequate amount of food given that there's still ham and grits still lyin' in my gut. For the next few hours, I alternate between half-heartedly watchin' nonsense on Netflix and dozin', thankful that my mind isn't given over to those weird, realistic dreams I was havin' earlier this morning.

Around 11:00 PM, I turn off the TV and go on over to the guest bathroom to take a shower and wash my hair again. As I'm dryin' off and puttin' my hair up, this time lettin' a few loose strands hang down to frame my face, it hits me, clear as day, that I'm actin' more like a love-sick woman preparin' to see her beau than a spiritual guide helpin' a lost soul join the Afterlife. I hear the voices of my Mamaw and Opal Gaspar in my head, scoldin' me for crossin' the line between aidin' a specter and makin' an emotional connection with one. They ain't wrong about the danger involved. Makin' such a connection increases the chance that the lost spirit will attach itself to me and never move on, which would be an affront to the natural order of things and a really tough situation to fix. It's also entirely possible that in tryin' to establish an emotional connection, the practitioner can lose their own soul in the process. The strange dreams I've been havin' and the changin' of my normal habits should be a cautionary warnin' to myself that things are spiralin' out of control, and that if I have any sense at all I would pack my things and leave the Southern Streams area immediately. But even the flashbacks I've been havin' over the miserable time I spent in prison over the Caleb Nash incident don't make me stop thinkin' about the ghost of the handsome Jonathan Sweet. In fact, I ignore everythin', even goin' as far as to dig through my belongins' lookin' for the only nice jewelry I own, an antique, gold chain with a single large pearl that my Mamaw gave me on my fourteenth birthday. I put it around my neck, and when I clasp it, a strange buzzin' feelin' tickles the insides of my ears. I write off this sensation as a response to my reflection in the bathroom mirror. The lady at the thrift store was right: I look as if I stepped out of an old-timey love story. My face goes pink and I look away. I return to the bedroom, and, havin' learned my lesson about walkin' long distances in flip flops, I slip my feet into a pair of cotton flats I've had for years and settle myself out on the lanai to wait patiently for some sign of my Johnny Reb.

A little after 1:00 AM I see a shimmer at the top of the berm, and I know without a doubt it's him. I feel his anticipation as if it's a livin', breathin' thing. Quietly closin' the screen door behind me, I head up the berm. It's more difficult than before due to my choice of feminine apparel this evenin', so I climb with caution. I stop a few inches from him, careful not to make any physical contact no matter how much I want to touch him. The one and only time we touched left me ill for hours, and tonight, I surely don't want to miss him showin' me where his earthly remains, along with Big Lucy's magical charm, rests.

His eyes go wide when he sees me, and his expression is one of complete and utter awe. *"You are surely a sight for these ole' eyes, darlin'. Ya're just about the most beautiful thing I've seen since I left ya' in Mississippi. I think I would trade my soul to be able ta' kiss ya, Sara Anne, though I ain't even sure I have a soul left to trade."*

Before I can stop myself, the words slip out. *"I'd like to kiss ya' as well, Johnny, but I'm 'fraid that would make for a very short evenin.' It's real important that you show me where your physical remains lie. I can't do a single thing to help ya' without knowin' your final restin' spot."*

He stares at me with love sick, hungry, blue eyes, and I almost don't care if I end up on my back for hours because my need to touch him right now is just as great. Thankfully, however, my trainin' suddenly kicks in, or perhaps it's my Mamaw here keepin' me on the straight and narrow, 'cause instead of makin' contact, I break the stare and take a step further apart. His expression instantly falls, first in disappointment, and then in acceptance of the situation. *"I don't think I'll ever get my fill of lookin' at ya', darlin...not in this life or even in the next."* He points to the jewelry around my neck. *"Ya're even wearin' your favorite necklace, the one your Mama and Daddy gave ya' on your fourteenth birthday. Ya' never took that thing off... not even when we was..."*

The specter doesn't finish his statement, but I'm too shocked even to think about what he means by that. I reach up and touch the pearl at my neck. *"You've seen this necklace before, Johnny?"* I ask in complete disbelief.

"Why sure, sweetheart. It was your favorite. Ya' wore it practically every day that I knew ya','" he answers.

This knowledge hits me like a brick to my head, and though I want to ask a million more questions...about the necklace...about his life with Sara Anne McKinney... about how I came to be part of this story over a hundred years later...I know that nothin' can move forward without my findin' the bones of Lt. Jonathan Sweet from Meridian, Mississsppi. *"Johnny, we can talk more about the necklace later, but before we go any farther, I need you to show me your final restin' spot.*

"Sure, darlin'. Follow me." He turns and starts to head down the berm onto the Southern Springs side.

Rememberin' how far he had me walk the night before, I stop him and ask, *"Just how far away is this spot, Johnny?"*

He scratches the back of his head before answerin'. *"I

suppose it might be a tad too far for your lady feet, Sara Anne. I ain't so good with the length of distance no more"

"Can you give me an approximate idea of where in this area we're headin'?" I question.

"It ain't too far from that stone swimmin' hole. You know... the one where I first left ya' the rose." He gives me the shyest of smiles. *"I've been wishin' since that day that you would go back there, darlin'. I admit to likin' very much how you looked in that bathin' outfit."*

His reference to me in my bikini makes me blush, and I'm glad that it's probably too dark for him to notice. Still, his mention of the swimmin' pool lets me know I'll need to take my car there. It's entirely too far for me to walk to the lodge and back, especially in the middle of the night. Plus, I can't imagine a specter drivin' along with me in my car. I'm not even sure it's possible to contain all that meta-physical energy in the small space of my Honda. *"You're right, Johnny. It's too far for me to walk along with you. How 'bout I drive there in my car and you meet me at the pool gate, okay?"*

"Sure thing, sweetheart! Though I can guarantee I'll get there faster than you." He fades straight away, and I head to my car sittin' in the driveway. I try to be as quiet as possible, but my engine startin' up in the silence of the neigh-borhood at night time sounds like somethin' akin to The Second Comin'. I drive without my lights on toward the lodge, parkin' in the empty lot. As I walk down the little path to the pool, I note that it looks strangely spooky in the dead of night and am relieved to see my special ghost friend standin' right in front of the pool entrance as we agreed.

"See...I told ya' I'd be here before ya'. Some advantages to bein' dead and all," he says with a grin.

"You're not buried somewhere inside the pool area, are you?" I ask, unable to keep the apprehension out of my voice. If Johnny's bones are under the pool, they will be impossible to reach.

"Not at all, Sugar," he answers. *"I'm over this way a bit."*

Relieved he's not in the pool area, I follow him away from there and past the fire pit and tennis courts. My relief is short-lived. Johnny stops in front of a locked, chain link fence. *"I'm right over there, Sara Anne, just under the left side of that long fishin' net."*

He points through the locked gate, and my stomach gives a nasty flip. It appears my poor Johnny Reb is buried somewhere under Southern Streams' Pickleball Court #5. The complete absurdity of the moment leaves me without proper words, so I stutter out the first thing that comes to my mind. *"Are ya sure?"* I ask.

The tall lights that illuminate the pickleball and tennis courts obviously stay on all night at Southern Streams. The glare and shadows from 'em make Johnny's face less distinct than when I see it in the complete dark, and I'm havin' trouble discernin' his expression. I hear him say, *"'Course I'm sure darlin'. I've been lyin' here for a long time now, though I admit I found it far more peaceful when it was woods above me and not this silly net. I never could figure what they's was hopin' to catch with it."*

"It's not for catchin' animals, Johnny. It's part of a game people play. They try to hit a ball over the net with paddles," I explain.

He nods his understandin'. *"That makes sense, I suppose,*

but 'tween you and me...them runnin' back and forth over me ain't very polite."

"No. I suppose it isn't, but in their defense, I don't believe anyone knows you're here. This is far from where the battle took place. Honestly, I was guessin' your earthly remains would be somewhere on the Rippavilla grounds, especially since ya' spend so much time there."

He steps into the shadows where it's darker, givin' his face more definition. I can see clearly a pained expression on his face. "I shouda' been with my unit in the outlay of the Big House that night. But Lordy, darlin'...I was pretty much starvin, so I wandered off in hopes of trackin' me somethin' I could eat. Got caught unawares by a Yankee boy and took a Minie ball to my gut. Never did make it back to my unit."

This admission clarifies to me how Johnny was able to see me at the pool and leave me the rose, his final restin' place bein' so close to it. What it don't explain is his connection to Rippavilla and his ability to travel so far from where he died. A specter's energy field usually stays close to where their life ended, or in the residual energy of someplace that once held great emotional appeal. His hauntin' Rippavilla doesn't make sense, and I ask him about it. "If this is where ya' met your end, Johnny, how come you're able to spend so much time at Rippavilla? This spot here where your bones lie is quite a ways from the Big House. Usually departed souls aren't able to do so much travelin'."

My handsome specter shrugs. "Can't rightly say what drew me to Rippavilla. Accordin' to Miz Ruby, the whole area 'round the Big House sits on some kinda' odd, magnetically charged lines, under the ground that is, where no one can rightly see 'em. I don't know much about such things, but I *figured it must work in the same ways as a compass does, pointin' me to that location. Miz Ruby said my spirit was drawn to the tremendous amount of energy there, same as hers. But that's all I know. In truth, I always liked imaginin' that I was the Master of such a grand place. Only thing missin' all this time was you, Sara Anne...in that house with me...with you as its Mistress... just like we planned."*

Upon hearin' these words, a strange memory comes over me, as if I'm positive I've heard these very words before at another time in my life. I suddenly feel short of breath and drop to my knees right there in front of the pickleball fence. I hear that strange buzzin' noise in my ears again, and in my mind, I see very clear mental image of me and Johnny standin' on a wooden porch in the early part of an evenin'. I'm wearin' a sweepin' dress with my pearl on a chain 'round my neck; I can even smell the overwhelmin' scent of night jasmine and magnolia right here in a spot that's devoid of any such greenery. Most absurdly, I remember the exact moment Johnny is describin'...which is impossible 'cause it never happened in my lifetime.

Chapter Twenty-Four

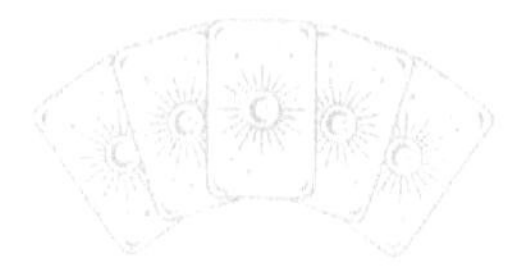

I FEEL MY SPECTER'S ENERGY SPILLIN' ALL OVER THE PLACE, obviously agitated over my current fragile emotional and physical state. In my head I hear him callin' to me, *"Sara Anne...Darlin'...are you alright?"* but the words sound like they are comin' from several feet away and not from right next to me. I know he wants nothin' more than to help me off the ground, but his touchin' me surely would only make things worse.

I raise up my arm, thinkin' I can keep him from layin' metaphysical hands on me while pushin' myself up off the ground, all wobbly legs and swayin' balance. I'm undoubtedly not appearin' very lady-like in my long, flowy dress that's now all tangled 'round my knees, and once I'm standin' upright, I feel as though my head has been split in two: me, Cordelia Mae Achley is livin' on one side, while someone entirely different is livin' on the other. The pearl chain 'round my neck feels heavy and warm against my skin. I think I'd like to remove it, but my arms don't seem to wanna' follow through, and I'm suddenly overwhelmed with a deep sense of fatigue, wantin' nothin' more than to stumble to my car, head home, and drop into bed to sleep for a couple of straight days.

Instead, I force myself to remember why I'm here. This lost soul is relyin' on me to help him move on to the Afterlife. *"I'm fine, Johnny. I just felt a mite strange for a bit... as if someone else's thoughts was inside my head. Explain to me again about that charm Big Lucy made for you and Sara Anne."*

Johnny moves back into the haze of lights, and thus, his expression is again lost to me. *"Like I already told ya, darlin, Big Lucy twisted those strands of our hair together and tied 'em with a white ribbon. She lit some black and purple candles and drew a circle 'round the two of us 'fore prickin' our fingers with a sewin' needle and squeezin' drops of our blood on the knot. Then she mumbled some words I can't much recall understandin'. When she was done, she gave the charm to me to hang on to. She said I had to always keep it with me for the hoodoo to work. I put it inside my Grandpappy's pocket watch knowin' it would be safe there; it was still there the night I died. I remember thinkin' as I lay on the ground with my blood pourin' out of me that the damn charm didn't do no good at keepin' us together, Sara Anne."* Though I can't see his face, the tone of his voice suggests he's emotional over the memory. *"But now I guess I was proved plumb wrong, 'cause here we are, darlin...back together just like Big Lucy said."*

I try to shake the feelins' of despair that are fillin' my soul right now. Previously giddy with the excitement and romance of the situation, I had erroneously believed I could locate Johnny's remains, secretly dig 'em up, retrieve the watch with the charm, and reverse the Vodou spell that Big Lucy had cast upon the couple, thus freein' him from his earthly chains. Now I realize what a ridiculous notion it all was, especially after discoverin' that my Johnny is buried under layers of asphalt, concrete and dirt in an open, public place. I pray that my charmin' specter don't feel my sense of hopelessness, 'cause it's obvious he's been waitin' a real long time for this moment.

Additionally, I have another issue I need to attend to as soon as possible. There ain't no doubt in my mind that I'm sharin' my head and body space with a second soul. My sudden change in tastes regardin' food and clothin', strange memories poppin' up out of nowhere, and the crazy, true-to life dreams are direct indications that somethin' metaphysical is takin' up a presence inside of me. For reasons I can't yet explain other than a sixth sense, I have a feelin' that this old pearl necklace of mine holds the answers. If I can figure out how I came to own this piece of antique jewelry that once belonged to Sara Anne McKinney, then maybe it will be possible to break the spiritual chains connectin' me to these Civil War ghosts. However, for me to even begin to solve all these ghostly problems, I'm gonna' need to rely on the help of two people who generally rub me the wrong way: my older sister, Rachel Beth, and the very demandin' Phyllis Bagley.

IN MY QUEST TO HELP POOR JOHNNY, I DECIDE TO START with the more difficult of the two conversations. My sister, Rachel Beth, is nearly ten years older than me. She and my brother, Colton, are from my Mama's first

MARRIAGE, WHICH WAS LONG OVER BY THE TIME I CAME TO be. We ain't never been close, not just because of the wide age gap between us, but more 'cause it was obvious I was Mamaw's favorite and that I'd been the one to inherit the family hoodoo gifts.

By the time I turned fourteen, Mama had been gone from our lives for seven years and us younger kids were left in the care of Mamaw. Rachel Beth was also gone from our household, she havin' married a local boy, Billy Yardley, at age 17, and them takin' a place of their own a few miles down from our farm. Even when she was part of our lives, Rachel Beth paid me little mind. When she did decide to acknowledge my existence, it was only to remind me that I was simply the by-product of our Mama's bad choices, and that I bore the Achley name 'cause no honest man would give me his.

I knew at an early age that my Mama and the man that fathered me weren't lawfully married in neither the eyes of the law nor the Church. It weren' hard to forget, bein' that folks let me know every chance they got. Still, it never bothered me much. I was fine with bearing my Mamaw's maiden name, "Achley," along with the special gifts that were part of her line. When I was old enough to understand 'bout the things that went on between a man and woman, I ventured to ask my Mama for my daddy's name but was scolded sternly and told that the less I knew 'bout "that no-good-son-of-a-bitch," the better I'd be. After Mama left, I tried bringin' up the topic with my Mamaw, but she told me in simple words that I needed to follow the path in front of me and not worry about the paths that already had been walked. After that, I stopped askin'. It just didn't seem important.

Despite Rachel Beth's personal disdain of me, she appeared dutifully at all the family gatherins' includin' my birthdays 'cause she knew better than to give my Mamaw anythin' to be angry 'bout. Honestly, I'm pretty sure my siblins' both loved and feared her at the same time. Her reputation as a "wise woman" was not to be messed with as talk of her skills had grown to mythical proportions. In my case, I loved her dearly. However, when it came to my trainin', she was a solid Taskmaster, not given to shows of affection, so I was mighty surprised when she gave me such a lavish gift as a pearl necklace on my birthday. I thought the pearl restin' in its old-fashioned settin' was the most beautiful thing I'd ever seen, and I proudly clasped it 'round my neck. Even today, I still remember Rachel Beth makin' cryptically rude comments 'bout it. "It figures you'd get somethin' old and used like that, Cordelia…considerin' the source," she said when the two of us was alone. At the time, I assumed she was referrin' to the fact that my Mamaw seemed to dote on me, but later in life I recalled the look of outright jealousy in her eyes. Now that Mamaw is gone, and none of us know for sure whatever happened to our Mama, Rachel Beth is my only source for gathering any information about the necklace.

I didn't bother callin' ahead to see whether a visit was okay. Knowin' Rachel Beth like I do, she'd find a million reasons not to be able to see me. I knew that after she'd lost her husband Billy in a freak farmin' accident a few years back, followed shortly by her eldest son, Jack's, death in a motorcycle collision, my sister basically became a hermit, rarely leavin' her house. Chances were good she'd be home, and once I was at her door, it would be hard for her to turn me away without causin' a scene in front of the neighbors.

After her tragedies, Rachel Beth sold her property in the Sevierville area and moved to a small frame house in Clarksville where her daughter and grandbabies live. Leavin' early the followin' mornin', I made the hour and a half drive without much trouble. However, I was more than a little nervous about needin' to discuss' an event with my sister that had been long put in the past. After the losses she's suffered, her favorite sayin' was, "Let the Lord's plan be as He meant it. It ain't my place to question it." I'm hopin' that since she already considers me to be a god-less sinner, she'll find it okay to talk to me about my perceived tainted past.

I know by her car bein' in the driveway that Rachel Beth is home. After takin' a long time to come to the door, she eventually answers my bell-ringin' with a face that looks as if she'd been sucking on the sourest of lemons. "Hey, Rachel Beth. Long time, no see. You're lookin' well. I like the new hair color," I say, tryin' to keep our initial conversation light.

"What do you want, Cordelia Mae? Ain't Clarksville a long way from Nashville?" she answers through clenched teeth.

"I'm not in Nashville no more, Rachel Beth. Haven't been for years. I'm livin' in Spring Hill now," I respond.

"Hmmm…no doubt you was run out of the Music City

after that murder trouble. What in the good Lord's name caused you to show up today on my doorstep?"

"I need to talk to you 'bout somethin' important, Rachel Beth. Can I come in? I promise I won't take up too much of your day."

She frowns. "This ain't a real good time, Cordelia Mae. If you'd a called ahead, I woulda' told ya' just that."

She starts to shut the door, but I put my foot on the stoop to keep it from closin' it. "This is really important to me, Rachel Beth. I drove a long way to get here." I pull the small pouch from my pocket, a last-ditch bribe I hope will gain me entry. "I made you some of Mamaw's tea. The one that ya'll said helped your headaches." I wave the pouch in front of her nose so she can get a good whiff of the herbs inside.

I can tell the bribe weakens her resolve. Rachel's suffered from migraines for as long as I can remember, and despite many visits to city doctors and specialists, the only thing that seemed to bring her any relief was the herbal tea my Mamaw used to make and to which I alone have the list of ingredients and steps. "You sure this is just like Mamaw's?" she asks.

"Absolutely," I promise. "I make it exactly like she taught me...usin' her special mortar and pestle."

She grabs the pouch from my hands and swings the door open. "I can only give you twenty minutes, Delia. Then my shows come on and I don't want to miss nothin'."

Grateful for even that tiny bit of time, I enter my sister's immaculate parlor and park myself on the edge of her sofa. She sits herself in a recliner across from me, the pouch with the tea leaves gripped in her hand. "Now... what's so all-fire important that you gotta' come botherin' me in my grief, Cordelia Mae?"

Knowin' I don't got much time, I get right to the point and pull the necklace from the pocket of my jeans. "I need to know what you know about this necklace, Rachel Beth...the one Mamaw gave me for my 14th birthday."

I swear her face goes a shade paler as she shakes her head. "Girl, I can't remember that far back! Why would I remember somethin' about a silly gift you got on your birthday several moons ago?"

Even if I didn't have any psychic abilities, I would know she was lyin'. Her eyes shift from left to right, and I see her squeeze the cloth of the pouch even tighter. I hate to use threats to get what I need, but Johnny's soul...and perhaps even mine...depends on this information. "Rachel Beth...you know I can tell when folks are lyin' to me. I suggest you tell me the truth or I will not be held responsible for what might befall ya'."

My older sister squirms in her chair. She grew up livin' with both my Mamaw and me, and though her faith don't allow her to go professin' her belief in the hoodoo, she knows perfectly well it exists. "You are the lowest of the low, Cordelia Mae Achley! Threatenin' your own flesh and blood like you're doin'!"

"I ain't got no other choice, Rachel Beth. Things have come up. I need to know where Mamaw got this necklace from. I've been told it's Victorian in design and an antique, so I know she didn't get it from anywhere local. Just tell me what ya'll know, and I promise I'll leave you alone. In fact, I'll even make you more tea whenever you need it. Just spill it!"

Rachel thinks 'bout it for a moment, then sighs and leans back in the recliner. "I suppose everybody involved is long dead, and Mamaw can't blame me from the grave if she hears that you're threatenin' me." She takes a breath and begins, talkin' faster than she usual. "The only reason I know about the necklace is because I was snoopin' in Mamaw's things and saw the letter before she walked in and caught me at it. She grabbed it from my hands and slapped me one good across my face."

My heart begins to race, knowin' for sure that Rachel knows more than she's ever said before. "What letter?" I ask

"The letter that came with the necklace…by post. Mamaw had to sign for it at the post office."

"Who was the letter from? What did it say about the necklace?" I question, anxious for the answers.

"Hold your horses, girl, I'm gettin' to all that. The letter was from the warden at Lauderdale County Prison," she says. "In Mississippi."

At the mention of Lauderdale, my heart jumps. It's the county in Mississippi that's home to the town of Meridian…home to Johnny and Sara Anne. "I know exactly where that is. Go on."

"The letter said that the necklace belonged to a lifer there at the prison who was dyin' of lung cancer and who had turned his soul around and accepted the Lord Jesus as his Savior. He'd asked the warden to hold onto the ugly thing and when he died to see that it got to his only livin' relative…a daughter in Sevierville…who he thought was livin' with her grandmother."

At this revelation, my hands start to tremble and the necklace once again feels warm to the touch. "Shit!" I swear. "That man in prison was my father?"

"See what happens when you go diggin' into things better left buried, Cordelia? Does knowin' that your own father was a horrible criminal make you feel better?"

I can't even think about that angle. I need to know the man's name, although part of me already somehow knows. I brush the idea away. Maybe the necklace was somethin' my father stole? He was, after all, in prison for life. "Did you see the man's name, Rachel Beth? Who was he…this man that sent me a valuable piece of jewelry?"

"Mamaw made me promise not to tell you, Delia. I can't break a promise to a dead hoodoo woman. Lord knows what might happen to me."

"Mamaw's long moved on to the Afterlife, Rachel Beth. But I'm still here and I'm just as skilled as she. You tell me what I need to know right this minute, ya' hear me? Or else! After all these years, I deserve to know who my damn father was!"

Rachel purses her lips and shakes her head. "Whatever, Cordelia Mae. It don't surprise me none that your daddy was a jailbird like you. You obviously take after him…like father…like daughter. Both of you criminals. It ain't no skin off my nose if you find out that some hoodlum by the name of Carter McKinney left our Mama with a little unpleasant surprise before takin' off and leavin' her high and dry with a baby in her belly."

Chapter Twenty-Five

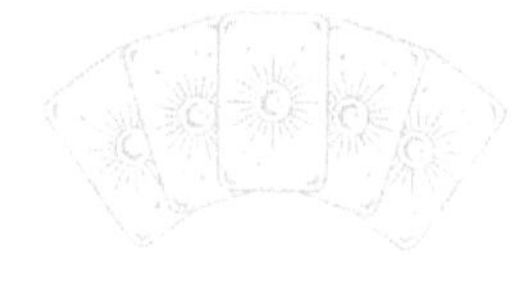

RACHEL BETH'S REVELATION HAUNTS ME AS I DRIVE ALL THE way back to Spring Hill. It's shockin' 'nough finally to discover the name of my daddy after all these years, but even more maddinin' to know that my Mamaw knew this important information for years and never thought fit to tell me. I know she must've had her reasons, but the fact that I had to learn this life-alterin' information from, of all people, Rachel Beth, sticks in my craw like a bur on a mule's ass.

If what my sister said is true, it may explain some of the deep connection between my Johnny Reb and me, and why I resemble his Sara Anne. What I need now is to learn where Carter McKinney falls on Sara Anne's family tree, thus findin' my own place. Despite bein' hungry and tired from my mornin' adventure, I drive directly to the Spring Hill library in the hopes of securin' some computer time, my need for answers greater than my needs for food and rest.

It's lunch time, and the library is empty, so I have no trouble claimin' a desktop. I immediately check the two most popular ancestry sites. Although both mention a Carter McKinney, neither goes back far enough to serve my purpose. I then find a link to a site run by a Confederate reenactment group that focuses on the ancestry of Civil War families of the Confederate South. Though believin' it to be a long shot, I click on the link and am surprised to be rewarded with exactly the information I'm lookin' for. In a page devoted to Mississippi, I locate the McKinney family tree from the town of Meridian. The first entry is for Patrick Arthur McKinney, born in 1808 in New Orleans, Louisiana, and died in 1842 at the young age of 34. He had married June Marie Turnboldt of Natchitoches, Louisiana, in 1829, and the two of them moved to Meridian in 1831, where they had six children, four of whom lived to see adulthood. I recognize the name of their eldest, a son named Thomas Turnboldt McKinney, having seen it during earlier research listed among the land records for Lauderdale County. At that time, I speculated he might be Sara Anne's father, and now I can verify that hunch. In 1850, Thomas married Mary Sara MacDonald, also of Meridian, ten years his senior and considered an "old maid" by Southern standards at that time. Thomas and Mary proceeded to have five children, with two dyin' in infancy. Their firstborn was a boy named Colin James, followed a year and a half later by a set of fraternal twins, named Arthur Thomas and Sara Anne.

I stare at the names for a long time, tryin' to sort out

my feelins' before goin' any further. When I do move on, I, of course, trace Sara Anne's family tree branch first, but I'm shocked at its short length and abrupt end. According to these family records, Sara Anne McKinney died December 3rd, 1864, at the tender age of 17. A funny chill runs down my spine as I realize that Sara Anne passed only a few days after Johnny. Had they not gone to Big Lucy for that castin' might they have eventually found each other in the Afterlife?

An odd pain rolls deep within my belly, and I'm not rightly sure whether it's from me not eatin' anythin' all day, or from the sadness I feel for my Johnny and his Sara Anne, along with the absolute proof that there's no way I am a direct descendant of Johnny's one true love like I came to the library believin'. However, there's still the chance that I'm related to the family somehow, and I lean over the computer to click on Sara's twin brother, Arthur, but hesitate. Somethin' is botherin' me about the dates. I scroll back up to an earlier page about Thomas and Mary, and that's when I see: the date connected to the youngest of their deceased infant children, a boy child named William John who was born and died the same day as Sara Anne…December 3rd, 1864.

I suppose it could be possible that the McKinney family suffered two awful tragedies on that same date, them losin' both their grown daughter and their newborn son at the same time. Medical practices in 1864 certainly were not what they are today. Yet, somethin' ain't addin' up here to me. Accordion' to the family tree, Mary McKinney was 30 years of age when she married Thomas. In 1864, she'd have been 44 years old when

William John was born...not impossible, but most unusual.

The pain in my gut increases, and without warnin', I'm suddenly relivin' mental images of myself in childbirth, my face sweaty and contorted with pain, as an older woman wearin' a *tignon* (creole headdress) presses on my abdomen and scolds me to push harder. I hear the weak, strangled cry of a newborn and then feel the most over-whelmin' sense of grief I can ever remember.

The computer screen in front of me blurs and I know I'm gonna be sick. I head to the Ladies room as quickly as possible with my hand over my mouth. I barely make it there before I empty my heavin' stomach of nothin' but bile. Spent, I lean my head on the cool metal door of the stall and consider the facts that have recently become clear to me: the boy child that died on December 3rd, along with its Mama...was not Mary McKinney's baby; it was Sara Anne's...hers and Johnny's.

Thankfully, no one disturbs me while I'm in the Ladies room. I stand up and walk to the sink, where I splash cold water on my face and rinse my mouth out as best I can using my hand as a cup. The face lookin' back at me in the mirror is pale and wan, and though it's the face I am sure I was born with, my reflection appears to me as a stranger's.

I return to the technology center, and true to the nature of the South, my purse is untouched where I had left it and the web page is still open to the McKinney family tree. Determined to have with me as much infor-mation as possible when I meet with Phyllis Bagley, I sit myself back down and get straight back to work, ignorin' my sick stomach and the beginnin' of a mighty powerful headache. Knowin' that Sara Anne's line ended with her and her child, I move on to her twin brother, Arthur. It takes a few minutes of scrollin' through a long list of his progeny to eventually find what I'm lookin' for in the 7th generation down from Arthur: one Carter Francis McKinney, born January 7th, 1959, and died June 18th, 1993.

There's no doubt in my mind that this man is the same Carter McKinney who sent me the necklace, since the dates line up just right; his dyin' in June of 1993 and me turnin' 14 in September of that same year. There's no mention in the family tree of Carter havin' any children in the family tree, but that don't surprise me none. I'm sure as rain that he and my Mama never officially married. It's a wonder he even knew about me at all, unless perhaps my Mama was houndin' him for child support money.

That would make me an 8th generation member of the McKinney family, a child born of Sara Anne's twin brother's line. It would explain why I resemble the woman so much, and gives meanin' to why I seem so connected to the family. What it don't explain are the dreams, the visual memories and the food cravins' that I've been havin' that are all new to me. This is a question I'm hopin' Phyllis Bagley can help me answer. Finished with my family tree research, I print the pages detailin' my family history and leave the library to head back to Rippavilla Plantation.

The docent is givin' a tour when I arrive, so I wander the gift shop bidin' my time until she returns, pickin' up books and flippin' through their pages, perusin' a rack of postcards, and rearrangin' a display of plastic Confederate soldiers; anythin' to keep my head centered in the present. Eventually, the tour enters the gift shop, along with its knowledgeable guide. Upon seeing me, Phyllis Bagley peers over her glasses and smiles but doesn't personally address me. Instead, she holds up a finger, signalin' that I should hold my peace until the tourists leave the gift shop.

It takes nearly twenty minutes for the last visitors to pay for their purchases and exit the building. Phyllis sighs. "Thank you for your patience, my dear. I'd rather not get into a discussion that possibly could be overheard. Dropping hints about our mutual paranormal friend is good for business, but the last thing we want to do is call negative attention to the house." She slides her glasses off her nose so that they hang on a chain around her neck. "I hope that your coming here means you've reconsidered my earlier request?"

I hesitate before I respond. If the Caleb Nash incident taught me anythin', it taught me to be cautious about how much I reveal regardin' my metaphysical abilities. I was thoroughly hounded and badgered for months after my acquittal of the boy's murder, and that experience made me "gun shy" when talkin' about the extent of my gifts. As it stands now, things have moved beyond the option of playin' it safe. If I'm gonna' be able to help Johnny and still keep my sanity, I need to go ahead and offer up some trust. "Things have...escalated regardin' our mutual friend, Miz Bagley. I'm afraid I need some advice on how to...proceed."

I don't miss the glint of anticipation and excitement in the docent's eyes. Her head swivels to the ornate grandfather clock standin' in the corner of the gift shop. "I have an hour until my next tour... a private group... Red Hat ladies from Springfield, Illinois on a Girl's Weekend to Nashville. I surely won't need a lot of prep time for that one. Follow me. We can talk in the break room."

I follow Phyllis back to the familiar room in which we spoke after she busted me for sneakin' 'round the house without permission. As she did before, the British woman puts a kettle on to boil and pulls out the same two mugs with the plantation's image on them and sits down across from me. "So, Miss Cordelia...how can we be of assistance to each other?"

Right away I understand that if she agrees to help me, I will be obliged to return the favor in her quest to document afterlife experiences. It's not like I have any choice; the only other person I would ever be able to seek help for this would be my old mentor, Opal Gaspar, who sadly is spendin' the last days of her life in a care facility sufferin' from advanced Alzheimer's, and I don't have enough time to research and vet another local psychic. Phyllis Bagley's business card states she received a doctorate from some fancy paranormal school in Scotland, which seems promisin'. "I'm not sure where to start, Ma'am. Things have been advancin' so fast I don't rightly know where to jump in."

The tea kettle whistles, but the elderly woman ignores it, too focused on the conversation. "Perhaps you should start by explaining why you now seem to be presenting double auras when previously you only had one."

The docent catches me off guard. To be able to see auras on other livin' beings requires a fair amount of metaphysical talent. Even I still struggle with readin' auras on certain occasions. It's clear to me now that my 'new partner' is more than a busy-body academic, dabblin' untrained in the spirit world. She has some genuine talent. "Then I presume you can see that they belong to two different people...me and someone else?" I ask.

"Clear as day, my dear, though I can tell there is an intimate bond between the two of you." she replies. "Just who is in there with you? It's not our cheeky house ghost...of that I'm sure. This second aura is definitely feminine in nature."

I nod. "You're right. She's a woman. But she and our mutual friend are connected...in a big way."

Dr. Bagley rises to fetch the tea kettle and spoons the loose tea into a strainer before adding it to the hot water. "Then, Miss Cordelia, you must start at the beginning and tell me everything you know about your new 'stowaway' while we wait for our tea to steep."

Once I begin, the words come pourin' out of me like a fast-runnin' creek. I describe the changes in my habits: the way I dress and wear my hair, my sudden hankerin' for foods I never ate before. I tell her about the necklace, and how I unwittingly inherited a family heirloom from a father I didn't know. Then I show her the copy I made of the McKinney family tree, and of my Daddy's place on it.

The docent listens to me without interruption, leavin' her tea untouched and goin' cold. When I stop to take a breath, without even gettin' to the huge problem of Johnny's bones and the Vodou charm buried beneath the pickle ball court, Phyllis shakes her head in amazement and pipes up, "I'm so glad you came to me with this, Miss

Cordelia. This isn't the first time I've heard a story like yours. Frankly, it's more common than most people realize, though a majority of the population accepts this strange phenomena as simple REM sleep activities. Nothing could be further from the truth. Tell me, my dear, have you ever heard of past life regression?"

Chapter Twenty-Six

I AIN'T ALTOGETHER COMFORTABLE WITH THE IDEA OF BEIN' hypnotized. I've read enough about past lives to consider that there may be some truth to the whole idea of souls reincarnatin' into different lives, though it goes against everythin' I was taught growin' up Baptist. My Mamaw and Opal Gaspar both were able to compartmentalize their faith beliefs and their hoodoo gifts into separate theories. I myself was never quite convinced that one negated the other. Rather, it's my humble contention that there's a whole lot more about the true nature of souls and the dealins' of the Universe than anyone actually understands, and thus I choose to keep an open mind.

It's not the spiritual theory that bothers me about past-lives regression therapy. My uneasiness rests in the idea that under hypnosis, I might unwittingly reveal my true feelins' regardin' my sweet Johnny Reb. With my training and life experience, I understand that I need to take a less emotional attitude when dealin' with specters; my job simply is to help them move on, not to develop romantic feelins' for them. Yet, from day one, I've been deeply attracted to this long- dead Confederate soldier, and even though I know it is my honored duty and sacred obligation to help him move to whatever awaits his soul, a big part of me don't want him to go and leave me.

Phyllis Bagley rents a townhouse in an expensive, gated community in Thompson's Station called Woodlawn Estates. The security guard at the front gate checks my name on a list before lettin' me in and directs me toward the west side of the complex. Despite the miles of look-a-like buildins', I find the docent's home by recognizin' the giant gazin' ball in her front yard that she told me to look for. She must see me pull up 'cause she meets me at the door, and I can tell she's pleased as punch that I'm actually going through with this hypnosis plan of hers.

Ever polite, she offers me a cup of tea or a soft drink before beginnin'. I'm far too nervous for that. "I'd rather we just got on with it, Ma'am, before I change my mind," I insist.

Phyllis leads me down a flight of stairs to a large room she obviously uses as a home office. The walls are lined with shelves of heavy books and an oversized antique desk sits at the far most corner, but what I notice first is a video camera setup on a tripod facing an overstuffed sofa. "You're recording our session? I ask.

"Well of course, my dear. I'd assumed you would want to review the whole experience when we're done. Some patients remember everything they tell me, but some others don't remember a solitary thing. Being that this is your first time, I wasn't sure how you'd react when you come out of the hypnotic state, so to be safe I'm set up to record. That is what you want, isn't it? To be able to view everything that is said and done during your regression?"

It makes sense to me, so I nod my agreement. "Yes, of course I'd like to hear what I say while I'm under."

"Good. Shall we begin then?" she asks. Not waiting for a reply, she points to the sofa. "If you'll take a seat there, Miss Cordelia. You can sit or stretch out...whichever way you find you're most comfortable."

I begin by sitting, but in this position, I'm forced to stare right at the camera which makes me self-conscious, so I kick off my sandals and lie flat on the sofa, a throw pillow under my head, starin' at the ceiling. "Now I want you to close your eyes and relax," the docent says. "Try to relax your mind and spirit. Empty your soul of all that anxiety and worry you are keeping bottled up inside. Take a deep breath in...and then...exhale. That's the way...nice and slow...in and out...letting go of your fear."

I am no stranger to centering my mind. It's the foremost step before beginnin' any hoodoo work and necessary when I communicate with the specters I engage. My usual technique is to picture a blackboard in my mind... crammed with hundreds of words that I slowly watch myself erase, which is what I do now while the British woman speaks to me. Her accented voice is now softer and far less clipped than during her normal speech patterns. "I want you to picture a door, Cordelia...a door with a knob. Do you see a door, my dear?" she asks.

"Yes, I can see it."

"Excellent. Tell me what the door looks like. Is it made of wood? Is it a shiny metal door?"

"It's a wooden door," I murmur. "An old wood door

with a brass knob." The woman's voice sounds as if it's getting farther away, and my breathing falls into a slow, regular pattern.

"That sounds like a wonderful door, Delia," the voice says. "I want you to grab the knob and turn it. You'll find that the door is unlocked and that you can step through it without the least bit of worry. Step through that lovely door, my dear, and into your past…"

THE RECORDIN' OF MY REGRESSION THERAPY WAS unnecessary. I remember every moment of the two hours, able to recall specific moments and their details like scenes from a favorite movie. On the other hand, my UK friend is thrilled with the results and happy beyond belief to have proof of such a productive session to use for her academic study. She asks my permission to share it amongst her colleagues. I give it to her, signing a consent form that stipulates that my identity, as well as that of the Sweet and McKinney families, must remain strictly hidden.

We watch the tape together, not so much as a way for me to remember things I related, but more as jumpin' off points in our discussion of where we should go from here, and how I can help my Johnny move on. Fortified with a glass of bourbon on ice, I admit to the docent that I have "feelins'" for our resident specter, that perhaps I'm even in love with him, and that despite understandin' better where those feelins' are comin' from, I am becomin' increasingly saddened and anxiety ridden over the thought of losin' him...apparently again.

The professor is sympathetic, obviously a true believer in the topic of her studies. "That doesn't surprise me at all, my dear. You and that particular lost soul have been connected for hundreds of years during which time you've experienced both extreme joy and heart-wrenching grief ...well...at least two lives we know of. I'd be extremely interested in seeing if this connection goes back even further than the lives we explored in this session."

I nix that idea. Right now, I am only interested in the problems surroundin' the here and now. From my experiences, I believe that unless I find Johnny's remains and retrieve the watch with Big Lucy's charm, my special Confederate soldier ain't movin' on...to anywhere. Not to Heaven, or Vahalla, or Jannah, or even to his next "life." Least that's what I conclude, but the truth is, everythin' about this specter, or my strange ties to him, break the rules of my previous metaphysical trainin' and any knowledge of ghosts passed on to me by my Mamaw and Opal Gaspar. Hell...I ain't even sure where the whole idea of reincarnation fits in my Baptist upbringin'. I am way out of my comfort zone on this mission to help Johnny, almost like a blind man tryin' to land a plane. "Maybe that's somethin' we can explore at a later date, Miz Phyllis. Right now, I need your help gettin' our specter friend 'found' and unearthed. As I explained to ya, he's restin' in a real terrible spot."

"And I will help you with that, Miss Cordelia. You have my word. But even you must be astounded at what we've uncovered this evening. I've done these types of regressions dozens of times before and discovered that it's very common for my patients to see familiar souls appearing in several past lives. There seems to be some type of repetition in grouping the same souls together in different life cycles. But this is the first time I've ever seen so many of the same life events in both of the past lives we explored. Scholars have always held to the theory that souls are sent back to new lives to learn from their past mistakes and to gain spiritual growth. But what I saw tonight was more like a repeat performance. Plus, all the souls involved in your lives seem to have a direct biological heritage. It's most unusual, my dear, and truly fascinating. It shatters so many preconceived notions scholars have held regarding the afterlife."

My throat tightens at her comment. I remember explicitly what the professor is speakin' of. Walking through that door to my past, I discovered that Johnny and I have known each other long before our first meetin' on the berm. Not only did we have an intimate relationship one hundred and sixty years ago, but another at the time of the American Revolutionary War. In both cases, a child was created from the union, and in both times, Johnny was called off to war only to end up dead while I and our child died shortly after giving birth. I don't need no video tape to remind me of the pain and loss of those moments. I recall every agonizin' millisecond as if it happened only yesterday. Up until now, I'd never given' much thought to becomin' a mother. The thought that I might end up bein' as bad in the role as my own Mama has always kept me from actively seeking the experience.

Now, knowin' what I know of our past, I can't help but wonder what it might have been like to create a family with Johnny.

Sadly, that's a door I'll never walk through. Even if I do find that Vodou charm and release my poor soldier boy's soul, it's unlikely I'll ever see him again. I'm no expert on how all this reincarnation stuff works, but I'm doubtful the Jonathan Sweet I'll be meetin' tonight on the berm will show up in my life again so soon after his soul's release. The regression therapy showed me that there was nearly a hundred years between our last two meetins'. Maybe, if things follow the same pattern, we'll both meet up again in 2123…but I won't be the same Cordelia Mae Achley-McKinney I am today, and Johnny won't be my sweet Johnny Reb. Instead, we'll both only be some past life memories in our new selves, and that thought literally breaks my heart. How can I even consider a happy life knowing my one true love, my fated destiny, is gone forever?

Chapter Twenty-Seven

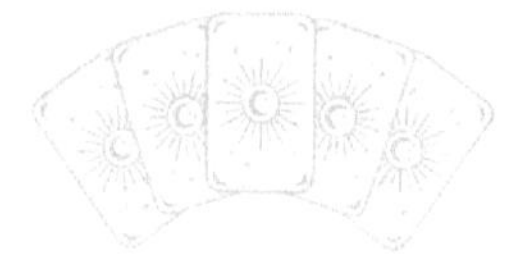

Miz Bagley gets up and adds more ice to her rock glass, followed by another splash of bourbon. Who would have thought a cardigan-wearin, tea-drinkin', British professor would be such a fan of American bourbon? I would have guessed she'd much prefer Scotch whiskey. "Would you like a refill, dear," she asks, as she holds up the bottle of Maker's Mark.

"No thank ya, Ma'am. I need to be able to drive home." I don't mention that I still plan on meetin' with Johnny in the wee morning hours, concerned that she'll talk her way into taggin' along. I wanna' keep all the time I have left with him for myself.

She nods and takes her glass to a chair across from me. "Now suppose we go over the logistics of where our soldier friend is buried. You mentioned it was on Southern Streams property?" she asks.

"Yes…in a very public spot with impossible problems to overcome," I explain. "Accordin' to Johnny, he's lyin' directly under one of the community's Pickleball courts… apparently several feet below the net."

"Is he sure?" the docent asks. "I would have guessed he was buried somewhere closer to Rippavilla with all the time he spends haunting there."

I take issue with her use of the word 'hauntin'. Johnny's behavior ain't nowhere near the level of true hauntin'. I've seen plenty of examples of troublesome specters. They far exceed in malice all of Johnny's playful attitude, but I've come for the woman's help, so I let her misconception slide. "I originally thought the same thing, Ma'am. About his bein' at the big house all the time. He explained that he draws energy from the ley lines under Rippavilla, more so than he can garnish from his final restin' place. But there's not the slightest doubt that he knows for a fact where he took his last breath. That's why I need your help. I was hopin' you would know the right people to contact about findin' him. I don't suppose the residents of Southern Streams will be very happy with us diggin' up their fine amenities. From my short time livin' there, I can tell they like that game very much. I see people usin' them courts all day and far into the evenin', them havin' lights over there and all. I wasn't sure who to speak to first…the people in charge of the community or the city of Spring Hill officials?"

The docent took a sip of her bourbon, obviously mulling the question over. "I would think we should start with the Southern Stream's HOA representatives, since this directly affects the residents of that community. I will tell you, however, if their board is anything like the one here at Woodlawn Estates, I expect it won't be an easy sell.

I have found that when you give people a bit of discretionary power, it tends to go straight to their egos. Nonetheless, I do have some contacts over there at Southern Streams, and a no-nonsense reputation. Perhaps it will be enough to convince the board members that the poor, unfortunate, soldier boy deserves a proper resting place. You do understand, though, Miss Cordelia, that we will be forced to make public your psychic abilities. I'm sure you have some reservations about that. Rest assured, my dear, there will be those that will show disdain for talents and gifts they don't themselves understand, Plus, they will no doubt google search information on you and bring up all that unfortunate old business with Caleb Nash. Are you ready for that level of scrutiny?"

How can anyone be ready for the personal attacks that I know will be heaped on me once my history with Caleb comes to light. Since moving south of Nashville upon my release from prison, I have carefully managed to avoid being recognized or connected to that awful murder. The thought of reliving it all makes me physically queasy. Still, after learnin' what I now know about our past together, my concern for Johnny's soul outweighs my personal fears. I have no choice but to move forward with my personal path. "I understand everythin' you're sayin', Miz Bagley, but where I'm sittin', I don't feel as if I have a choice. My Johnny is dependin' on me to help him. He's been waiting for nearly one hundred and sixty-three years. How can I possibly let him down knowin' the truth about how much we've always meant to each other?"

I HAD SOUGHT PHYLLIS BAGLEY'S HELP WITH THE intention of figurin' out what the hell was goin' on with my sudden change in personality; the strange dreams, the unusual food preference, and a completely different sense of fashion. Her past life regression therapy was supposed to help me figure out whether the deep connection I have with my ghostly soldier boy is the same one I experienced with him in a previous life when I truly was his beloved Sara Anne. Now, drivin' back to Spring Hill, I am more confused than ever.

All my life, I have believed that when a soul finishes their time among the livin', they follow the light and move onward. My belief was that you went to the Great Beyond, the Afterlife, Heaven, or Akhirah; the name didn't matter, the key point was that your spirit went there and STAYED. There were no second chances...no "do-overs"...no extra chances to "get it right."

I wasn't alone in this belief. The various Baptist preachers that made their way through Sevierville always made it perfectly clear that once you finally made it to Heaven your soul rested there for all eternity. Even the hoodoo trainin' from both Mamaw and Opal Gaspar taught the same thing. If they was here now with me, I have no doubts they'd absolutely concur that all those lost spirits I had helped to move on weren't in no way gonna' turn around and come back in another body. Both ladies, who had accumulated a whole helluva' lot of metaphysical knowledge in their lifetimes, would call Phyllis Bagley and her new-fangled beliefs a steamin' pile of donkey shit.

Truthfully, despite what I saw on the docent's video tape, and the events of the past few days, I am still havin' an extra hard time swallonin' this whole reincarnation theory. Most confusin' of all is that I know what I saw on Miz Bagley's video recordin' is straight from my soul. I wasn't faking the memories I was recallin', whether they were joyful or painful. I still feel 'em now. That means that either I am crazier than a loon, or my eternal soul has been returned to earth at least twice before for a purpose I can't begin to fathom.

Thinkin' 'bout this all has given me a terrible headache that I can't even blame on Miz Bagley's bourbon alone. I'm hoping if I get back to the Kozinski's home by 11PM, I will still have time to take a few Tylenols and lie down until it's time to meet up with Johnny. This rendezvous also causes me a bushel of anxiety. I'm unsure of what I'm actually gonna' tell him about what I've uncovered. I contemplate whether or not I should try and explain to him that we two have had feelin's for one another long before he ever met and fell in love with his Sara Anne, but I don't rightly understand it myself. I imagine my specter will have an even harder time tryin' to make sense of reincarnation, 'specially with him bein' a good 'ole country boy, from the 1800s, raised with the Bible like any proper Baptist. How do I even begin to properly explain a multiple lives theory when I don't know much 'bout it myself, or even how Big Lucy's Vodou charm fits into this whole scenario?

Plus, there's the further question about whether I should say anything to my devoted specter about the two children we have supposedly conceived and lost. In all of our time together, Johnny has never said a single word about he and Sara Anne producin' a child. I'm guessin' he was long gone with his regiment by the time she learned she was pregnant, and mail delivery weren't so regular during the war. Maybe she even chose not to tell him. To lay this news on him now, so long after the fact when nothing can come of it, seems incredibly cruel. Still, the more pieces of the puzzle the two of us can put together, the more it's likely that we can figure out how to stop this recurring cycle of lost love and heartache.

I pull into the dark and quiet community of Southern Streams a little after 11:00PM. As I pass the pickleball courts, still brightly lit, I think about my Johnny Reb lyin' under them, lost and forgotten. It gives me a tight, achy feelin' in my throat. If for nothin' more than the sake of his personal dignity and the value of his sacrifice to a cause that was forced upon him, I am more determined than ever to see that his remains are finally found, identified, and buried with the respect he deserves...even if it means losin' him all over again.

I AM STILL SLIGHTLY GROGGY WHEN I MEET JOHNNY ON THE berm behind the Kozinski yard. I'd done exactly what I had planned to do when I got back from my adventure with Phyllis Bagley; I took two Tylenol and laid across the bed, clothes and all. I'm mighty glad that I had the foresight to set an alarm 'cause when it went off at 3:00 AM, I found myself in a deep, dreamless slumber, and even with the alarm blarin' next to my head, I had the hardest time pullin' myself from my bed.

With only enough time to splash some cold water on

my face, and run a comb through my long hair, I look and feel decidedly more like Delia Achley than Sara Anne McKinney, which makes me feel a little more confident than I had felt earlier in the evenin', unsure of who I actually was. The early, pre-dawn sky is overcast and dark, and initially I'm unable to see any manifestation on the berm. I feel an overwhelmin' sense of panic, thinkin' that somehow Miz Bagley's hypnosis and regression therapy has ended my ability to see my favorite ghost. But as I walk closer to the incline, I can barely make out a male figure as a shadow in the thrown-off light comin' from the neighborhood street lamps.

I turn around and look behind me to make sure that the houses circlin' this berm are all dark, though I'm not sure that I'd change my direction even if someone was watchin' me. The pull to spend time with this dead soldier boy is too great to ignore. He waves to me and I wave back as I clamber up the overgrown berm. It seems with every time we meet, my specter manifests more and more details about his physical, earthly self, lettin' me notice somethin' new about him each time we're together. Tonight, it is a tiny mole on his neck under his left ear. I desperately want to reach out and touch it, but I don't, fearin' the reaction I'd have would surely put an end to our time together tonight.

"It's so good to see ya', darlin," Johnny says, grinnin' with hands in his pockets and lookin' sweeter than honey on a biscuit. *"Waitin' for you these past few nights seems harder than it's been waitin' all these years...this knowin' ya're so close, but unable to be together all the time."* I notice that he's staring intently at my hair, which unlike the last few times

we've met, I've left long and straight instead of braided and pinned up in the style favored by Sara Anne. He must note that he's been caught rudely starin' so he explains, *"I am most taken with your hair like that, Sara Anne. It makes my heart race faster."* Then, realizin' the irony of that statement, he adds solemnly, *"I mean it would if I still had a heart that could beat. Truly darlin' it's most...fetchin'. With all that beautiful red hair, hangin' down on your shoulders all wild like, ya' remind me of the stories Big Lucy would tell me about the 'Fue Follets,' the mystical Cajun fairy folk who were supposed to live in the bayou. Them women fairies were so beautiful, folks said they could steal a man's heart forever...just as you have surely stolen mine, Sara Anne."*

I feel shaky, like my knees won't be holdin' me up much longer, so before I topple over, I sink to the ground and pat the spot next to me. *"Let's sit a spell, Johnny. I've learned a few things today I need to share with ya'."*

The specter sits as close to me as we dare, careful not to make physical contact, though the energy that hovers between us is so strong it takes every ounce of our willpower not to give in to the need to touch. *"I think you've been right all along, Johnny. I suppose I am your Sara Anne, though not in the same way as ya' might remember."* I go on and try to explain the whole concept of past lives to him in the simplest terms I can manage, describin' the trance-like state the Rippavilla docent put me in, and what was revealed to me durin' that experience.

His sky-blue eyes go wide, and he subconsciously shakes his head while I go through the whole story, as if he's findin' my words hard to accept. *"Are you sayin' that we have always been destined to be together, darlin'?"* my specter asks. *"That somethin' like that is even possible? It goes against everythin' the Bible says, Sara Anne. Still, if you say it happened then of course I believe ya', darlin'. I know ya'd never lie to me."*

"I can only tell you what I have firsthand knowledge of, Johnny. The hows and whys of it I don't understand myself. All I can determine is that Sara's soul moved on in this form, in my present life like ya' see me now, but I'm guessin' yours stayed behind 'cause of Big Lucy's spell."

Johnny looks off in the distant dark. *"I do remember thinkin' that very first day I met ya' on July 4th, that somehow, we'd met before, but how or when I couldn't explain. At the time I just passed it off as wishful thinkin', the fancy of a boy pinin' for a girl, but perhaps there was more to it than that, if what ya'll are tellin' me is true. All I know is that I've always loved you, Sara Anne McKinney...still do...and if I hadn't been called off to fight them damn Yankees, we would've married and built us a family and a home."* He looked at me with a face full of longin' and hope before asking, *"Do ya' think we'll be together again, darlin'...once you find Big Lucy's charm and I move on? Is somethin' like that even possible?"*

My throat is so tight I can barely squeeze the words out. *"I don't know, Johnny. I just don't know what comes after... and that's the honest truth."*

Chapter Twenty-Eight

As promised, Phyllis Bagley has managed to get us an appointment with the Southern Streams HOA Board of Directors. I meet up with her at the community's lodge, which is a very busy place on this Thursday mornin' in June. People are comin' and goin', and every room in the place seems to be hostin' a group or a club. True to the hospitality of the South, the residents wave to us and say hello as if we are all the best of friends. This should give me a good feelin' about the task at hand, but it don't. Instead, I feel a big 'ole ball of tension windn' around my gut. I have no doubt that the professor was correct in her warnin' that it's likely the Caleb Nash incident will become a topic in our discussion about findin' Johnny's remains, and the thought of havin' people look at me like some kind of freak is far from appealin'.

The lady at the front desk is different from the one I'd talked to earlier in the week about the wild roses. The name tag on her perfectly pressed gingham blouse reads "Bunny," but her general disposition is neither sweet nor cuddly like her namesake animal. She peers up at us over her tortoise frame glasses. "May I help you?" she asks, though her expression reads the opposite.

I've decided to let Phyllis take the lead on this whole project. I expect that my British docent is perfectly capable of goin' toe-to toe with not only the stern "Bunny," lady, but with any hard asses we may face on the Board as well. "Good morning, dear lady," Phyllis says. We have an appointment with the HOA Board. I spoke with Donna Martin yesterday afternoon."

Bunny seems put-out by this information. "And you are...?"

"I'm Phyllis Bagley. Dr. Bagley, actually." She opens her handbag and pulls out her business card which she slides across the counter toward the receptionist, who picks it up and spends an enormously long time examining it.

Finally, Bunny hands the card back to the docent. "You're a long way from home, Dr. Bagley. What brings you to our little community?" she asks.

Phyllis smiles like the sweet old lady she is not. "I'm afraid I'm not at liberty to discuss that with you, Ms. 'Bunny.' Any information on the subject will certainly have to come from the Southern Streams HOA Board."

Bunny had just seen the professor's business card listing her as having a doctorate in "paranormal studies," so I have no doubt as to why the woman's eyes go wide at this comment. I'm bettin' by tonight every soul in Southern Streams will hear that the Board met with an expert on the paranormal. The woman comes out from behind the desk. "Follow me" she instructs.

The receptionist leads us down a hallway to a heavy

wooden door with a placard above that says "Board Room." She opens it to usher us in, then reluctantly closes it behind her with a look that says she would rather have stayed. I don't quite know what I was expectin' but it wasn't such a formal settin'. The focus of the room is a large semi-circle wooden table around which sit the nine members of the Southern Streams HOA Board, each with a large nameplate in front of them. The four women and five men give us the once over, then the lady Phyllis had called the day before, Donna Martin, acknowledges us. "Welcome, Dr. Bagley and associate. The Board and I are extremely curious over the concerns you brought to me yesterday. If you and your guest would have a seat, perhaps, for the sake of clarity, you could explain why you believe Southern Streams has somehow 'disrespected the history of this property.' I can assure you that according to the builder and the town of Spring Hill, this land was wholly approved for the multi-home community that exists here, and all of us on the Board are confused at the urgency of your request to meet."

I can easily read the auras of the people around the fancy desk: the Southern Streams HOA folks are showin' varyin' levels of apprehension, stubbornness and hostility, and despite Phyllis' warm yellow aura of confidence and leadership, I don't feel good about this meetin' leadin' to anything fruitful.

As I expected, Dr. Bagley doesn't show one iota of self-doubt or intimidation. While I obediently sit myself down in the chair that President Martin has assigned me, the professor remains standin', and in fact, steps right up to the table to address the board members. "Let me begin by saying how pleased I am that this board is willing to hear my concerns. I am quite sure that the blame for this egregious error lies directly with the community's builder and Spring Hill's Zoning commissioner."

At the words "egregious error," several of the board members look at each other with concerned expressions. A portly man with a bad toupee speaks up. "And what 'egregious error' do you believe they've committed, Mrs. Bagley?"

"It's Dr. Bagley...," she states, then examines his own nameplate and adds, "...Mr. Carvelli. And if you bear with me, I'll be happy to explain everything so that the entire matter is perfectly clear. I'm sure you all would like to know a little more about me and why an old woman from across the pond would have issues with a 55 Plus community in Middle Tennessee." Phyllis withdrew additional business cards from her tote and personally hands one to all nine members. She waits patiently for them all to read the card, while I note that a few of the members, the male ones especially, nudge each other, obviously over the professor's field of expertise.

"As you can see," Phyllis says, "My field of study is the paranormal, which I can assure you means more than your usual understanding of 'the things that go bump in the night.' I've been studying the alternate realms of spirituality and life energy for more than thirty years, and without sounding like a braggart, I'm considered somewhat of an expert in the field of post-death experiences."

I feel the tension in the room rise and one elderly lady with silver-blue hair actually giggles, though I can tell it is completely out of nervousness and not humor. For most people, talkin' about what happens after a person dies is an uncomfortable conversation. Beliefs are often dictated by religious trainin', while the film industry has done a pretty good job of scarin' people about specters and lost souls. Another gentleman who looks a tad younger than the rest of the group shakes his head and puffs out his chest in a self-important manner. "I mean no disrespect… **DR**. Bagley…" He stresses the word doctor like he takes issue with the title. "Surely you haven't called this board together over something as silly as a 'ghost' problem here in Southern Streams. I can tell you right now, Ma'am, I am a one hundred percent, a long-time atheist who doesn't believe in any of that bearded-man-in-the-sky nonsense, and I'm more than a little put-out that I gave up my 10:00 AM tee time to listen to this drivel."

"Oh Mr. McMann, you misunderstand," Phyllis pleasantly says." I'm not here to convince any of you to believe in the paranormal. I am well aware that preconceived prejudices run deep, especially here in the Southern part of the United States, and lord knows, as someone of my advanced years, I understand how hard it is to teach an old dog new tricks."

I have to bite my lower lip to keep from grinnin' over the professor's double "dis" of the pompous ass's attitude. McMann's face goes red and a few of the board members gasp, while several look away. Donna Martin doesn't seem pleased with either of them. "Dr. Bagley, I will remind you that the board called this emergency meeting specifically at the request of The Franklin Battlefield Trust Association, of which both the mayor's wife and I are founding members, as a way of showing our appreciation for your generous donation to our work refurbishing Rippavilla. However, I still expect you to do your part in helping to keep these proceedings civil. I ask you to please refrain from making any further…incendiary remarks."

The British woman doesn't seem in the least bit perturbed by the scolding. She smiles blandly and says, "I do apologize Madame President. I'm sure it came out sounding worse than intended. I suppose I've grown rather prickly over the years when it comes to naysaying regarding my wholly scientific study."

The Carvelli gentleman offers this suggestion. "Dr. Bagley, why don't we expedite these proceedings and get right to the point of why we're here. What is it you want from the Southern Springs HOA?"

"I agree wholeheartedly, Mr. Carvelli. There's no reason to spend any of my time or yours working to convince people that paranormal activity is as real as the nose on your face," the professor said. "The matter at hand has to do with some grievous and disrespectful actions that have been recently brought to my attention."

"And what actions might that be, Doctor?" Carvelli asked.

"Your community, Sir, has dishonorably built your Pickleball Court #5 directly over the remains of a poor, deceased Confederate soldier! How one could build homes on land with this type of tragic history without first checking for such possibilities is beyond my imagination! It's quite shameful."

All at once, there is a symphony of shocked denials and confusion over the docent's insinuations. It don't surprise me none. In general, lots of the livin' get squeamish regardin' talk of burial rituals. I suppose it's 'cause they're afraid of their own Afterlife. Unfortunately, the discussion gets loud and argumentative causing President Martin to use her gavel to regain everyone's attention. When the room settles down, the board President turns her attention to Phyllis. "Dr, Bagley, that is a highly controversial accusation! Do you have any concrete proof that our pickleball court is built over this poor man's remains?"

"I have it on the best authority, Madame President," the docent answers. "Straight from the horse's mouth, as they say." Phyllis points to me, and adds, "The ghost of Pvt. Jonathan Sweet of the Confederate army has personally told my associate, Delia Achley, where his remains can be found."

Every eye in the room lands on me before pandemonium takes over. A handful of board members are arguing loudly with President Martin over the idea that an "emergency meeting" has been called to discuss "bogus claims made by imaginary ghosts." The man with the 10:00 AM tee time begins to bundle up his things as if to leave. The Boss Lady ain't havin' none of it, and I can see why Phyllis chose to call Donna Martin in the first place. Just like the professor, the President of the Southern Streams HOA is tough as nails. She ignores the four people harpin' on her, and once again bangs her gavel on the wooden desk top. "Order! Order! I will have order in these Board proceedings!"

The people all stop what they're doing and give Martin the floor. "Every member of this Board should be thoroughly knowledgeable regarding the bylaws and guidelines of this organization. If you find yourself unable to adhere to them, I will accept your resignation immediately." She lets this threat hang in the air for a moment, then continues. "That being the case, I strongly suggest everyone sit themselves down and use self-restraint until this meeting has been formally adjourned."

With the chaos over, the President turns her annoyance toward Phyllis. "Dr. Bagley, you know that I respect your work and your commitment in helping to keep the flavor and history of this area free from commercialization. However, you can surely understand how ludicrous this all sounds to people without your background of study. Do you have any other proof that our pickleball court is covering this soldier's remains? Historical documentation, perhaps?"

"I'm afraid I don't, Madame President. I've been aware for a long time that your community's neighbor, Rippavilla Plantation, has hosted several specters over the years. There's been quite a lot written over the years about the supposed 'haunting' of the old house and the land surrounding it. That's not surprising considering the energy brought on by all the tragedy of war that's happened here, but I've come to discover that there was one specific spectral energy that especially favors this location. I, myself, have felt his presence, but he's never manifested himself to me."

Properly scolded, the board members are careful to follow Robert's Rules of Order. A man who has been quiet until now raises his hand and waits to be acknowledged. "The Board will hear from John Typer," Donna Martin acknowledges.

"Thank you, Madame President. I would like to know what Dr. Bagley means by manifestation. I am not up on 'ghost protocol.'" He asks this with a perfectly straight face, but I get the impression he's poking fun at both Phyllis and President Martin.

It doesn't seem to bother the professor in the least. "That's a terrific question, Mr. Typer. Manifestation means that the spectral energy shows itself in a physical manner...something you can see with your own eyes. Not everyone is able to see manifestations. It's a hereditary gift. My associate is highly sensitive to such energy. She's been able to see and speak with him on several occasions, and still continues to do so."

"She can talk to him...like we're talking now?" the man asks, his tone incredulous.

"As the specter has no physical body parts, Mr. Tyler, the two of them speak telepathically," Phyllis explains.

This is all too much for the senior citizens on the Board to take in. There's a lot of eye-rolling, and a handful of disbelievin' faces, and I hope, with everything I hold dear, that the professor don't start goin' on about the role my past life experience might have on the situation, or about the Vodou charm that's keepin' Johnny's soul stuck here. Even Ms. Martin seems less than convinced over the news that I can see and speak to ghosts.

A lady member wearin' a Chicago Cubs T-shirt has been starin' at me intently since Phyllis mentioned my name. She's also been rudely pokin' around on her cellphone instead of listening. She raises her hand to speak next. "The Board recognizes Mrs. Velma Cleary," the President says.

The lady leans back in her chair. "This question is for Dr. Bagley's associate… Ms. Achley, I believe I heard that was your name?" She spells it out. "A-C-H-L-E-Y…is that correct?"

I get a bad feelin' 'bout where this conversation is goin'. "Yes, Ma'am," I say.

She glances down at the cellphone on the table and narrows her eyes at me. "Hmmmm," she murmurs. "And do you sometimes go by the name 'Cordelia'?" she asks.

I know exactly where this is leadin' up to, but there ain't no way I can stop my past 'dirty laundry' from becomin' part of this discussion. "Yes, Ma'am. I do sometimes use the name 'Cordelia'…on occasion."

"I knew I'd heard your name before," Mrs. Cleary smugly states. "You're the same Cordelia Achley that was involved with that child murder in Nashville about ten years ago, aren't you? Caleb Nash was the little boy's name."

My tongue feels like a lead brick in my mouth, knowin' that my past is gonna' be a roadblock to recoverin' Johnny's remains. I find it too hard to speak, so I just nod instead.

"Is that a yes, Ms. Ashley?" Board member Martin asks, though there's no doubt she already knows the answer.

"Yes, Ma'am, " I admit, "I'm that same Cordelia Achley." And just like that, Donna Martin's Robert's Rules of Order gets flushed right down the proverbial toilet.

CHAPTER TWENTY-NINE

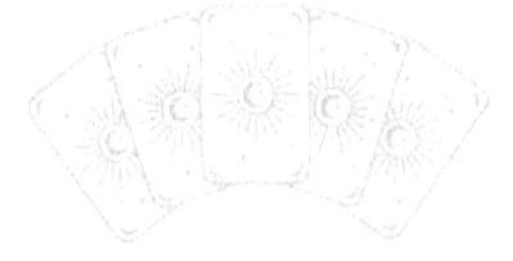

Over lunch at the Olive Garden on Main Street, Phyllis don't seem in the least perturbed by the fact that the Southern Streams HOA has just flat out turned down our request to dig up Johnny's remains. I, however, am seein' red over the group's less than sympathetic behavior, though I get that they undoubtedly had a hard time believin' his ghost personally told me he was buried under their Pickleball Court. Most folks have a hard time comin' to terms with the trappins' of what happens after ya' take your last breath.

Instead, the docent's attention is firmly focused on butterin' her bread stick with a preciseness seen only in the paintin' of masterpieces. "Aren't you just a little disappointed?" I ask. "They took less than five minutes to discuss the matter before turnin' us down. Frankly, I felt like they'd all dismissed us before we even got started."

"As I presumed they would," Phyllis said, as she daintily bites into her coated breadstick.

"If you figured they'd turn you down, why did we waste all mornin' tryin' to talk some sense into 'em?"

"Because we must appear to be faithfully following what you Americans so drolly call 'chain of command.' We mustn't come off as having 'thrown a wobbler,' Miss Cordelia. That would just accomplish the wrong type of notoriety. If we wish to be taken seriously, we must plot our advances in a completely logical way," the docent explained.

I wait for the waiter to drop off our entrees before continuin' the conversation. When he's finished dustin' our food with parmesan cheese and walks away, I lean over the table so I don't have to speak loudly over the din of the crowded restaurant. "I'm not followin' you, Ma'am. If the HOA don't give us their formal approval, I don't see how we're ever gonna' dig Johnny up on our own. Me and you with shovels in the middle of the night ain't gonna' cut it. It's surely will take some heavy equipment to get through those layers of concrete and asphalt."

The British woman laughed. "Oh, gracious me, Dearie. I have no intention of retrieving those boy's remains on my own. There are much easier ways to go about that," she countered.

I am about losin' my last thread of patience with this lady and her talkin' in circles while my Johnny languishes in his earthly prison. "I mean no disrespect, Ma'am, but ya'll talk a good story without movin' forward. I need to know exactly how you plan on helpin' me release poor Johnny's soul, otherwise our deal is off."

Phyllis puts down her fork and looks over my shoulder behind me. "Patience, Miss Cordelia. I do believe the help we seek is on her way to our table at this very second."

I turn around to see an attractive woman in her mid-forty's headin' our way. I notice that the lunch crowd seems to be payin' an enormous amount of attention to her arrival, but I personally don't recognize her until she pulls out a chair and sits herself at our table. "This better be worth it, Phyllis. I passed on a possible love-sick jumper over on Broadway to meet with you here in Green Acres," the woman complains, all without pausin' for any polite greetins' or introductions. Up close like this, I immediately recognize her; Edwina "Eddy" Rooney, News 5's evening anchor and Nashville's most infamous investigative reporter.

"As I said on the phone, Ms. Rooney, this is a juicy one. You're going to want first claws on this story," the professor said.

I am far more shocked over the professor's statement than the reporter bein' here. According to the terms Phyllis and I had worked out before I agreed to be part of her academic study, my personal information and interactions with Johnny were to stay absolutely confidential. Now, here the professor was offering Nashville's most doggedly ambitious news woman an opportunity to cash in on things I'd hoped to keep private. I give the British woman my best "stink eye," which she obviously pretends not to notice.

The anchor woman waves over the waiter and orders a glass of red wine, then leans back in her chair. "Okay... you got my attention. Tell me more."

The docent proceeds to tell Edwina Rooney the story

of how I came to be communicatin' with Private Jonathan Sweet of the Confederate Army and the role Rippavilla Plantation plays in the story. The journalist takes notes in a spiral ring pad she pulls from her handbag. Thankfully, Phyllis leaves out the part about my past life regression and the possibility that I might have had a relationship with this particular spirit through several different time periods. She also don't mention my experiences with Caleb Nash. At least not right away.

Miz Rooney looks up from her writin' and asks. "Just how long have you been chatting with ghosts, young lady?" She puts the point end of her stubby pencil to the page. "By the way...what did you say your name was again?"

"Achley," I say with hesitation, "Cordelia Mae Achley." I'm feelin' more than a little guilty for bein' ashamed' to say my own name. My Mamaw gave it to me when I was born, long before either she or I ever came to find out that I was really a McKinney, and it ain't no one's fault but my own if my actions ten years ago sullied it.

Rooney taps the pencil against her lip while she works over the information. "Achley? Hmmm...Why does that name sound so familiar to me?"

Miz Bagley don't wait for me to explain. "Because, Edwina, my dear, this isn't Miss Cordelia's first encounter with controversial ghosts. You may remember another 'spirit' incident...about ten years ago...concerning the murder of a young boy. Caleb Nash was his name."

The reporter drops her pencil in her lap. "Are you saying this is the same woman? The one that helped the police locate the body of that poor dead child and then was arrested for his murder?"

"The very same," Phyllis stated, not workin' too hard to keep the gloat out of her voice. "Our Cordelia has a proven track record in helping lost souls find their way, Edwina, and she's one hundred percent the real thing. Trust me, I've seen my share of charlatans and this girl is not one of them. She's speaking one on one with a dead Confederate soldier whose remains have gone undetected for well over a century."

Eddy Rooney appraises me as if I was a pullin' mule she was fixin' to buy. "I remember that case," she says. "I was new to Nashville and was relegated to being a lowly 'feature reporter,' so I didn't have the opportunity to work that story. But as I recall, there were a lot of people who thought you were guilty as hell, Ms. Ashley. I believe they called you the "Murdering Ghost Girl," and were convinced you were Winston Frazier's secret accomplice."

Even after all these years, I feel my face go hot. "That's a complete lie, Miz Rooney. I never met Winston Frazier and I had nothin' to do with that child's murder. I was his tutor and he reached out to me after his death 'cause I had always been kind to him in the livin' one. That's all there is to it. Nothin' more."

"Oh, I believe you, young lady, and after I get done with my expose on this case, so will all of Middle Tennessee. This is like the perfect storm...two ghost stories coming to a head out here in the boonies of Nashville. I see an ACJ award in my future!"

"Does this mean you're interested in taking on this

story, Edwina?" Phyllis Bagley asks, barely containin' the desire to rub her hands together in outright glee.

"Absolutely," Rooney said. "I'd like to get the first segment taped later today if I can get the copy together and round up my favorite crew. I'd like this first segment to be in front of the pickleball court in question."

"You know you'll need to get permission from the HOA, right?" Phyllis asked.

Rooney smiled and picked the pencil back up. "You leave that all to me, Professor. There's this little old thing called the First Amendment." She paused and addressed me, "Now, let's begin by discussing how you first came to meet this soldier boy ghost, shall we, Ms. Achley?"

ONE DOESN'T NEED "THE GIFT" TO KNOW THAT EDWINA Rooney's newscast from Southern Streams is gonna' rattle a few cages. Turns out that the TV journalist had been personally and officially invited onto the property by a local woman resident who Edwina's mother played canasta with every Tuesday at the Lodge. The gung-ho reporter was set up and halfway through her spiel before anyone on the HOA Board got wind of what was goin' on, but by then, a good-sized crowd had already gathered in an attempt to figure out just what the hell was happenin' near the pickleball courts.

"This is Edwina Rooney with News Center Five at 5:00. I'm live here in the Southern Streams community with respected paranormal scholar and historian, Dr. Phyllis Bagley, whose research has recently discovered that the neighborhood's popular #5 pickleball court sits directly upon the remains of a deceased Confederate soldier. Dr. Bagley, how sure are you of this information?"

The professor smiles calmly at the camera, her trademark cardigan buttoned up to her neck despite the summer temperatures. "Oh...I am very sure, Ms. Rooney. I have no doubt that several feet below this athletic structure lie the bones of one Pvt. Jonathan Sweet of the Confederate Army. He was a soldier who lost his young life during a skirmish with Union troops just prior to the Battle of Spring Hill."

"That's quite a remarkable statement, Dr. Bagley...and one that's sure to brew a lot of controversy," Rooney calmly states for the camera. "Are you one hundred percent sure of your facts? How could something like this happen? After all, this area of Spring Hill is historically noted as being the location for Hood's encampment in preparation of the advance of Schofield's Union troops. Wouldn't it be safe to assume that an adequate search of the land was done in advance of the planning and building of this community for this very reason?"

"Yes," replied Bagley, with a sad smile. The old woman was a master at this game. "One would certainly think so, being that the battle site is just a mile away and this property sits so close to Rippavilla. It's hard to imagine how this poor boy got himself missed." Phyllis pauses for effect and sighs "Of course, in all fairness, Pvt. Sweet was away from his unit at the time of his death. The poor lad, like many of his fellow soldiers, was near to starving to death. Young Johnny was just out hunting down something to eat when he lost his life."

"That's an amazingly detailed story, Dr. Bagley. How can you be so sure this all happened like you say?" Edwina asked, never taking her eyes off the camera.

The picture of perfect composure, the docent blinked behind her owl-like glasses, "How you ask? Why…it's because he told us that's exactly how it happened."

The crowd of Southern Stream folks, who had up until now had been generally polite, began murmuring to one another over the idea of the dead soldier speaking. Ignoring them, the reporter continued her questioning, "Let me see if I understand you correctly, Dr. Bagley. Are you saying that this 'Johnny Reb' who died over 160 years ago, spoke to you and 'told' you how he died?"

The professor laughed, a sweet, old-lady-like giggle that I'm sure was meant to disarm the crowd, who seemingly was gettin' more and more agitated as their numbers increased. "Of course not, Ms. Rooney. I can't talk to spirits. But I know someone who can. A young woman psychic spoke with Pvt. Sweet. He told her his whole sad story, word for word, and then she told me."

This statement causes the residents of Southern Streams to start loudly complainin'. Off in the distance, I see several cars pull into the parking lot closest to the tennis and pickleball courts. A woman jumps out of a silver jeep and starts headin' directly toward where Miz Rooney is conductin' her interview. As she gets closer, I can tell that it's the President of the Southern Streams HOA, Donna Martin, who we'd met earlier this mornin'. She looks madder than a wet hen, and even from this distance, I can see that her face is all scrunched up and turin' red. Apparently, the news reporter sees her as well, 'cause she quickly concludes her broadcast. "What a fascinating tale, Dr. Bagley. We all look forward to hearing more. Join us at 10:00 for more on this exclusive, breaking story. This is Edwina Rooney, News Center Five," the journalist concludes, making a swipin' gesture at her neck to the two fellows holdin' the cameras.

CHAPTER THIRTY

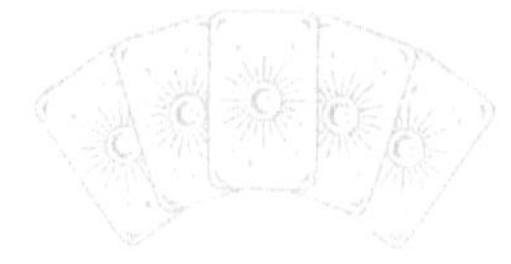

THINGS FROM THAT POINT PRETTY MUCH PROGRESS THE WAY ya'll might expect. President Martin threatens to have Miz Rooney arrested by the Spring Hill Police, while the strong-minded journalist refuses to back down, giving the irritated HOA lady an earful about her First Amendment Rights and askin' what it was the HOA was tryin' to hide from the community. This causes a lot of ears to perk up, which was not much of a surprise. People tend to be interested in secrets, 'specially when it might concern the value of their property. Still, the growin' crowd of residents are generally split over the opinion of who was right and who was wrong, though none of them seemed especially excited about the possibility of anyone diggin' up their pickleball court.

Phyllis extracts herself from the argument between the two women and walks on over to me, takin' the offered bottle of water I hand her. "Well...that went pretty smoothly, don't you think Miss Cordelia?" the professor asked. I looked over to where Miz Rooney's crew is packin' up their equipment. The men didn't seem too worked up about what was bein' said, though I suppose when ya'll worked with someone like Edwina, you got used to lots of angry confrontations.

"I'm not sure I would say it went 'smoothly', Professor Bagley. The HOA lady's gone all red in the face. I can't imagine she'll be welcomin' any of us back real soon," I comment.

"Doesn't matter," Phyllis says in between sips. "We won't be back until everything's in place to dig our ghostly friend up. By the time that happens, there won't be much the HOA Board will be able to do about it."

"You really think they're gonna' let us dig up that pickleball court?" I question. It's no secret I don't harbor the same conviction regardin' the outcome that she and Edwina share.

"By the time our work here is done, Miss Cordelia, the naysayers will be holding the shovels for us," Phyllis jokes.

I think the British scholar is bein' overly confident but I don't get the chance to tell her as much. A group of residents are walkin' toward the courts from the pool area, led by a familiar face I recognize from our earlier meetin' with the HOA Board. It's that Velma Cleary woman. The one that let the Caleb Nash cat outta' the bag. There's no doubt by her determined stride that she's a lady on a mission. I'm guessin' that she's come straight out of the pool 'cause she's drippin' water from under her polka dot cover-up onto the shoes of the bystanders. She turns 'round to point an accusatorial finger at me and I find several sets of eyes suddenly glarin' my way.

It's more than crystal clear that it's time for me to

high-tail it out of there. I surely don't want to be here if and when the city police or the county Sheriff arrives. Just the mention of Caleb Nash is sure to get me a ride to the station for' additional questionin'. Phyllis promises to come by the house and explain the rest of the plan as soon as she clarifies things with Edwina Rooney. Truly, I wish she'd just go back to her home or even back to Rippavilla. The events of the day have given me a hell of a bad headache, and all I want to do is take a few Tylenols and nap until it's time to see Johnny.

Luckily, no one hounds me to my car and I slip out of the Lodge parking lot without a police escort. I relax a bit, only to turn onto Sprockett Springs and see my neighbors millin' about outside their houses in small clusters. This is most unusual as I have determined early on in my stay that no one in Southern Streams is outside their homes during the late afternoon summer heat. I pull into the Kozinski driveway and no one says a single word to me. Sylvie Weathers gives me a slight wave and a sad smile as I unlock the front door, and I answer with "Hey, Miz Sylvie," before I step inside and lock the door behind me. I don't even have time to take a breath or make myself a cup of tea before my cell phone starts blarin' from my handbag.

<hr>

"I'M SO SORRY IT WORKED OUT THIS WAY, CORDELIA," THE voice on the other end admits. "I still think you're a real nice young lady, but I think it's better this way." She pauses, soundin' more than a trifle guilty for askin' me to leave. "You know how people can be...and we still have to live there the rest of the year. It's very difficult at our age when your neighbors shun you."

"No worries, Miz Kozinski. I wholeheartedly understand your position," I reply. There's no reason to get all snarly with the poor lady. She's been nothin' but kind to me and has now generously offered to pay me through the dates of our agreement even though I won't be stayin' here. I wish I could turn the offer down, but without that little bit of income I'd find myself destitute. "I'll just pack up my things and be out of here by evenin', Ma'am."

I look out the front window and there are a lot more people gathered in front of the house, includin' a news van from Miz Rooney's competition. Leavin' without bein' harassed might be a problem. It's then I see Professor Bagley's Volvo comin' up the street. She parks in the driveway behind me and heads to the door without a single word to all the folks yellin' questions at her. I let her inside and she shakes her head in sympathy. "I'm sorry about this, dear. Maybe it would be best if you come stay with me awhile."

I for sure don't want to move in with Phyllis. Too much time with her opinionated ways is apt to make me crazy, though I don't see that I have too many other options. She sits on the end of the bed while I clear out the few possessions I've stored in the guest bedroom. I reach for the wilted wild rose still in the vase thinking to throw it out, but change my mind. It was my first token from Johnny and I can't bear to part with it. Instead, I put it between the pages of the rom-com paperback, the one about the tooth fairy I took to the pool that day and never found time to read, and now gifted to me by my recent employer. A deep sense of melancholy sweeps over me and when I pick up the quartz crystal, also a gift from my Sweet Johnny Reb, I am overwhelmed and the tears come from somewhere deep inside of me.

I slide to the floor, alternatin' between rockin' and sobbin', the rose in the book and the crystal pressed to my chest. I close my eyes and images flash in my mind, some from this present time, but most from several different pasts. Phyllis tries to comfort me but I push her away. I don't want to be interrupted. In this moment, I want it to be just me, alone with this trunk full of memories, most of which I've never personally experienced. The professor seems to understand my state, She gets up from the bed, turns out the light and lets me be, closin' the door behind her and leavin' me with the ghosts of my memories.

I'M NOT SURE WHEN SLEEP KICKS IN AND THE RANDOM images in my head turn to full-on dreams and nightmares. When I finally pull myself out of the dreamy state and into consciousness, the room is the semi-golden color of sunset and my cheek is tear stained and rashy from bein' pressed into the woven bedroom carpet. My head feels fuzzy and I have a bad case of cotton-mouth.

I find Phyllis Bagley sittin' at the island watchin' a video on her cell phone of Edwina's earlier broadcast. When she sees me, she puts the phone down. "I'm so glad you woke on your own, dear. I would have hated to rouse you out of such a sound sleep you so sorely needed. Do you feel rested?" the older woman asks.

"Not really," I reply. "Honestly, my whole self feels rather exhausted...as if I've led several lifetimes all at once. There were dreams...so many of them..." My voice fades off.

"It's to be expected," the professor explains. "You've obviously awakened memories that were buried deep in your psyche. After effects like yours are unusually rare in patients who undergo past life regression, but it does sometimes happen. Anything you wish to share?" she asks hopefully.

"Nope," I answer. I'm not ready to talk about what I saw and dreamt." The researcher in her looks so disappointed, I add, "Least not yet. Who knows...maybe I'll change my mind goin' forward."

She nods her understandin' and changes the subject. "I do hope you're up for Edwina's interview," Phyllis comments. She looks down at her phone to check the time. "It's far later than I thought. She's expecting us at Rippavilla in forty-five minutes or so to go over the questions she intends to ask beforehand. The idea is to broadcast live from the plantation, so there won't be any re takes."

This is the first I'm hearin' 'bout any interview and my stomach does a flip flop at the thought of talkin' publicly about any of this. "I never agreed to bein' on television, Miz Phyllis. I'm in no frame of mnd to be talkin' about Caeb...or Johnny, for that matter." I state.

"But my dear, don't you want to see your Johnny's remains found...along with that watch and that damning

Vodou charm? It's been your goal all along, hasn't it? You wanting to help this poor unfortunate soul to move from this earthly plane to the Afterlife? You…speaking live on camera…is what it's going to take to finally get the job done. You realize that, don't you?"

The British woman's statement leaves me momentarily stunned and now questionin' everything I thought I already knew. Is this truly what I want? Johnny leavin' the here and now? Leavin' me to live my present life without him…never knowin' for sure if I'll ever see him again or if he'll go on rememberin this "me," Cordelia Mae Achley? Suddenly, nothin' seems so clear anymore.

CHAPTER THIRTY-ONE

My interview with Miz Rooney is viewed as a success. 'Least that's what Phyllis and the lady reporter tell me. In my own mind, I look like a stutterin' fool, a crazy woman who done lost her last touch with reality. However, Edwina's 10:00 PM segment with me goes over big with the folks in the Nashville viewin' area, and is quickly picked up by the national networks. After that, things move quicker than I could have ever imagined. By the followin' afternoon, my story 'bout what happened with Caleb and the current situation with Johnny's remains is all over social media. Traffic 'round Rippavilla is backed up for three solid miles with people curious about the paranormal goin' ons, and the Trust that holds ownership of the landmark is forced to cancel tours of the house until further notice. Every media outlet is camped out on the front lawn of the historic plantation, requiring the Maury County Sheriff's office and the Spring Hill police to provide crowd control, traffic duty, and general security.

Truthfully, I don't give a rat's ass 'bout any of the fame. My goal was, and still is, to free my poor Johnny's soul from his earthly prison. As part of the deal I worked out with Edwina and Phyllis in exchange for my interview, I've been allowed to stay at the big house until I can see my goal accomplished. The two women don't tell me how they accomplished this feat and I don't ask. Phyllis even manages to get a local plumber to come in and hook up the water in one of the house's old 1950's style bathrooms so I can at least have somewhere to wash up. The only thing I care about is the extra time I can now spend with Johnny.

Durin' the daylight hours, I can feel his presence but the sun's energy keeps him from materializin' to the point where I can actually see him. I spend a lot of my time durin' the hours from sunrise to sunset in the room with the Ruby Davis' paintin', readin' my cards for insight and nappin'. Sometimes I fall into a deeper sleep and dream things from the past. Upon wakin', these watery images always leave me melancholy, achin' for somethin' I've never had and undoubtedly never will. It's the nights with Johnny that make the long, dreary days, worth it. We laugh and talk. He tells me stories from his childhood and I tell him some 'bout mine. We have stopped talkin' 'bout Sara Anne all together, and he don't call me by her name any more.

'Course he don't call me Delia either. Just "Darlin". I don't mind. The way he says it sounds much sweeter to my ears than any other name.

I've moved passed the achin' desire to touch him. That's what I tell myself anyway. Despite all that's happened, I haven't forgotten my hoodoo trainin'. Ghosts are pure energy. It ain't like they got a physical form, only the image of one. Knowin' this, I'd be a complete idiot to go and touch somethin' akin to a downed power-line. Johnny's energy is stronger than most lost souls I've met. Contact with him would knock me clear on my ass. I can tell by the look in his sky-blue eyes that he has similar feelins', but is afraid of harmin' me as well. So, we sit together with an invisible line separatin' us. In truth, we're only a few inches apart, but it feels like the whole damned Grand Canyon is there, stretchin' between us.

We also never acknowledge that big 'ole elephant in the room. Once Johnny's remains are dug up and I locate the watch with the Vodou charm, neither one of us is quite sure what will happen next. Based on what I know and my past experiences, I'm guessin' that Johnny will move from this plane to the next as soon as I properly break Big Lucy's charm. I've been doin' a lot of research on the subject using the computer in Phyllis' office, and it don't seem like it's a terribly difficult castin'. Still, one never knows what's involved in love charms like this one.

Plus, accordin' to my past life regression, it seems like the connection between my soul and Johnny's goes way beyond a single charm cast by a New Orleans Vodou woman in the 1800s. The few times Johnny is willin' to talk about me breakin' the charm, he swears that if my new castin' don't work, and it appears that he will remain stranded in this in between stage, he's more than willin' to stay right here at Rippavilla so that we can still be together in the same way we have been.

It's a sweet thing, and it melts my heart, but I know

deep-down it's the wrong thing to consider. Even if I could somehow stay here in Spring Hill for the rest of my earthly days, I would grow old while Johnny would forever manifest as this young soldier boy. Even more distressin' is the idea that when the time for my earthly existence is over, there's no guarantee that I'd be able to stay here in spirit form and not move on like I'm meant to.

Wouldn't that just leave my Johnny still trapped on this plane, alone and waitin' all over again? It's a question that keeps me up at night.

AND JUST LIKE THAT, IT APPEARS AS IF JOHNNY AND I DON'T have long to wait for the Universe to set our course. Edwina's story about poor Pvt. Jonathan Sweet bein' buried under a Southern Streams' pickleball court has garnished plenty of local and national attention, with people sittin' on both sides of the fence about how this situation should be handled. Even Tennessee's Governor has gotten into the mix, along with the Daughters of the Confederacy, an organization that got its start right here in Tennessee. On the other hand, there's an equal number of people who don't think any special attention should be afforded this dead "traitor to American democracy." They think Johnny's remains ought to be quietly and privately dug up and returned to his survivin' family, who amazingly enough, still live in the Meridian, Mississippi area.

The question of whether someone is actually buried in that spot is no longer a quandary. The first thing the community HOA Board did was to hire a firm to come out with special equipment that could penetrate the pickleball court and through multiple layers of Tennessee clay and stone, sendin' images back of what was below. It didn't take long for this company to affirm that there were indeed human remains exactly where my soldier boy said they were. From then on, it was just a question of when, how, and who would pay for the exhumin' of these remains, as well as who would cover the cost of returnin' the community's space to what it was before. In the end, it was the Daughters of the Confederacy that ended up fundin' the project with the stipulation that they could put a plaque commemoratin' Pvt. Sweet's service and their part in retreivin' his remains. That's not to say there weren't a lot of folks who were decidedly unhappy with that agreement, but it satisfied the Governor, the voters in Southern Streams who were countin' the days until they could use their beloved Court #5 again, and the long dead soldier's existing family who wanted to give their ancestor a proper burial, and, as it worked out, the opinions of those folks surpassed everyone else's.

During the two weeks leading up to Johnny's exhumation, I keep a low profile, hangin' out at Rippavilla and grabbin' precious moments with my Johnny Reb. An attorney hired by Edwina Rooney's network saw to my right to privacy, makin' sure I couldn't be exploited by the media.

According to the terms of my contract, I would give her network exclusive rights to the story, and in return, I would be allowed to attend the actual exhumation, allowed first access to the mysterious watch should it be located, and paid a fair rate for any future interviews. The money don't mean a dang thing to me. I only agreed to the whole legal eagle shit 'cause I wanted to be absolutely sure I'd be there when they dug my beloved Johnny up.

As the days got closer to that moment, there was less talkin' between Johnny and me and a whole lot more weepin', at least on my part. Havin' no physical body, my sweet soldier boy couldn't shed actual tears 'long with me, but his grief and pain was as real to me as his ghostly manifestation. We make desperate promises to each other to try and make contact from whatever location he moves on to if that's how this all ends up goin', but in my heart, I know it is an unlikely scenario. I don't pretend to know everythin' about the Afterlife, but it has never been my experience for souls to make contact once they have moved on from this earthly plane of existence. That don't mean I'm labelin' all those famous mediums who say they've spoken to the dead as liars. It just hasn't been what I've come to know.

On the night before the scheduled exhumation, Johnny and I meet in Miz Ruby's room for what might be the last time. It's a bittersweet and heartbreakin' moment for both of us. I try and explain to him the ritual of the castin' I plan on using to reverse the Vodou curse laid on the hair charm, but my beloved soldier boy seems distracted and not much interested in the mechanics of my hoodoo work.

"I'm sorry, Darlin'. I don't mean for it to seem like I don't care about all your effort. I appreciate your burnin' desire to try and help me. Truly I do. But now that I might be close to actually movin' on, my poor soul wants nothin' more than stay right

here where I am. With you. Just like we're doin' now. Seems kinda' cruel of Heaven to drag me away so soon after all these years of waitin' to be with ya' again. I can't imagine the Lord Almighty bein' so mean-spirited. As of late, I've been wonderin' if all of this ain't just some form of divine retribution for us puttin' stock in Big Lucy's dark magic."

The purple light of early dawn is beginning to filter into the room. Johnny sits across from me as close as he dares, and even without us touchin', I feel his energy brush up against me, makin' the hair on my arms stand straight up. The air 'round us is charged with ghostly static electricity and my heart hurts in my chest while my tongue feels far too big for my mouth. *"We already talked about this Johnny. It's not a matter of cruelty on the part of the Creator, and it sure as Hades ain't no punishment. Love is bigger than any ole' breakin' of church rules. Least that's what I've always believed. After your journey on this plane is done, your soul movin' on is just the way things are supposed to work in the Universe. The fact that yours is still wanderin' in this same plane after all these years is ..."* I can't make myself say it. I can't call it a mistake, nor will I let myself believe that my meetin' Johnny and fallin' in love with him was nothin' more than a cosmic oversight wrought by a wise-woman's spell. *"A rarity,"* I say, completin' the sentence.

"Your love for Sara Anne...for me...somehow anchored your soul to this place. I wish I could explain it better, Johnny, but I can't. Maybe when you leave here," I reply, my voice hitching, *"and you reach the Afterlife, somebody there can help you make sense of it."*

My soldier boy turns away. Even though his mani-fested image is slowly fading in the coming light of the new day, I sense his frustration. He is silent for a minute or two, and when he speaks, the words are heavy with sorrow. *"I don't give a single red bean about any answers, Darlin'. Or even recevin' my eternal rewards in Paradise if it means I won't be with you anymore. I swear on every one of my lost bones that if Ole' Scratch himself came up from Gehenna and offered me a deal, I'd trade my soul for more time here with ya.'"*

"Oh, Johnny," I moan. It's all I can manage with my throat all closed off and achy-like.

His image is barely a whisp now as he stands up and tucks his hands in his pockets. I want to believe it's so he doesn't forget and accidently touch me, though I wish with everything I am that he would. *"I'm gonna' go now, Darlin' before I'm no more than an empty voice in your head. If you can remember the day I left you to join my regiment, then ya' know how I feel 'bout long goodbyes."*

I have faint, painful memories of that moment from my regression session with Phyllis Bagley, and I choke out a sob. *"I remember, Johnny. You tucked a wild rose behind my ear and kissed my cheek... all shy-like 'cause your parents were standing there behind us. You said it was bad luck to say 'goodbye,' so ya' said 'see ya' soon, Darlin', instead."*

His ghostly image flares for a moment and I'm treated to one last dimpled smile. "It makes me happy to know that you remember. The smile begins to fade, along with any type of solid form. All that stands in front of me is a muted, gray mist. *"No matter what happens later today I will always love you. I only know what the preachers done told me, but if God is as merciful as they say, I pray he won't make me wait another eternity to see ya' again."*

Tears are runnin' down my face. He puts a hand out to brush them away, but stops himself before actually touchin' me.

"Will I see you tomorrow? At the exhumation?" I ask, in barely a whimper.

"I don't expect ya' will, Sweetheart. It bein' durin' the daylight hours, with all those livin' people around, there's probably a good chance I won't be able to 'manifest,' as ya' call it. Besides, I'm not sure this ole' heart of mine could handle seein' ya' find nothin' but my dusty, 'ole bones in that hole. You go ahead and try to undo Big Lucy's castin', and if it somehow doesn't work, I'll be right here waitin' for ya', happy as can be. But if that scenario ain't in the cards for us, and I move on like ya' think, then I want you to have a good life. Find someone who loves ya' almost as much as I do and make a home together. Now, just like the last time, I ain't gonna' say goodbye 'cause it seems far too final of a thing to actually say. It's steeped in bad luck, so let's us just leave it as 'see ya soon, Darlin'.'"

The gray light continues to fade until it's just a few tiny specks, not unlike dust motes floating in the sun light. *"I love you, Johnny. Always and forever."* And as the last speck of my sweet Johnny flickers out, I whisper, "See you soon, my love," to an empty room.

I slump down the wall behind me and weep silently as the sun completely rises in the east. When I finally stop, I decide to pull my cards from my backpack along with the pressed wild rose and the quartz crystal. I pour every ounce of my energy into a traditional card spread for assessing a relationship. The first four cards I turn over tell me nothing that I don't already know.

The Two of Cups, the Star, and the King of Cups tarot

cards indicate that Johnny and I have a deep, spiritual connection, romantic fulfillment, and are spiritually driven. The 4th card is the Queen of Wands, which symbolizes a very intimate and passionate relationship. As we have never even touched, I can't attest to anything more than the erotic dreams of the past that have filled my nights, in addition to the unfulfilled longing I feel every time we are together. All of these signs I disregard as obvious. They do not give me the hope I'm seeking. The fifth card in the spread is the most important and the one that holds the most anxiety for me. It's the one that focuses on the future of the relationship.

I hesitate for a moment, and with shaking hands, turn over the Wheel of Fortune card in the upright position. This card, shown in this pose, symbolizes that life is cyclical, producing good times and bad, and that Fate cannot be controlled by mere mortals. In a relationship spread like this one and as the fifth card, the Wheel indicates that change is coming to me and Johnny. As if I didn't already know as much. Frustrated and disappointed at the lack of clear wisdom from the Tarot, I sweep the cards up and shove them back in the box.

Chapter Thirty-Two

On an overcast, clothes-stickin-to-ya-kinda-mornin' in late June, I gather with a small group of observers to witness the exhumation of Pvt. Jonathan Ezra Sweet, an early casualty of the skirmish between the Union and Confederate troops in Spring Hill, Tennessee. Security has been hired to keep the curious from entering the private community, and a makeshift fence has been put up to keep the gawking residents and the myriad of news people and cameramen away from the actual dig. Only a specially designated group of people have been allowed access to the excavation spot. Besides the members of the construction crew that's doing the diggin', the group includes; forensic archeologists who have been hired to handle the actual remains, our Governor, who never misses a photo op, the Mayor of Spring Hill, three representatives from the Daughters of the Confederacy on site with their own photographer, two elderly woman who are said to be descendants of the Sweet family of Meridian, Mississippi, Donna Martin, Southern Streams

HOA President, the Chairman of the Battlefield Trust Committee, Conrad Listle, Rev. Miles Sharpley, a Baptist minister from the local church, Phyllis Bagley, Edwina Rooney with her camera crew, and me.

Someone, I'm not sure who, has hired a small brass band standing just outside the fence to play "Dixie" as the remains of the Confederate soldier are removed from their original resting place. The circus-like mood makes me queasy, or perhaps it's just the dismal mood that hangs about me on this fateful morning. The Governor says a few words followed by one of the ladies from the DOTC, and then the construction crew begins their assault on Pickleball Court #5.

It takes nearly forty-five minutes until enough of the court is removed, as well as a few feet of mud and gravel. People are overly warm in the heat and humidity. Some of the crowd outside the fence leave their posts to return to cooler homes, and chairs are brought for those of us at the excavation site. I am too damn nervous to sit. I pace back and forth, sending out metaphysical feelers in case my Johnny Reb has decided to watch his own exhumation. We'd talked about that in the days leading up to this, and though he'd given me a definitive answer the night before on whether he wanted to attend, I wondered if at the last moment he would perhaps change his mind. I feel nothing, so I suppose he's made the decision not to be here. I am half relieved. This is hard enough for me to bear. I can't begin to understand how Johnny himself might feel.

Eventually, the excavation crew reaches a point deep enough that is based on the readings of how far down the body actually is. They pull out their equipment and the forensic archeologists take over. After another thirty minutes of hand digging and sweeping, one of the specialists climbs out of the hole to announce that they've found what they believe to be the soldier's remains, in the exact location the scanning images forecasted they'd be. He shows us a tarnished, mud-encrusted belt buckle with the raised letters "CS" standin' for "Confederate State of America". The buckle is irregularly shaped and consistent with the types worn by a low-rankin' soldier like my Johnny, so the archeologists are confident they've found the remains we are lookin' for based on my conversations with the ghost. Before I can even lay a hand on it, the buckle is placed in a bag to be returned to the family as all the legal eagles have arranged.

As of yet, the pocket watch I'm seekin' has not been found and my anxiety level grows higher as the work continues and it's still not located. At one point, I walk over to the hole and look down inside. I catch sight of a femur bone picked clean of all flesh and knowing it belongs to Johnny makes me sway on my feet. So much so, I find it necessary to lower myself to the ground and stick my head between my knees. The last thing I want is to fall apart before I can lay hands on the cursed charm inside that watch. I can do my sweet Johnny Reb no good from the gurney of some emergency room.

Upon feeling well enough to stand, I head back to my chair to wait some more, blaimin' my little incident on the overwhelmin' heat. Phyllis tries to engage me in conversation, but I remain silent, unwilling to share any of what I'm feelin' with her. Then, finally, the lone female archaeologist comes topside holdin' something in her hand. She seeks me out and says, "I've been told you have a court order allowing you first access to examining this relic. It's highly irregular, but I'll comply with the law." She hands me a pair of silicone gloves to put on before she's willin' to hand it over. A barrier between my skin and the item hurts my chances of gettin' a good metaphysical read on the piece, but there's no escapin' this woman's directive, so I tell myself it's worth my compliance if only to reach the damn hair charm I need inside the watch.

I put the gloves on and she lays the item gently in my hand. I feel nothing at all from the watch itself, though that doesn't alarm me, as I expected as much. I walk away a few steps to allow for a little privacy while I open it. This upsets the archeologist and she attempts to follow me, but Phyllis stops her. I stand with my back to the group, fubblin' around because of the awkward gloves. The timepiece is difficult to open, its latch all rusted and filled with packed dirt, but eventually I am able to pull the two pieces apart.

Time in the ground and the harsh elements of nature have not been kind to Johnny's beloved pocket watch. The crystal on the timepiece is fogged so badly the time can't be read. Yet, it's the other half of the watch that shocks me. I can tell that at one time this side held a photo, perhaps of a young woman, but it is blurred and water damaged beyond any recognition. Even worse is the fact that the compartment itself is completely empty except for a few strands of brittle cloth, most likely part of the charm's bindin' ribbon. Any hair that once made up the Vodou charm has completely decomposed, leavin' nothing behind but the slightest tinge of green slime.

With a feelin' of complete and utter hopelessness, I can't help but go weak in the knees as I slide to the ground, weepin' in frustration and despair. With the Big Lucy's hair charm completely gone, how can my Johnny's soul ever move on?

My reaction to the empty pocket watch has several people rushin' to my side to help me up. I have no words for what I'm feelin'. Up until now, I had never let myself think 'bout what it would mean if the charm wasn't there in the same way Johnny described it. Findin' it gone like this overwhelms and confuses me. If the charm has long dissipated, why is my Johnny still trapped on this earthly plane? I have no answers.

My sadness and frustration is too much to bear in the presence of all these gawking people. I need to escape. Without explanation, I dash across the lodge lawn to the parking lot. The media people, who have been takin' in all this drama from behind the fence, immediately note my departure and rush to follow me, yellin' out their questions. I jump in my car and pull out of the parking lot, swervin' to avoid the camera people determined to get their all-important shots. A few news trucks try and follow me, but I doubt that any of them know about the back dirt road entrance to the Rippavilla property which is safely protected by a keypad entry. Even if a few news hounds manage to track me here, there's little chance they'll be able to get beyond the gate.

In the car, I try and pull up my metaphysical "feelers" in an attempt to get some sign of Johnny's presence. There is nothing...just a large, empty void. I fight off the panic I'm suddenly experiencin'. In this highly emotional state, I am doubtful of my psychic abilities. I know from Opal Gaspar's trainin' that in my present confusion, I am incapable of makin' any kind of spiritual connection. I tell myself that it will be better when I am in the confines of the old house. Johnny's presence is always so strong in that place.

I manage to lose the news vans on the Saturn Parkway, thus makin' my arrival at the back entrance before they can catch up to me. My hands are shakin' so bad that I have to put the keypad numbers in twice before the gate opens for me. I drive through and the bar comes back down, sealin' the entrance off for any unwanted company. I expect that Phyllis and Edwina will eventually make their way here, along with the Franklin Trust people, but by then I will hopefully have had a chance to give my Johnny Reb the bad news about the Vodou charm in person. Alone like I am, I can no longer lie to myself over my mixed emotions regardin' this turn of events. Part of me is worried and upset that I haven't been able to help this poor lost soul move on, which I realize is the deep-seated responsibility tied to my metaphysical gifts. On the other hand, I cannot deny that a big part of me that has strong feelins', love even, for this long dead soldier boy, is secretly happy for the inability to reverse the charm, thus keepin' him tied to Rippavilla and me.

I understand this kind of thinking is highly selfish on my part. This poor lost soul don't belong still walkin 'among the livin', and my reason for wantin' him to stay is entirely based in my desire to keep him near me. In order to keep my growin' guilt at bay, I reason that at some point the Universe may let me know how to help Johnny move on. When that time comes, I will do my rightful duty and help him find his place in the Afterlife. In the meantime, however, there ain't no reason for us to deny the connection we obviously share. I am willin' to stay true to my sweet Johnny Reb for as long as I have him here with me, even if it means giving up what society deems a normal life with husband and family. I learned a long time ago that love always comes with strings attached.

AS I ENTER RIPPAVILLA THROUGH THE STAFF ENTRANCE, MY stomach is tied up in emotional knots. In the past, I have always felt some part of Johnny's spirit reachin' out to me the moment I stepped foot on the plantation's property. Today, the atmosphere surroundin' the house feels stagnant. Traces of older metaphysical energy still linger in the air, but they lack the vibrancy of my Johnny's presence. I leave the modernly created space that houses the staff areas and gift shop and enter the older parts of the building, all the while tryin' not to panic over the lack of what I should be experiencin'.

"Johnny," I call out, both physically and mentally. "It's me Johnny...Delia. Sara Anne. We need to talk." My voice echoes in the empty space. No one answers. I take the stairs to the second floor and head for the room with Miz Ruby's picture. I feel minute traces of lingerin' energy from our time here last night, but my lost soldier boy is not present in real time. Even the portrait of Miz Ruby looks more faded than I seem to remember. A thought comes to me, and I fumble with the back of the paintin', searchin' for the drawin' of Sara Anne. I somehow know in my heart that I will find it gone before I even begin to look, but that don't stop the tears from comin' when my instincts prove true. The drawing is no longer there.

I slump to the floor and let the grief wash over me in unstoppable waves. This was a possibility I had never truly planned for, though I've always understood that there ain't no set rules for when or how a lost soul moves on. Sometimes they linger on the earthly planes for reasons the livin' can never fully understand. It now seems clear that Big Lucy's charm had no bearin' on my Johnny's hangin around for all these years, and I consider that maybe once he'd been truly "found" there under that damn pickleball court, his soul felt free to move on.

Still, none of it explains my role in this whole experience, nor does it shed any light on the memories I unearthed during my past life regression session with Miz Phyllis. With Johnny now gone, I'm not sure I'll ever have the answers. Another thought crosses my swirlin' mind, and I check that I still have Johnny's gifted quartz crystal. Relief settles thick 'round me as I find the stone right where I put it. I pull the lovely token out of my pocket and place it in front of me, but it offers no solace, nor do I feel any energy radiatin' from it. Still, it was a gift from my true love and I will, nonetheless, treasure it always.

With a sense of desperation, I rummage through my bag for my Tarot cards. I realize any readin' I do in this highly emotional state is subject to great misinterpretation, but I am without a clue as to how I should proceed after this heartbreak. I hear the sounds of people and traffic from outside the window and I know my privacy is limited. There is no time to do a proper spread, so I center myself as best I can in this grief-stricken state and draw a single card, hoping against hope for some sense of direction. I flip the card over to reveal the Wheel of Fortune, once again in the upright direction, a symbol for change and destiny. I am in no mood to have the Universe wag a "told ya so" metaphysical finger in my face. I view this card as a "no-answer- answer." Forcefully shoving the card back in the deck, I shuffle them with even greater conviction. Then, satisfied I have mixed them completely, I select again, willing the Universe to advise me. With a flick of my wrist, I find myself staring yet again at that same damned Wheel of Fortune. With a groan of total frustration, I kick the remaining stack of cards with my foot, scattering them across the room just as I hear Miz Phyllis's voice calling me from below.

"Cordelia? Are you up there?" the docent asks.

"Yes, Ma'am. I'm up here. In the pink room," I reply.

She appears at the door, concern apparent in her normally poised demeanor. "Are you alright, Cordelia? You gave me such a fright back there, first fainting, then running off like that." She takes in my anguished expression and the scattered Tarot cards. "Cordelia, dear, what's wrong?"

I can't help but to rush into the elderly woman's arms sobbing, "Oh Miz Phyllis...he's gone...truly gone. I'll never see my sweet Johnny Reb again."

DOING HER BEST TO SUPPORT ME, THE BRITISH WOMAN arranges for me to stay day and night in the big house, just in case I am able to make contact again with my lost soul. The media blitz about Rippavilla havin' an honest to goodness ghost has increased tourism in the area by leaps and bounds, and now, every tour at Rippavilla is booked solid day after day. During the daylight hours, I spend my time alone in the wooded property surroundin' the house, searchin' for answers that don't come. At night, I wander each and every room, lookin' for any new sign of my beloved soldier boy. In my heart, I know my Johnny is gone from my reach, but it gives me comfort to spend time in the place he called home for so long.

Miz Phyllis offers to try another past life regression, but I decline the offer, worryin' that I might discover that I was the final step in Johnny's soul's progression, and that the cycle of connection between the two of us is finally over. If that's true, then I would rather not spend the rest of my days with that heart-breakin' knowledge. Instead, I tell myself that I am content to go through what remains of my life knowin' that I've been loved by the same sweet soul for nearly 250 years. That's more than most people can say.

After three weeks with no sign from Johnny, I decide it's high time I move on. Miz Phyllis kindly invites me to stay with her at her lovely Thompson's Station town-house, but I refuse her generous offer. I need time and private space to determine what I want to do with the rest of my life, a future that I have decided will not include anything of a metaphysical nature. I know my Mamaw would tell me that it is a grave injustice against the ways of the Universe, me turnin' my back on my gifts, but from personal experience, my so-called "gifts" have left me with nothing but heartache. I toss all of my hoodoo paraphernalia, including those damned traitor Tarot cards, into a dumpster behind the Target on Rt. 31 and leave Spring Hill for good.

Travelin' further south, I take what little money I have left and rent a tiny studio apartment over a laundromat in Pulaski, Tennessee. Luckily, I seem to go unrecognized in the small, workin'-class community, something I'm eternally grateful for. I've had enough of bein' in the media limelight to last a lifetime. Instead, I take a part-time job in a small coffee shop during the day, while my empty nights are spent with memories and dreams belongin' to Sara Anne and the woman that came before her. As the days and weeks pass, those hauntin' night time images seem to grow fainter as time marches forward. All things considered, I take this as a true blessin'. The less I remember of my Johnny and what we had together, the better off I'll be.

Chapter Thirty-Three

FOUR MONTHS LATER...

There is a lot to say about the comfort of havin' the same routine day in and day out. My life in Pulaski is as dry as week-old cornbread and I am perfectly content to leave it that way. I keep to myself, makin' only the barest of attempts at buildin' any connections with the livin' folks around me, and even then, only out of necessity. As for the non-livin', I keep them as far away as possible. I sage cleanse my personal spaces twice a week, decorate every corner of my apartment and the coffee shop with ghost-bustin' symbols, and am never without a spirit deflectin' crystal somewhere on my person. I leave no wiggle room for any passin' lost soul to misconstrue the fact that Cordelia Mae Achley, Ghost Whisperer, is totally out of business.

This clean slate also includes no contact with the people that played a role in everything that went down in

Spring Hill. I have completed my interview commitments with Edwina, and thankfully, as is her nature, the journalist has moved on to newer stories. I have received text messages from both Sylvie Weathers and Mrs. Kozinski which I delete without reading. Poor Miz Sylvie doesn't seem to take the hint, so eventually I need to change my cell number. It's not like I want to be cruel. I appreciate that my old neighbor is a kindly lady who cares about my welfare. It's just that I need to make a clean start here in Pulaski and the over-abundance of her weekly sympathetic texts don't help to accomplish that.

On the other side of the spectrum, bein' a woman who says what she means and means what she says, Phyllis Bagley has left me completely alone to figure things out on my own. I know I made a promise to someday help her with her dissertation on the Afterlife, but the professor understands it can't be right now and is satisfied to wait until I feel emotionally stable enough to do so. That's why I am so utterly shocked when she walks into my coffee shop one rainy October morning. She settles herself at one of the small cafe tables and waits for me to come to her. I don't bother bringin' her any coffee. I already know the British woman prefers her Breakfast tea. I grab a little pot of hot water and a few tea bags and wander over, though I fully admit to bein' a tad frosty in my greetin'. "You promised, Miz Bagley, that you wouldn't follow me here. I gave you, and you alone, the location of my whereabouts 'cause I took ya' at your word that you would leave me be for a while. In all honesty, Ma'am, I got my feathers in a ruffle seein' you here like this."

"I understand completely, my dear," she states as she

goes about makin' her "cuppa" as she's known to call it. "I think it's very wise of you to take some time to digest all that's happened. But something came in the mail for you in care of Rippavilla and I felt it was extremely important for me to make sure you received it." She pulls an envelope from her purse and hands it to me.

"As I explained to you when I left, Miz Bagley, I need some time away from Rippavilla and my memories of what took place there. So far, I've been doing a fine job of pushin' that heavy burden from my head. I'm hardly havin' any of those past life dreams at night. This clean start idea is workin' out just fine for me. I don't see why ya'll felt like ya' needed to muck it all up." I shove the envelope in the pocket of my apron without even lookin' at it.

I can tell that the elderly woman is disappointed in my reaction. She turns her attention back to her tea, but adds, "You of all people should understand that you can't hide from your destiny, Cordelia Mae Achley. You're just fooling yourself if you think you can."

I am in no mood to trade philosophical barbs with a university professor, so I leave the table without another word. Phyllis finishes her tea, then pays for it and leaves the shop without even a goodbye. I take deep, cleansing breaths and try to tap down the hurt and sadness that's wantin' to take up residence in my heart. I especially don't bother to look at the envelope or its contents until my shift is over and I'm in the safe space of my apartment. It's a good thing I waited. The name on the return address in the upper left-hand corner of the cursed envelope alone makes my heart race.

CHAPTER THIRTY-FOUR

3 WEEKS LATER...

ON THE NEARLY FOUR-HOUR DRIVE TO MERIDIAN, Mississippi, I almost turn back on two separate occasions. At one point, I actually do drive back north before getting off at the next exit and headin' back south once again. I've been a mixed bag of shiftin' emotions ever since Miz Bagley brought me that damned letter three weeks earlier, and even though I made my decision to go ahead and do this, it don't mean I ain't completely shook up about it.

The catalyst for this trip was the letter from a woman by the name of Priscilla Sweet Buckingham, claiming to be the great, great grand-daughter of Elias Johnathan Sweet, my Johnny's youngest brother, apparently born sometime after Johnny left Meridian, when his mother was well-advanced in her child-bearin' years. It seems the remaining family members had left the Meridian area shortly after the Civil War, which is why I didn't find notice of Elias in the Lauderdale County burial records.

The letter was an invitation for me to attend the ceremony commemoratin' the interment of my Johnny's remains in the family's burial plot in Meridian. He was to be buried next to his parents with all the honors and respect that he should have received upon his tragic death. Miz Buckingham went on to say that since I had been so instrumental in findin' the poor boy's lost restin' place, she had hoped that I would be interested in seein' him finally "home again."

I won't lie. I cried for days after readin' that letter, waiverin' back and forth about whether I should attend. I never formally replied to the woman's invitation, afraid that it would leave me unable to change my mind. But here I was, on my way to Meridian. In the end, I felt I owed it to my sweet Johnny Reb to see that he finally made it back to the home he so dearly loved. At least he'd be near the restin' place of his beloved Sara Anne and the son he had never known. I considered it a final act of love on my part.

Still, I never gave much thought about the date of the internment, but it eventually dawned on me that the family had oddly chosen the 31st of October for the ceremony. In hoodoo lore, the 31st of October is considered *Samhain,* or as modern culture deems it, All Hallows Eve, a day when the veil between the world of the livin' and the dead is exceptionally thin. At first, I instantly consider that there might be some metaphysical workins' in place with that choice of dates, but then I pull out the copies I made of the Lauderdale County records and realize that

October 31st was my Johnny's birthday, and thus a reasonable date for the family to select for a ceremony of this type.

Carefully timing my departure from Pulaski, I arrive at the Meridian church cemetery just in time for the ceremony. The Baptist church itself was a remnant from another time, and the headstones around me bear witness to the many years that have passed since the last soul was buried here. There is a surprisingly large crowd gathered for the event, including several old gentlemen in Confederate officer's apparel. A folded Confederate flag rests on what must be Johnny's polished oak casket, and I think to myself how present-day history and culture wouldn't possibly understand this group's remembrance of our Country's sad and troubled past. Still, havin' known the deceased on a personal level, I find the trappins' of the ceremony somehow appropriate in this specific case.

I stay in the background, hopin' to remain unnoticed. I've changed my hairstyle since leavin' Spring Hill, losin' my long locks to a more modern swing cut, so I am hopeful that I look different from the haunted, spirit-talkin' woman that every news outlet carried photos of five months earlier. I listen to several people speak on Johnny's behalf, and though they try very hard to capture his essence, none of them comes close to describin' the Johnny I knew and loved. When a young boy bugler begins the mournful notes of solemn Taps, and they finally lower the casket with my Johnny's bones inside, I no longer can contain my grief. Hot tears slide down my cheeks and though I try as hard as I can to remain silent, a few gasping sobs escape my mouth. A few people turn around and notice me, nudging one another and whis-perin' amongst themselves.

I take their attention as my warnin' to leave. The last thing I want is to be bombarded with questions about how I came to know where Johnny's remains were located and what it's like talkin' to ghosts. That story is old news and I desperately want to keep it that way. I turn and head to my car with the intent to disappear. I am suddenly glad that I decided to book a room in advance at the Comfort Suites just outside of the Meridian city limits. I feel far too shaky and exhausted to safely make the four-hour trip back to Pulaski, Tennessee.

I almost successfully make my escape when I hear a male voice callin' behind me. "Miz Achley? Cordelia Achley?"

Initially, I pretend I don't hear it and keep on walkin' to my car, but the footsteps behind me speed up and the voice becomes louder and more insistent. "Miz Delia, Ma'am, please…stop a moment. I really need to speak to ya.'"

With a hand on my car door, I stop. Somethin' in the sound of his voice, the insistence in it, makes me turn around. The man closes the space between us and when I look up at him, my knees go weak, and my heart races in my chest. I suddenly go warm all over despite the chill of the late autumn weather. The man standin' in front of me looks the splittin' image of my sweet Johnny Reb.

Undoubtedly, on closer inspection, there are major differences. This man is shorter and a bit stockier. His hair is cut in modern style with a side part and his Patag-onia jacket screams modern, urban hipster. Still, it's Johnny's blue eyes, his dimpled chin and high forehead that causes all the air to suddenly be sucked from my lungs. I begin to feel strange, all woozy and lightheaded, and I need to put both my hands on the car to keep from slidin' to the ground.

"Whoa there, Darlin'...let me give you a hand. You look like ya' suddenly seen a ghost," the modern Johnny says, as he puts his hands around my waist in an attempt to keep me from hittin' the concrete pavement of the parkin' lot.

It's not his touch that catches my attention and instantly snaps me out of my faint, but his words. "What did you just call me?" I ask.

He blushes a deep shade of pink. "I'm sorry, Ma'am. It just sort of slipped out. I don't mean no disrespect. Honest." His drawl is crazily familiar. "Not even sure why I said it," he stammers. Seein' that I appear to be less wobbly on my feet, he lets go of my waist and sticks a hand out to shake. "Robert John Sweet, at your service, Ma'am. I wanted to thank you for bringin' our missin' family member home."

"Oh," I mumble, my mouth suddenly feelin' like it's filled with cotton. "You're related to the late Private Sweet?" I ask. It's a dumb question. Of course, he's related.

"Yes, Ma'am. Jonathan was my great uncle, several generations removed. Priscilla Buckingham is my sister. She's the one who organized this ceremony and wrote to invite you to attend. You have no idea how honored we all are to have you with us on this auspicious occasion. I know my Uncle Johnny must be smilin' ear to ear from his seat in Heaven."

That thought of Johnny happy makes me tear up again.

"I'm glad it all worked out this way, Mr. Sweet. I'm so very glad that your uncle is safely back home where he belongs." Behind Robert, I see a crowd of people heading our way. "Look, Mr. Sweet…"

He cuts me off. "Please call me Bobby, Miz Achley. I grew up Bobby John and the 'Bobby' part just sort of hung on."

"Ah then…Bobby it is. Honestly, I don't mean to be rude, but I'm really not up to meetin' with all these people. I hope you understand. I've been tryin' to keep a low profile since this all happened. The focus needs to be on your lost uncle and not on me. I am doing my best to not be recognized."

"I understand completely," Bobby replies. "Is that why you went and cut your hair? It's still quite lovely, you know." He notes my startled expression and once again turns red-faced. "Jeez, I apologize. That was quite inappropriate again. I don't know what's gotten into me today. Must be meetin' you in person that's got me all discombobulated. To be honest, I was fascinated with your whole story. It was a damn shame 'bout the Caleb boy." Then noticin' that the crowd from the grave site is almost upon us, Bobby says, "Oh hell, I'm babblin' again. Honest, I'm usually not such a total dufus 'round beautiful woman. Are you stayin' long in Meridian," he asks.

I think about lyin' but somethin' in my heart tells me not to. "Just for tonight," I answer. "I plan on leavin' for Tennessee the first thing tomorrow morning."

"Can I buy you a drink, then?" the modern Johnny asks me.

I laugh. "It's 11:15 in the morning. That's a little early for a cocktail, don't ya think?"

Bobby John blushes again. I find it so stinkin' cute. "I guess you're right 'bout that Miz Achley," the man admits. "How 'bout a cup of coffee then? Or breakfast? Or even lunch if you like real food better than the breakfast stuff?"

He's so adorable, so earnest and hopeful, that I'm findin' it hard to think of reasons to say no. Plus, I need to get out of this parkin' lot pronto if I don't want to be stuck for a long ghostly question and answer session with the rest of the Sweet clan. I stick my chilled hands in my pocket and find that the quartz crystal token from my sweet soldier boy is unusually warm to the touch. I might have wanted to deny my gifts, but them gifts have a certain way of takin' charge when they need to. I go with my gut feelins'. "I am a bit hungry. Breakfast sounds wonderful, Mr. Bobby John." I say, as I hand him my car keys "But you drive. You probably know Meridian better than me. Plus, today...I feel like finally puttin' someone else in the driver's seat for a change," I say as I make my way to the passenger side of the car and slide in.

EPILOGUE

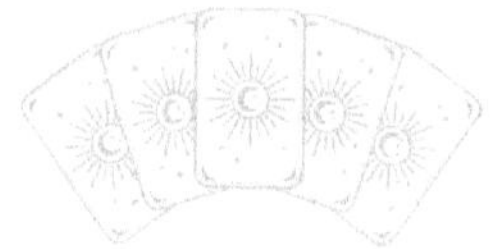

TWO YEARS LATER...

THESE DAYS, WHEN PHYLLIS BAGLEY COMES TO VISIT, I AM A much better hostess than I ever was before, intent on showin' the dear lady some of that Southern hospitality folks is always talkin' about. While the professor cuddles my infant son, I fix her a pot of fresh English Breakfast Tea and a plate of the homemade biscuits I made earlier this mornin' in anticipation of her arrival. She coos at my John Robert with a sweetness that's not normally part of her usual stiff upper lip personae. "Such a wee beautiful boy, you are, sweet child. So very alert for such a tiny thing."

I pour the steeped tea into her cup and saucer and take the baby from her arms to settle myself in the rocker near the table. "I do think he's gonna' be a genius some day in the future," I brag. "Ya' can tell by the way he watches everythin' so carefully."

"Spoken like a true mother," Phyllis jokes. She takes a sip of her tea and looks at me intently for an uncomfortably long time.

"What?" I ask, her staring at me makin' me suddenly antsy.

"Oh nothing, dear Cordelia. It's just that I've never seen you look this happy. Your aura is actually glowing a brilliant pink yellow."

I smile serenely and look down at the baby beginning to doze in my lap. "I am happy, Miz Phyllis…deeply and wonderfully happy. These past two years have been like a wonderful dream I don't ever want to wake up from.

"There's no doubt married life and motherhood agree with you, my dear," she replies. Ever the scientist, she asks, "And those past life memories…are you still having them?"

I shake my head in the negative. "Not very often. Occasionally, I'll be doing something and I'll feel an overwhelming sense of *deja vu*, but then, the feeling passes quickly and I forget what caught my attention in the first place. I almost never have those night time dreams belongin' to someone else anymore, and frankly, I'll wholeheartedly admit that I prefer living in the present rather than the past."

"I can understand that, Cordelia. Still, you were a fascinating case study on past life regression. I'm hoping I'm able to convince you to try it again…when you're ready of course," the professor says.

"Maybe someday, Ma'am, though like I said before, I have this solid feelin' that Bobby John and I marryin' and havin' John Robert was the end of the cycle for our two wander-weary souls. It appears that we two have finally managed not to be separated by the forces of war, nor were we made to carry the burden and grief of a lost child...at least not so far. I've been tryin' to focus on the blessins' of the here and now without gettin' mucked up by tragedies of the past. But as I promised, if I feel the time has come to try a regression again, you'll be the first one I call."

"That's quite sensible of you, dear girl. Tell me though...how much of your past history together is your husband aware of? It must be difficult for him to contemplate, especially if he's not blessed with the metaphysical wherewithal that you, yourself, possess," the British woman questions.

"Well, Bobby himself has said that he was instantly and deeply attracted to me the moment he saw me on television when I did that interview with Edwina at Rippavilla. Plus, I can't tell you how many times in the past two years the dear man has said he feels as if he's known me his entire life. But as for me tryin' to convince him about the possibility of past lives and reincarnation...well...that might have to stay on the back-burner. Bobby John is a tried-and-true Christian, a Baptist no less. He accepts my bein' able to talk to ghosts and such; he considers it as some kind of 'blessing' sent down from Heaven, but I don't know how open he'd be to any other explanation. Maybe someday he'll go and figure it out on his own. However, if he don't, it's perfectly fine with me. It don't matter much what a person wants to believe 'bout the meanin' of life, or what name they wanna' give their belief system, Miz Phyllis, 'cause I have discovered the key to understandin' it all."

"All, dear girl? That's quite a broad statement," the scholar replies with a smile. "Go right ahead and tutor an old woman, Cordelia Mae Sweet. Tell me what you have discovered is the key to all things in the Universe."

"It's very simple, Miz Phyllis," I explain. "Astoundingly genius in its simplicity. It all comes down to the exchangin' of love, Ma'am. Nothin' more. Nothin' less. Love's the supreme gift the Universe generously bestows on all us simple souls that makes everythin' and everybody part of its connected magic. The very truth of the matter is, no matter how you read the cards, love is the guiding force behind every spin of that timeless, mystic Wheel of Fortune. It's the light along each of our paths and it never dies. Not completely. Like energy, it just changes form and moves through time. I know this to be true 'cause I'm livin' proof of it," I murmur quietly as I kiss the top of my precious child's head, "me and my one and only, sweet Johnny Reb."

More from Serenade Publishing

Songbird series

By Sarah Williams

Songbird

Heartbeat Song

Our Song

Brigadier Station Series

By Sarah Williams:

The Brothers of Brigadier Station

The Sky over Brigadier Station

The Legacies of Brigadier Station

Christmas at Brigadier Station

Heart of the Hinterland Series

By Sarah Williams:

The Dairy Farmer's Daughter

Their Perfect Blend

Beyond the Barre

The Outback Governess

Primrose

By Tanya Renee

Prairie Sky

Prairie Nights

Prairie Fire

Prairie Hearts

Prairie Sound

Prairie Rain

Prairie Prestige

Prairie Roads

Prairie Charm

Prairie Rose

With The Band

By Tanya Renee

Finding Direction

Love Notes

On The Edge Of Forever

The Spring of Love

By Virginia Taylor

Forever Delighted

Forever Amused

Forever Heartfelt

For more information visit:

www.serenadepublishing.com

ABOUT THE AUTHOR

Victoria Rocus is a retired educator, accomplished miniaturist, and full-time author living near the home of country music, Nashville, Tennessee, USA. When she's not writing new adventures for her imaginary friends, catering beach parties for mermaids, or finding homes for orphaned dragons, she's building and rehabbing one-of-a-kind dollhouses and accessories, just like her favorite character, Dr. Rosie Parker. Many of her multiple miniature buildings are 1/12 scale replicas of settings from her unique fantasy stories.

Victoria started her writing career as a weekly blogger while still teaching middle school language arts. Now retired from the educational field, she's been able to make writing a full-time adventure, penning several fantasy and romance stories she hopes readers will enjoy with both a sigh and a smile.

Find out more at: victoriarocusauthor.com

instagram.com/victoriarocusauthor
tiktok.com/@victoriarocusauthor

ACKNOWLEDGMENTS

Unlike the actions of my so many of my beloved characters, the stories that you love to read don't magically appear in your online bookstore. They are truly the product of several people pitching in to make the "magic" happen.

Long after I've typed "The End" on the bottom of the last page, my story has been through multiple readings and edits, along with discussions over cover design and marketing. In that spirit, I 'd like to take a few lines to thank the may souls who have made *Once Upon Our Time* a reality.

Applause and grateful and whole-hearted thanks goes to Serenade Publishing and CEO Sarah Williams for the monumental support you continually offer for each and every book. You are an inspiration of dedication and hard work, and an awesome mentor.

To my dedicated Beta Readers: Carol Peden Fuller, Donna Gentile Ruth, Daniel Caddigan, Kaia Viney, Michele S. Kaspar, and Gail Hoder. I am thankful for your commitment to making each publication the best it can be. No one does it better than you guys.

To my own personal cheer team, the folks that celebrate each new release with me: Dan and Chris C, Steve and Gail H, Roy and Denise P, John and Paula D, Shannon and Ryan B, Erin A, Jean H, Marcia W, Debbie P, Bill and Carol F, Betty M, Lorraine R, Linda F, Bonnie M, Cindy J, Christine M, and everyone who isn't mentioned here by my fault alone and who I will surely remember right after this book goes to press. I will never be able to thank you enough for your support.

I would be remiss not to express gratitude for my wonderful family: my husband, Victor, my children Steven, Michael, Allison and Kaia, and my sweet, little granddaughter, Valerie James. You are the souls that own my heart.

Lastly, a multitude of thanks to my loyal and generous readers who have supported me with each and every book. Words alone can't tell you how grateful I am for your gracious and committed support.